THE
LAST
STRAW

J. JOSEPH MAWEK

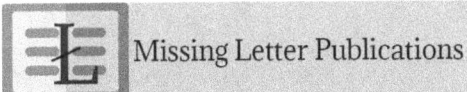
Missing Letter Publications

Missing Letter Publications
PORT WASHINGTON, NEW YORK

ISBN-13: 978-0-69287-582-7

Cover and interior by Gary A. Rosenberg
www.TheBookCouple.com

To my wife, Patricia, family,
and inspiring friends.

In memory of Michael Crichton.

CHAPTER 1

Sundays

Springtime in the not too distant future.

Ron Billings looks out from his porch overlooking Hempstead Bay, straining to see Morgan Park across the water on the Glen Cove peninsula less than a mile away. A more perfect place for watching the Grucci fireworks display is not possible, along with the added bonus of avoiding the huge crowd gathered in the park and the resulting traffic and parking hijinks.

It's the end of a beautiful day, and now, just minutes before darkness and the start of the fireworks, he walks out on his lawn and sits in a chair to relax and reflect on the perfect, clear warm evening. A cloudless, calm, teal blue sky is to the west. Only the steady rumble of firework displays already in progress disturb the calm. That rumble and the distant but steady dog barks break the evening peace as he sits in his lawn chair, sipping a glass of Malbec. A Padron Principe burns in the ashtray as Ron's music favorites can be heard playing from the garage.

Then, without any warning and in an instant, it is there. Barely breaking the calm of the moment, to Ron's left, not more than fifteen yards away, stands a full-grown Doberman pinscher, a beautiful, muscular creature with a dark shiny coat, eighty pounds of "best in show" becoming interested in the man in the lawn chair.

The Doberman looks up and stops its wandering upon being discovered by the man in the chair. Ron thinks it best to keep still and let the dog pass on its way. *Just keep it in your peripheral vision,* he tells himself, *and it will realize it doesn't belong here, and it will find its way back to where it does belong.* Here in Sands Point, neighborhood dogs are walked on a leash and never let run wild, and he'd never seen anyone walking a Doberman.

The Doberman is frozen in its stance as Ron begins turning his attention back across the bay to feign a sense of calm and security. But then, a second dog appears in his periphery next to the Doberman. In similar fashion, it too in an instant stands frozen, as majestic as the first, but not a Doberman, a Rottweiler. A fully grown adult, the Rottweiler appears to push the scales to 100 pounds.

"Jesus Christ," Ron says softly, trying not to look, but he has to confirm that his peripheral vision is not to blame for the doubling of dogs. "Oh, crap." He decides to make for the open garage, just ten to fifteen yards from where he sits. He slowly turns in the chair, readying himself as the two marauders begin a growl and shifting about as to telegraph their intentions to party down with their newfound friend.

Ron knows he has to make a quick sprint for the garage and pull the door closed in a single motion to have any chance of escaping untouched. He doesn't like his chances, but if he just stays put, these two appear to be getting ready to make dog chow out of him.

He bolts toward the garage, flinging the chair in the direction of the dogs. It does little to hinder their flight.

The quicker Doberman reaches him as Ron grabs the garage door. It bites hard into Ron's right hamstring and causes him to lose his grip as he falls to the floor in a wrestling contest with the biting Doberman. And then, as quickly as it began, it ends, as Ron, still gripping the now-broken wine glass in his right hand, swings decidedly, plunging the glass deep into the side of the dog, causing it to yelp and retreat, and waking Ron from this less than refreshing unplanned nap.

"Holy shit." He sits up. Stunned and slowly moving to the corner of the bed, he rubs his head and eyes and begins to recall that he had traveled to Greeley, Colorado, earlier that day, and is in his room at the Best Western Hotel. Traveling as often as he does occasionally messes up his sleep. He sometimes wakes in the middle of the night and is totally confused about his whereabouts. At first it was a bit scary; now he is becoming used to it. He'll sit up in bed and tell himself to stay calm and you'll remember in a few seconds, and of course he comes out of it and realizes where he is and how and when he got there. This afternoon's nap nightmare, however, is something new.

His head is aching from the nightmare as he reaches down from the bed and grabs the newspaper lying on the floor. A jolt of real life to help himself snap back, he tells himself. "So what's new in Stinkytown?" he asks out loud to himself while opening the paper.

Greeley, Colorado, is "fondly" and appropriately nick-named Stinkytown due to the foul smell of the air from the nearby beef slaughterhouse. Greeley is one of those many "big little" towns you run across if you travel for business as Ron does. Of course, characterizing a town or city as big or small is just a matter of perspective. How many times has someone said that this or that city or town is big, and then when you're there or really look into it, you discover it's kind of puny?

New York is big, LA is big, Paris is big. The rest? Ah, not so much. All you have to do is look at the population and you realize that what the locals' idea of big is, is way, way off. Just look at New Orleans, a "big" southern city slammed by hurricane Katrina in August of 2005, a disaster wrought upon a city of less than 400,000 residents, although the lives of more than a million living in the area were affected by the storm.

Not to belittle the ferocity of Katrina or to say New Orleans isn't a big city; it is when compared with others like Atlanta or Nashville, both which are a half million each. But if you really want to talk about big, you have to look at New York or one of the others. The city of New York alone has a population of over 8 million, and taking in the surrounding metro area, there's almost 19 million people residing within roughly 100 miles of Central Park in New York City. Now that's BIG!

But out along the eastern front range of the Colorado Rockies where Greeley is, there are only small cities and towns. Heck, even the capital city of the state, Denver, has a population of just 600,000, and in all of Colorado there's just a little over 5 million people. And that population is spread out across over 104,000 square miles, the eighth largest state in the USA, including Alaska, which is the largest, having over 660,000 square miles of area. Alaska is a BIG state. New York? Not so much, with just 54,000 square miles.

Meanwhile, the good city of Greeley, Colorado, just fifty miles north of Denver and with a population of around 94,000, is like many small cities and towns along the eastern front range of the Colorado Rocky Mountains. Greeley, however, is blessed with a multifaceted culture, which, when woven together, makes for a brilliant fabric of present-day western life. Besides the always-present backdrop of the magnificent Rocky Mountains to the west, Greeley is rich in cowboy and cattlemen history and culture, dating back to 1862 when it is first called the Cherokee City Station, a lazy sort of stagecoach station halfway between Denver and Cheyenne, Wyoming, fifty miles to the north.

Off about thirty miles to the west of Greeley, the eastern front of the Rockies presents one of the most spectacular and mesmerizing sites one will ever come to lay their baby blues upon. The first time out there, with that grand picture off in the distance, a person simply cannot stop looking at the magnificence of the eastern Colorado mountain range. It is truly hypnotic, downright intoxicating, much more so than the first time resting one's eyes upon Albert Bierstadt's painting of Lander's Peak in Wyoming in 1863, which he painted after his first trip to the West. Bierstadt's magnificent painting sits in the New York Metropolitan Museum of Art. It is equaled in magnificence only by the great Dutch masters' paintings hanging in the Rijksmuseum in Amsterdam, and is often compared to Frederic Church's 1859 painting *Heart of the Andes.*

But Bierstadt improves on Church's, inasmuch as the granite peaks and fantastically illuminated clouds float above a tranquil, wooded scene which brilliantly includes in the foreground the campsite of a tribe of Native American Indians. The size, beauty, and scope of material captured by Bierstadt is astounding and transports the viewer for a short time to another time and place—i.e., nineteenth-century Rocky Mountains.

While Bierstadt's magic is comparatively short-lived within a museum visit, passing from Denver along the eastern front of the Colorado Rockies to Greeley can be virtually endless. You drive, walk, or bike along the Front Range, as it's called, and can't stop the incessant gazing off to the west as if you're going to miss something. When you arrive at your destination by car and step out, immediately your head turns to the west as if to check that the Rockies are still there with that picture-perfect blue sky perfectly framing the view. From Greeley, just thirty or so miles away, it's just stunning. "'Tis distance lends enchantment to the view, and robes the mountain in its azure hue," Thomas Campbell wrote of the Scottish Highlands around the late eighteenth century. The view of the front range of the eastern Rockies from the plains is nothing short of Mr. Campbell's summation.

Greeley has that view going for it, alright, and along with a host of other elements of western life, it's very much a welcome place for business and pleasure. It's not lacking much of anything with its cowboy culture complete with a grand rodeo that annually culminates in a two-week long shindig called the Greeley Stampede. The event dates back to the late 1800s and features pro-rodeo bull-riding and kids' rodeos, country and classic rock concerts, a demolition derby, 4th of July parade, a carnival, Western Art Show, free stage entertainment, and loads of festival grounds activities mixed with food and fun galore. Close to 450,000 visitors attend the Stampede annually.

Now that's not to say it's all a cowboy's life in Greeley. On the other end of the spectrum, there's the Hewlett Packard Co., which built and operates a computer manufacturing plant in west Greeley. Then there's the University of Northern Colorado campus, which is also the summer training home of the Denver Broncos. Topping it all off is a wonderful little downtown area of both new and old shops, hotels, restaurants, etc.

One of the largest employers in Greeley, and reflecting on its long tradition of cattle raising, is the beef plant located in the northeast part of town, immediately adjacent to the downtown area. This operation was owned and operated by the Monfort family since 1930, until 1987 when it was sold for $300 million to the ConAgra Foods Company of Omaha, Nebraska. Warren Monfort and his son Ken Monfort were innovators in the meat-packing business, starting out with feedlots and later, under the guidance of Ken, who is best known for moving meat-packing plants to where his cattle were being raised, eliminated expensive shipping costs associated with transporting cattle to Chicago, Kansas City, and other big meat-processing cities. Several other innovations introduced by Ken Monfort changed the way the cattle raising, slaughter, packing, and shipping process is operated today. By the time ConAgra took control in the early nineties, the Monfort family had several beef plants in Colorado, Texas, and Nebraska, the largest by far being in their hometown of Greeley, Colorado. All told, the thousands of head of cattle, pigs, and lamb would generate over $5 billion in annual revenue.

The meat plant in Greeley, however, like many grand things in this western culture, is a double-edged sword. By the 1990s, the beef plant was by far the largest employer in Greeley, as well as in Weld County. Its positive economic effect was clearly visible all the way to Denver and surrounding cities. Trucking companies, meat wholesalers, etc., all benefited from its success.

But a meatpacking plant isn't without its environmental

difficulties. "Stinkytown" is its nickname and for a very good reason. Every few days, to rid itself of the tremendous waste generated by the slaughter of thousands of animals, mostly cows and pigs, the plant, through what it calls "rendering," permeates the air with a stench of what could only be compared to raw sewage. Although it has a distinctively different odor, it is equally as repelling and, in Greeley's case, could be detected for many, many miles from the plant. In most cases, the local residents got used to the regular stench and appreciate the jobs and other economic and cultural benefits of the business. In the end, most everyone agreed with the Monfort's philosophy in that the stench is "the smell of money."

Besides jobs and economic benefits, the Monforts also brought an important sports element to the culture of Greeley. Not only are they partners in the Colorado Rockies baseball team, but they were also instrumental in bringing the Denver Broncos to the University of Northern Colorado Greeley campus for summer training camp. Having John Elway and other stars in Greeley for several weeks in the summer made UNC Greeley an attraction for many miles around.

So all told, having the Broncos in town for training, along with the Stampede and the natural beauty and allure of the eastern front, Greeley is a pretty decent place to visit in the summer or to live year round. That's not to take away from the other three seasons, especially in winter where several world-class ski resorts are within a few hours' drive. Spring rafting, fall hiking and leaf peeping, biking, hunting, and fishing are all top-notch and add to a well-rounded assortment of outdoor activities for all seasons.

So when Dr. Panalla Reddy, the chairman of the Intergovernmental Panel on Climate Change (IPCC), decided that

UNC Greeley, Colorado, would be the site to host the IPCC work conference, the climate change scientists converging on Greeley, Colorado, were overjoyed, but less so once the rendering operation was experienced. No doubt it had the effect Dr. Reddy was looking for, especially among those scientist collecting air samples.

The UN created the IPCC in 1988. It is the leading international body for assessing climate change. Its purpose is to provide the world with a clear scientific view on the current state of knowledge in climate change and its potential environmental and socioeconomic impacts.

The IPCC is a scientific body that reviews and assesses the most recent scientific, technical, and socioeconomic information produced worldwide relevant to the understanding of climate change. Thousands of scientists from all over the world contribute to the work of the IPCC by reviewing and assessing new scientific data pertaining to air quality, observed changes in ocean temperatures, changes in sea levels, and anything else related to climate change.

Ron Billings is an information technologist at the IPCC reporting directly to Dr. Reddy. Now, as his head begins to clear from his afternoon nightmare, he is sitting on the edge of the bed, reading the headline newspaper story and thinking to himself that, once again, the local police are getting it wrong.

The story is of a dead man found in his office by the cleaning lady, and includes details of the police report made by officer Tom Battan. The dead man sits at his desk with his pants down around his ankles. No evidence of foul play is found, although the reporting officer speculates that another man may have been in the room, indicating a twisted homosexual love affair may have played a roll in the dead man's death.

The young officer's report includes a list of typical office items that were found at the scene: two computers and ancillary devices, including a wireless router, mouse, printer, and display; writing devices, pictures, calendar, CDs, reading glasses, magazines, etc. Also noted, and characterized as being out of place and adjacent to the body, a pair of warm, medicinal, soft cold packs lie on the floor next to the dead man. The identity of the man is withheld, pending family notification.

Ron moves to sit on the corner of the bed, having finished reading the article from the front page of the *Denver Post* now laid out on the floor in front of him. The bedsheet is draped around his naked body, his head hanging down, still shaken from his bizarre dog dream and frustrated with the afternoon's activities. *That's odd,* he thinks about the cold packs in the *Post* article.

In the background he hears his music player, John Lennon singing out, "Fixing a hole in the ocean . . . trying to make a dovetail joint," and he thinks, *No way to fix this fucking problem,* meaning his relationships with his live-in girlfriend of eight years, Gwen, and his lover, Pat.

Still hanging his head, he studies the green and tan geo-design of the hotel floor rug as he lets the frustration run through his head, down across his shoulders, into the bridge of his nose, and back into his head where the sensation then repeats. There is no escaping; he hasn't a clue what to do. Somehow, he finds some comfort in staring at the pattern in the rug and letting it all wash out through his gaze and onto the rug.

The phone rings and adds to his despair. He doesn't want to answer it but knows he has to.

Not so much as flinching, he continues to sit, hanging his

head, with the *Post* sprawled out in front of him on the rug where it has been since before Pat arrived hours earlier. He sits and waits to answer the phone. *I don't give a crap, so why answer?* he thinks, before a sudden impulse to be in touch moves him to extend his body to his right and reach for the phone on the night table. His brother, Zach, is returning his call from earlier in the day. He hits the green button and says in a somber voice, "Hi, Zach. What's up?"

"Ronnie boy, you're still out there in Stinkytown?"

He hated being called that—Ronnie, Ronnie boy, even Ron. He wanted to yell out, "My fucking name is Ronald!"

"Yeah, I'm almost done supporting the air sampling project the IPCC is doing, but I'm going to stay until the environmental theater I told you about is done." He pauses a second before continuing, as he hears Zach's wife, Carrie, in the background. "So I guess you're returning my call?"

"Yeah, what's going on?"

Ron had called earlier to ask if they would have the approaching Easter holiday dinner this year. Ron had almost all the family holidays at his house, but at Gwen's insistence, he had agreed to call Zach to see if they would have the holiday.

Zach and Carrie, however, were not the party-giving types. They were always terrific party guests and fun to be with, but having parties was just not something they did. And when, occasionally, they did, they did not do it well. Their parties were like a college frat house party: not much food, lots of booze, occasional marijuana, and accompanying bad behavior. It didn't matter to them that they were in their early sixties. They only knew one way to have a party, and it was to party hard like the old days.

Their lifestyle was its own mural. No children, retired with lots of money, settled in suburban Westchester thirty minutes outside of Manhattan, they lived a life many of their friends and family envied.

"Are you having Easter this year? Gwen and I were wondering."

"Oh, you're not having it? Well, let me talk to Carrie." Zach had assumed Ron would have everyone over again this year. "Crap, Easter is next Sunday. There's a lot to do, you know. Ron, I wish I'd known earlier that you didn't want to do it."

"It's just with me away in Colorado this year . . . I won't be home till Friday night, and . . . anyway, why *can't* you do it this year?"

"Ah, there's just a lot to do. . . ."

"Hey, don't make it such a big deal. No one expects you to be slaves. We'll all help out, and it's easier for Dad too."

Dad, now ninety, had in the last year sold his house in East Hampton and unexpectedly moved to an assisted-living facility just thirty miles from Zach and Carrie's.

"Yeah, let me talk to Carrie."

Zach and Carrie weren't very good at giving dinner parties, partly because they insisted on keeping their guests satisfied to the point where they felt and acted like they were not part of the party at all, but rather the help. For them it was a day of cooking and serving, wedged in between a day of cleaning and prepping, followed by another day of cleaning up after the holiday. Zach honestly felt the only way this could be reasonably accomplished was with recreational drugs, alcohol, and music. If he were to be reduced to the "help," at least it would be fun.

Carrie, on the other hand, was not of the same thinking. For her, it was simply three days of work, especially the day of the party, which she'd spend most of it in the kitchen, worried and looking over the food preparation and miserable while attending to it. Failure was not an option, especially in the kitchen, and cooking for parties drove her mad with anxiety. Her mindset just wouldn't allow her to place that part of her responsibility in a box and go out and mingle with her guests. Not until the dinner was served and everyone was eating could she relax a bit—until the cleanup began, when she'd be off again into worker mode. Finally, after all the guests had gone, she'd be off to bed almost immediately, exhausted mentally and physically. Zach would continue to party.

Ending the call with Zach, Ron returns to his position on the corner of the bed, his head hanging like a ripened piece of fruit ready to fall from its limb. His gaze moves between the paper and rug as he returns his thoughts to his impossible situation with Pat and Gwen.

Earlier that afternoon, Pat had again stormed out of Ron's hotel room. Their afternoon of sex had ended badly, again, with Ron admitting to Pat that he is unable to break it off with Gwen. For several months now, he had been "shacking up" with Pat on Sundays before heading into the workweek. The usual pattern: Fly into Denver International Airport Sunday morning, arriving in Greeley before noon to spend the afternoon in bed having sex with Pat. Monday morning meetings were followed by work groups all week. Friday mornings, he'd depart for DIA and back to Gwen in New York until Sunday, when he'd be back again to Pat in Greeley.

The relationship with Pat had gone on much longer than any of his other travel-related flings, which were usually over within weeks. This one he knew was different. He knew he was unable to draw himself away. The sex had become a drug, an addiction, and he knew he couldn't end it. Exasperated, he didn't know what to do. So this Sunday afternoon, he thought that for the time being, he'd do nothing and clear his head with a forty-mile bicycle ride to Fort Collins and back.

The ride had relaxed him and, to an extent, released him of his earlier anxiety over Pat. But now, sitting on the bed and recalling the afternoon sex, the nightmarish dream, and bizarre news story, he feels again like the proverbial 500-pound gorilla is on his back. He thinks he's in love with Pat and is unable to end it, and he is at a loss with how to end it with Gwen. His cell phone rings. It's Gwen.

"Babe? Yeah, I just got back from a bike ride. What have you been up to?" "Babe" is his usual way of addressing Gwen.

A second call is coming in. It is Panalla Reddy; he has to take the call.

"Babe, let me call you back. I have Panalla Reddy on the other line, OK? Love you." He switches to the incoming call. "Dr. Reddy, how are you this beautiful evening?"

"Hello, Ron. I trust your trip from New York was OK?"

"Uneventful, just the way it's supposed to be. I even got in a nice bicycle ride to Fort Collins this afternoon; I'll sleep well tonight." He knows he is lying; there is way too much on his mind to count on that happening.

Panalla continues, "I want to meet with you as early as possible this week to discuss several items. Do you have an hour tomorrow? Maybe we can meet for breakfast at the Best Western before our day gets underway."

"That's fine! Not too early. Maybe around eight-thirty?"

"Good! I'll see you in the dining room."

"Is there anything specific I should bring or prepare?"

"No, I want to discuss and share some new reports I've received concerning ocean sea level changes and get a brief update from you concerning the lab environment you are working on. Related to that, I have someone in IPCC returning from sabbatical who I think will complement your rollout."

The word "rollout" makes the hair on the back of Ron's neck bristle. He is months away from "rolling out" the lab environment. "Sounds interesting," he comments to Panalla.

"Yes, I know you are months from rollout, but I want to share this new info with you and get your thoughts on testing, prototyping, and having the right resources to help with roll-out. The returning associate I think will be a big plus to your team; she's brilliant and has excellent hands-on experience."

Ron wanted to ask, "Do you have a picture of her?" but of course he couldn't. Instead, he agrees to the breakfast meeting with Dr. Reddy. "OK, I'll see you at eight-thirty. What's the sea level thing about?"

"Well . . . I was in a conference last week with the ocean-ographic work committee, and you know, Ron, usually . . . ah, their reports and discussion are concerned with rising sea levels. And the data is very tricky to interpret; the trend models they produce are of very long durations, some of them decades. Lately, however, over the past couple of months, some of their reporting stations are indicating falling sea levels."

"*Falling* sea levels?" Ron emphasizes the word "falling." "I speculate the data is bad. Has it been confirmed?"

"Well, that's the thing I want to involve you with, since you're also using these reporting stations as a subset of the data feed to the lab environment."

"Yes, of course. How consistent is the data? I guess since there's a concern, you're not ready to categorize it as isolated."

"Not at this point," Dr. Reddy confirms. "NOAA collects sea level and tidal movements, as well as tsunami warnings from hundreds of global reporting stations, as you're aware. Sea levels are very carefully monitored, focusing on places with the highest tidal movements."

"I can name several of these stations," Ron interjects. "The Bay of Fundy tops the list in North America, Cook Island Inlet in Alaska, Binic in France. Yeah, all of these NOAA stations are included in the LET." LET is the acronym for the developmental product Ron is working on, the "Living Environmental Theater."

"Well, several of them have consistently been reporting lower-than-normal tidal ranges, which is felt to be a leading indication of a *falling* sea level," says Dr. Reddy, also stressing the word "falling."

Ever since Ron joined the IPCC some twenty years earlier, melting icebergs, shrinking glaciers, and their corresponding rising sea levels had been the mantra of the IPCC and climate change.

"Ron, I have to go now. I'll see you for breakfast. OK? Thank you. Goodbye for now."

Ron confirms the breakfast meeting and hangs up.

CHAPTER 2

Monday

The Intergovernmental Panel on Climate Change (IPCC) concentrates its activities on tasks allotted to it by the World Meteorological Organization (WMO) Executive Council, and by the United Nations Environmental Program (UNEP) Governing Council resolutions and decisions, as well as on actions in support of the UN Framework Convention on Climate Change process.

The role of the IPCC is to assess on a comprehensive, objective, open, and transparent basis the scientific, technical, and socioeconomic information relevant to understanding the scientific basis of risk of human-induced climate change, its potential impacts, and options for adaptation and mitigation.

Review is an essential part of the IPCC process. Since the IPCC is an intergovernmental body, review of IPCC documents involves both peer review by experts and review by governments.

The IPCC is a huge and yet tiny organization. Thousands of scientists from all over the world contribute to the work of the IPCC on a voluntary basis as authors, contributors, and reviewers. None of them is paid by the IPCC.

The IPCC makes major decisions at plenary sessions of government representatives. A central IPCC Secretariat supports the work of the IPCC and is the central coordinating workhorse of the IPCC. It supports the IPCC chair and other members of the executive committee, and the IPCC bureau by ensuring that the IPCC work program is implemented consistently with the *Principles Governing IPCC Work*. It manages the IPCC funds consistent with WMO regulations and rules, and manages contractual and legal matters; organizes and prepares documentation for sessions, meetings of the executive committee, and working groups; and supports the groups, the Task Force on National Greenhouse Gas Inventories (TFI), and any other task force constituted by the IPCC. It provides information management for the IPCC in cooperation with the Technical Support Units (TSUs), and it contributes to the implementation of the IPCC protocol for addressing possible errors, provides the principal point of contact for members of the IPCC and observer organizations, and liaises with the two parent organizations, WMO and UNEP.

The TSUs of the IPCC take their lead from the IPCC Secretariat. IPCC TSUs provide scientific, technical, and organizational support to their respective IPCC Working Groups (WGs) and the TFI. A TSU may be formed to support the preparation of a report or any other task force constituted by the IPCC.

Ron Billings manages one of the TSUs. His breakfast meeting with Dr. Reddy includes a very detailed discussion of the data sources reporting lower sea levels along the European Atlantic and Mediterranean coastlines. In addition, Dr. Reddy informs Ron of recent seismic readings in an area called the Madeira Basin located some 250 miles north northeast of the island of Madeira, off the coast of Spain, where several deep-sea plains known as the Seine Abyssal Plain, the Tagus Abyssal Plain, the Horseshoe Abyssal Plain, and the

Ferradura Abyssal Plain provide direct access to the tidal waters passing through the Strait of Gibraltar and into the Mediterranean Sea.

Much of the meeting is to review the mapped portions of the seabed in these areas and encompasses the eastern section of the Tagus Abyssal Plain where the continental shelf of Portugal reaches, and to the western section of the Madeira-Tore Rise. On the south, an olistostrome, the remains of a landslip from the Gorringe Ridge, has deposited chaotic sediments, such as blocks and mud that accumulates as a semifluid body. *Olistostrome* is a term that is derived from the Greek word *olistomai*, which means to slide. Olistostromes are fragments of rock of all sizes, contained in a fine-grained, deformed matrix formed by gravitational sliding under water and accumulation of flow as a semifluid body with no bedding. In most of the Tagus Plain the crust is 8 kilometers thick; however, in the north it is only 2 kilometers thick.

The Horseshoe Abyssal Plain extends south to the Ampere Seamount and Coral Patch seamount, the Madeira-Tore Rise in the west, and the continental slope in the east. The crust below this plain is 15 kilometers thick. Crustal shortening has been accommodated in the plain by reverse faults every few kilometers.

Ron is comparing maps produced twelve months earlier to fresh maps he's extracting in real time on his notebook computer. He notices that a seamount from an ancient volcano known as the Seine Seamount has collapsed and created a rupture in the crust of the Earth running north through the Horseshoe and Ferradura Abyssal Plains and into the Tagus Abyssal Plain, 175 miles long and 58 miles wide at its widest.

"Ron, do you think this rupture might be swallowing sea-water from the aforementioned basins and possibly resulting in the sea level change?"

"Dr. Reddy, I'm no more of a geologist or oceanographer than you are. I can't say, but I'm going to continue to validate the sea level data and mapping data."

"I think that's a good idea. I'll make a couple of calls to involve the people we need to help us understand what we're seeing here. I'll call you in a few hours for an update."

They end the meeting. Dr. Reddy heads to his office, which is located a few minutes north of town in the prior Montfort of Colorado corporate headquarters. Ron returns to his room at the Best Western to collect documents for the LET project before making the fifteen-minute drive to his office at UNC.

As Ron is walking toward the UNC building entrance, he catches a glimpse of his reflection in the mirrorlike glass structure of the building and pauses for a few seconds to admire his looks. He's in his mid sixties, having turned sixty-four several weeks earlier. He's smiling at his image in the glass and admiring himself as he turns to the left, then to the right before coming back to center. He passes through the revolving door and passes through the main lobby before heading toward his office, which is down the center corridor. Halfway down the corridor, he sees Pat approaching. As they approach one another, he calls out.

"Hey, listen, I'm . . . I'm really tied up with this holographic issue right now . . ."

His work with holography and the LET prototype have the attention and support of several IPCC TSUs. The key innovation of the LET relies on modern holography to process and interpret data beyond 3D length, height, and width, including relative mass of targets being re-created to effectively produce what in a few years' time will become an early framework for developing Star Trek transporter-like technology. The new holographic science is a breakthrough that the IPCC sees as a communication enabler to present climate change simulation to audiences around the world in a dramatic lifelike experience.

The integrated holographic system within the LET is expected to present to an audience a climate change event close up, as if the audience were to be "transported" to the actual location. The LET is designed to reproduce weather-related forces one would experience in an event like a flood, a hurricane, an earthquake, etc., in an environmental setting matching the characteristics of where the event is happening or has happened, like in a jungle, a seacoast village, a city, etc.

Ron's LET is expected to enable the IPCC to demonstrate to a room full of people the actual forces a climate-related event unleashes, using dimensional holographic forms, along with new sensory emitting devices to emit sound and energy to deliver to the audience a never-before-seen, lifelike, real-time experience.

The key enabler of the LET, which Ron has named the holographic energizer, or HOE for short, is its ability to collect information and data about the room in which the machine is being used and then determine how much energy to use in its display capabilities to present a relative proportion of the disturbance associated with the actual climate event. Ron is quoted by *InsideClimate News* (ICN), an independent, non-profit, non-partisan news organization covering clean energy, carbon energy, nuclear energy, and environmental science, as saying, "It's like trying to create a small hurricane or earth-quake in a conference room." He further described the new technology in this interview with ICN saying that the HOE takes information and data about such weather events, and effectively produces a real time resemblance on a smaller scale (i.e., in a conference room or similar location).

The HOE enables the user operator to make changes to the holographic model as in a "what-if" modeling style, by increasing or decreasing the variable intensities related to any kind of climate-related component on the planet, like wind, temperature, barometric pressure, and even seawater tempera-ture, ocean currents, etc. in its theater. It is a brilliant piece of engineering resulting in a tremendous new capability. The IPCC is very eager to begin using it to demonstrate climate change–related events to the general public. Regular press releases concerning the development of the LET track the progress Ron and his team are making.

Pat barely stops walking, just a pause to say, "Yeah, me too."

It might as well have been a loud "Fuck you," Ron thinks. He stands in the corridor watching Pat walk off. *OK, OK, not too bad,* he thinks. He turns and slowly continues down the corridor toward his office. The initial feeling of relief soon leaves him and is replaced by anxiety over his newfound sexu-ality: having a homosexual lover. He thinks that he's become comfortable with the idea that he's taken a man as his lover, but is confused and wonders if, at this age, and still feeling as masculine as ever, *Am I . . . gay? Bisexual? Is it a phase?*

It scares him, as he recognizes his feelings for Pat are as strong as any he'd had with female partners in the past. He remembers their first time, later telling Pat that he thought he was going to have a heart attack when he reached orgasm. It was like no other sexual experience he'd ever had, and each time they were together, the feeling was the same. He wants to be with Pat, but is confused and helpless about what to do about his life with Gwen.

CHAPTER 3

In the Beginning

It's a beautiful, sunny Sunday morning in May. The soft, chilly spring breeze blowing through the hotel room window in Granada, Spain, brings a smile to Eddie Gerber's face as he rubs the sleep from his eyes, thinking about the weekend he and his wife, Camilla, are enjoying in this magnificent city of Ferdinand and Isabella, Columbus, Boabdil, and the Muslim empire that ruled here for 700 years and built such brilliant palaces as the Alhambra.

The Gerbers love Granada, its ancient history and architecture, geography, open-air restaurants, marketplaces, and street life. It is like no other place in the world. It is clean and safe with warm, comfortable Mediterranean weather. However, for the Gerbers, it is time to return to their apartment in Huelva after almost three weeks of roaming and absorbing the beauty of Andalusia.

"Camilla?" he calls to his wife from the bedroom.

"I'm out on the porch, Eddie."

He finds her on the porch reading and drinking her morning cup of tea. "Honey, listen! It all came to me this morning as I was waking up. I mean, this whole Andalusia stay, especially the last few weeks. I'll be right back. Gotta pee."

Eddie is excited about his early morning revelation. He

stands peeing with the bathroom door open so Camilla can hear him.

"And here in Granada it's all beginning to make sense . . . well, a kind of sense."

He wraps and ties his robe around his waist before walking through the bedroom and out on the open-air porch where Camilla, still in her robe, is reading a book and enjoying a peaceful morning tea. She marks her place and puts the book on the breakfast table to give him her full attention. Not realizing he is coming through the opening, she yells out, "What? I didn't—" then stops, realizing he is entering the porch, which looks out across the courtyard below. Off in the distance are the bristled, sunbaked hills of the Sierra Nevada.

As Eddie looks out across the hills at the distant mountains, his waking thoughts are fresh in his mind like an early morning dream. Lying in bed, he speculated if it is karma, destiny, or some unknown force that had brought him to this place, Granada. The final piece of it coming the night before when he and Camilla decided that, before leaving Granada, they would have to visit the Gate of Elvira.

It was already dark when they left the restaurant, but for Eddie Gerber it didn't matter that they were walking through the winding, narrow, dark streets of Granada late at night. It was as if he had been hypnotized; something drew him as they stepped away from the restaurant and decided to walk to see this place where, in much fanfare, Isabella and Ferdinand had accepted the keys to the city from the last Muslim sultan, Boabdil, in 1492. Glorified in several paintings through the centuries, it alone is arguably the single-most defining moment representing Western civilization's determination to go east by going west and, accidentally, discovering America.

Now, Eddie is all over it. It is clear to him that they will definitely sail back home to the States. Flying back is no longer on the table, at least not for him. He will sail back, and furthermore, he'll take the southern crossing, following Columbus's route. It's crystal. It is why he was driven to the Puerta de Elvira the night before, the place from where Western civilization turned and went west to find a new way to Eastern spices, the place from where Isabella subsequently sent couriers to retrieve the departing Columbus who had left the frontier of Granada for France after she had earlier refused several of his proposals.

"Honey, listen . . . I decided that I'm sailing back to the States, not flying. It kind of hit me this morning waking up," Eddie says matter-of-factly while looking out from their balcony. He continues, "The Alhambra, the royal chapel, seeing Columbus's tomb in Seville . . . and then the gates of Elvira last night!" His voice is charged with excitement as he turns to look at Camilla staring up at him from the table chair. "Christ, our apartment for the last few weeks in Spain is in Huelva!" he says with excitement. Huelva is where Columbus lived while courting Isabella and Ferdinand to sponsor his trip to America. "Isn't it as if we were compelled to go there last night?" he asks Camilla. "Christ, we walked so far . . . and in the dark. But the gate was brilliant! Thank god it was illuminated. That would have been disappointing had it been just a streetlight."

The Arco de Elvira, as it is also known, is well lit, and a plaque describes its importance as a Granada landmark. The Gerbers were enthralled that they were able to visit this place in history, and just in the nick of time before leaving Granada.

"I loved seeing it, too, Gerber. After seeing Padilla's

painting of that moment in history . . . it really made it very alive for me, too."

Eddie sits across the table from her now. "Doesn't it make you want to sail back? We'd take the same route!"

"Well, let's look into it when we're back in Huelva," Camilla says and smiles as she stands and finishes her tea. "Right now we have to pack and check out by ten and grab some breakfast at the corner shop."

"It'll be terrific," he continues on about the idea. "There's a zillion things to do, but we have enough time."

"Cup of tea for you, Gerby?" Camilla asks.

"Finding a boat is at the top of the list; learning the local waters, the route . . . we'll get some help from that sailing club back in Huelva. Ah . . . no, no thanks. I'll have some coffee downstairs."

"How about you? Packed already?" she asks.

Eddie stands up and says, "No, but I'm fast. Everything is right here, so I'm good to go in an hour." He touches her arm and kisses her, and then, taking her hand, he leads her across the hall and back to the bed, saying, "Maybe an hour and a quarter."

He closes the apartment door, and they slip back into the king-size bed for a quickie before departing Granada and returning to the ancient city of Huelva along the Gulf of Cádiz.

* * *

Helle Pinzón is not a man who has lived an easy life, although at this stage of his long life, he is taking it easy and making plans to retire—again. A man of considerable years, married several times, children, grandchildren, a large accumulation of wealth from a successful business adventure over the past eight years, Helle has many passions with which to enjoy his wealth. He is winding down his business in Gibraltar and enjoying life while residing along the coast in Punta Umbría, which is just outside Huelva, the capital city in the Spanish province of the same name.

Over the course of his many years as a resident of this part of the Spanish coast, Helle is more than just a proficient sailor; he has written several pieces on sailing and boating, and is a regular contributor to the *Nautic Press, Maritimas, Windsurfer,* and several other publications, the latter being a new passion for him, windsurfing.

Like the mythical Ziusudra, Helle is blessed with genes that enable him to age "gracefully." Still athletic enough to take up windsurfing, he looks a spry fifty but is well beyond that age. His once-reddish hair has now turned to salt and pepper, but is still full and at shoulder length. With light-colored eyes and natural tan complexion, slight build, yet physically a strong man of six feet in height, most women would describe him as being handsomely European or Mediterranean. A widower for more than two decades, his seafaring adventures are responsible for many broken hearts.

A lovely May evening, Helle has cut short a sunset sail to attend the local sailing club meeting being held at the University library in Huelva. He's fifteen minutes late as he walks in and quietly sits in the back near the door as the meeting is already underway. He listens as a newcomer engages the fifteen sailing enthusiasts who make up the club. They sit around a large conference table with a map of the local waters attached by Velcro to the whiteboard at the front of the room.

The newcomer, Eddie Gerber, has the attention of the group as Helle listens in.

"Actually, I've looked at his sailings quite a bit," says Eddie, referring to Christopher Columbus's sailing to and from America. "I'm going to sail to America . . . I mean, Camilla and I."

The group isn't quite sure what to make of Eddie but they are focused on him, as he shares his plan to end a year of vacationing in Europe and sail home to Hoboken, New Jersey.

"Yeah, his first crossing . . . ah, I want to take his crossing," Eddie tells them. "He is a navigator and an admiral for Spain. . . ."

Not for Spain, but Castile. Eddie knows that, but he wants to talk about the sailing, sort of air it out and work out some of the details here. What better place than the library sailing club's forum? The audience is focused and knowledgeable. It won't necessarily be in one night, but he figures it's the best way to prep the trip. After all, he is just a guy from Hoboken, New Jersey. How would he otherwise get the help he needs?

"Actually, he made four voyages to the Americas, first in 1492 . . ." Eddie goes on at length.

Actually, the evening of August 3, 1492, Columbus departed from Castilian Palos de la Frontera with three ships, *Niña*, *Pinta*, and *Santa Maria*. The ships were the property of Juan de la Cosa and the Pinzón brothers (Martín Alonso Pinzón and Vicente Yáñez Pinzón), the monarchs forcing the Palos de la Frontera inhabitants to contribute to the expedition.

Eddie is planning to sail the same route. He wants to buy a boat in Palos de la Frontera, sail the local waters and become familiar and comfortable with the boat, and take Christopher Columbus's route to America. Having sailed across the northern route to Europe a year earlier, Eddie is confident he can make the southern sailing once he's comfortable with the boat.

"It's been done a zillion times. Like Columbus—first stop, the Canary Islands."

Ah, the Canary Islands. Eddie is just hitting his stride.

"Actually the Canaries were ruled by the Crown of Castile. So like Columbus, everybody stops, including us, to restock provisions, make repairs . . ."

Eddie goes on as Camilla daydreams about the Alhambra's majestic gardens and towers. She is not looking forward to sailing back; the trip across the Atlantic to Europe was enough sailing for her. She is planning to fly home.

But Eddie is now hell bent on sailing back—witness the library conference. Not a big group, but in the town of Huelva, getting twenty people together in the library on a Tuesday night, it is the biggest single gathering in town, and for Eddie, having easily assembled fifteen knowledgeable sailors to discuss his plans, brilliant.

Camilla knows he is sailing back; he, however, doesn't know she isn't. She tells herself that, in the end, it doesn't matter any more than if they had decided to take different routes home from Manhattan to Hoboken. Like, "OK, sweetie, see you at home; I'm stopping at Macy's."

Eddie goes on and on for another twenty minutes about winds, currents, and routes. "While securing provisions from the island of La Gomera, Columbus received word that three Portuguese caravels had intentions of capturing him . . ."

Camilla excuses herself for the restroom as Helle takes a seat at the conference table. He has been listening intently and is interested in Eddie's knowledge of Columbus's voyage and hearing more about his impending sail to America.

Helle is an unusual human—over 100 years old. He is of a breed of people very small in numbers who don't get sick, stay healthy and safe. They possess a rare gene that enables them to live beyond normal mortality. They protect and hide their identity from the public, but instinctively are aware of others like themselves, yet avoid contact. Helle is fascinated by Eddie Gerber's discussion with the group.

"On September sixth, he departed San Sebastián de la Gomera for what turned out to be a twelve-week voyage across the ocean."

"Five!" Helle calls out.

The group's focus hesitates for a moment.

"So what kind of boat are you going to sail?" one of the club members asks.

"Well, I'm looking for a forty footer. It's gotta have size to hold all the crap—ah, I mean provisions and equipment . . . ah, pretty special."

"Well, it really doesn't have to be special," Helle says. "People have made it across the Atlantic in a twelve footer."

Again, the group goes quite. Helle is right. People have done it in small boats.

Helle continues, "You know, there was a time when a proper blue water cruiser had chines, a ketch rig, and self-steering gear at the stern. But that is a perception, and perceptions change. Numerically, the most common transatlantic yachts these days are ordinary production cruisers with standard kit."

Now Eddie's ears are open. This fellow who just walked in knows about sailing. *Good*, he thinks. Here is someone he can talk to about sailing across the south Atlantic.

"Hey, there's no real mystery to sailing three thousand miles downwind. The toughest part is getting across Biscay."

"I'm not taking the northern route," Eddie says.

The Bay of Biscay is the large gulf off the northeast Atlantic Ocean, located south of the Celtic Sea. It lies along the western coast of France. Eddie, having taken the northern route sailing from the United States, is familiar with this large body of water, which is directly north of Portugal and Spain and west of France.

"I'm headed to the south, Christopher Columbus's route."

"Well, whatever boat you have right now, the chances are that, with a bit of extra prep, she'll be fine for an Atlantic crossing. Ah, a watermaker, a generator, SSB radio—but you know every additional item adds complication and service cost, time. . . . So apart from a sound boat, all you really need is water, food, fuel, and a copy of the Atlantic, the southern part."

Eddie is impressed.

Helle has sailed across several times over his life, which had begun a long, long time ago in this very region in Spain, and earlier, like Columbus himself, in Genoa, Italy. "You know, it's important to keep it simple. It's all about consistent speed, twenty-four hours a day—no downtime."

"Really? Are you familiar with the ARC rally?"

"Yeah," Helle replies. "But never did that sailing with them . . . but I've sailed across. There's no need to fiddle around with twin headsails, twistle rig, or an asymmetric spinnaker. A main and poled-out Genoa 'barn doors' setup will do fine."

Just then the meeting coordinator, Captain Rodriguez, announces that he has to interrupt the meeting until next month. Two hours have come and gone, and the library will be closing in fifteen minutes. He thanks everyone for coming and asks everyone to join him next month at the same time when his friend, retired Admiral Architzela of the Royal Navy of Spain, will join them. The room quickly begins to empty.

Eddie wants to continue discussing sailing with Helle. "Excuse me," he says to Helle as they walk from the room. They shake hands, and Eddie introduces himself and Camilla. "I'm interested in hearing more about your sailing adventures, particularly the Atlantic crossings to the US."

"When are you planning to depart?" Helle asks.

"No later than August, maybe earlier."

"When did you sail over?"

"We sailed here last May and have been traveling across Europe and Central Asia since. Now I'm focused—*we're* focused—on sailing back. I've been planning and looking at boats since mid-February. Now it's May, and I'm ready to buy a boat and get underway, just a little time in the Atlantic getting used to the new boat, and then sail home."

"Well, just keep an eye out for chafe, and be sure to set up a preventer on the boom and a foreguy topping lift, and down-haul when poling out the headsail so you can furl in quickly when that nighttime squall hits."

"Which it will," Eddie says with a chuckle.

"Have a good night. Maybe see you next month if you're still here," Helle says as he waves and heads toward the exit.

"You, too."

Looking at Camilla, Helle smiles and says, *"Buenas noche, señora."*

She acknowledges this by smiling at him, replying, *"Y a usted, señor."*

Helle walks briskly to his waiting Uber as Eddie and Camilla straggle behind before reaching their Uber for the quick ride back to the apartment.

"Gerber, I can tell your heart is set on sailing back to the US. You're becoming obsessed with it. Why can't we just fly back, make it easy on ourselves?" Camilla thinks it is a good time to confront him on the issue before he finds a boat. "Eddie, you know I'm planning to return to work shortly. There's a lot for me to become reengaged with at the IPCC. My sabbatical ends in August."

Although he is looking at her and wearing a smile, Eddie is only half-listening. He thinks for a minute before answering. Camilla is looking out her window with a worried look on her face. He lightly clasps her hand. She turns and returns his smile.

"Sweetheart, it's a mystery to me as well. I mean, why I become compulsive over some things . . . like this. I feel as if I'm standing in the center of a hurricane and life's riches are circling. I only know that I'm strongly compelled toward certain ones and feel that I stand the chance of missing them as they're being sucked away by this storm called life. Don't you ever feel this about life . . . that it's like a moving target, a swirling thing made of people, places, opportunities that come and go?" Eddie is working himself up.

Smiling but sounding a little annoyed, as if she has heard this before, Camilla says, "I'm . . . sorry Eddie, I don't sense this. For me life's waters are calm. There's no storm, just several rivers that flow in various directions."

The driverless Uber car turns and announces that they will arrive at their apartment on Calle San Sebastian in two minutes.

"Honey, it's not like that for me at all. Life is like something swirling, moving quickly like a carnival ride. And just like the carnival, at times it is surreal, and I wonder whether this thing we know as life is life . . . or something else. We don't know 'cause we've not experienced death. Maybe this is death."

"You're talking crazy now, Gerber, and you're scaring me a little too." Camilla's smile dissolves to a look of concern.

"I know. I'm getting a bit carried away with the life-death stuff. That's just the junk that comes sometimes when I smoke pot. Let's go eat something and talk about the sailing."

Gerber makes an entry in the Uber's display that reroutes them to Palos de la Frontera. In a few minutes, they are across the Rio Tinto. They pull up to the curb several blocks short of the restaurant and decide to stretch their legs by walking the rest of the way to Sergio's tapas bar.

Palos de la Frontera, with a population of 8,415, is a small town situated eight miles from Huelva. It is from here Columbus set sail on his historic voyage in August of 1492. A town of long seafaring tradition, Palos de la Frontera is the cradle of the discovery of America, since it is from its port that the three caravels set out, to arrive two months later at the remote and strange lands of the New World.

Today's port of Palos de la Frontera has lost some of the sociopolitical drama that it enjoyed 500 years ago, since it is nowadays situated inland due to the 1755 Lisbon earthquake that altered the coastline, and also more recently, due to the construction of the docks that shelter the port of Huelva. However, despite these changes, everything in this town recalls the 1492 adventure.

A small monolith stands across from the Mudéjar doorway of the church of San Jorge from the fourteenth century, with the engraved names of the seventy sailors from Palos who took part in the discovery of America. In the town's main street is the house that belonged to the Pinzón family, now restored and bearing its coat of arms. In the outskirts is the Fontanilla, a Mudéjar fountain that was declared a National Monument, where Columbus supplied his caravels with water for the long journey. In the vicinity of Palos, on the banks of the Rio Tinto, is the monastery of La Rábida, where Christopher Columbus stayed. Inside, the frescoes by painter Daniel Vázquez Díaz depicts scenes from Columbus's discovery.

The Gerbers have been enjoying Europe ever since sailing a year earlier from Hoboken, New Jersey. It has been a well-deserved vacation, one during which they've enjoyed sailing, skiing, motorcycling, sightseeing, and the great foods of the continent. It soon will be coming to an end, and in its place, weeks at sea, if Eddie Gerber succeeds in his quest to follow Columbus's adventure.

But Camilla only sees the cathedrals, palaces, frescoes, monasteries, and countryside of southern Spain. For her, the idea of weeks at sea is worse than going back to work after vacation—much worse. She likens it to having to face serious surgery. Not only is it something she doesn't want to do, but also it scares her, the idea of being at sea for so long. Things could, and do, go wrong, not to mention weeks again with just the two of them alone at sea and dealing with Gerber's rants, the arguments, his stubbornness. She tells herself that she can't go through it again; it'll drive her crazy, and there's no way they both will step off the boat in America. She tells herself that she's not going to make the trip with him. She just hasn't decided when or how to tell him, although they both know that she has every right to say no and fly back home. This they had agreed to before sailing to Europe.

Now, as they walk toward Sergio's, her feelings about

sailing back home shift again. The romance of the trip stirs within her; the palaces and cathedrals, frescoes, monasteries and countryside, all of it would be encapsulated in sweet memories and completed by their days, weeks, in deep blue water as they sail back home. Ah . . . it is like a book, and she is caught up in the romance of it all, and, at least for the moment, she doesn't want it to end. But Gerber, she reminds herself, is now talking of sailing routes, buying a sailboat, prepping it, and sailing again. That is the reality of it, and she tells herself to snap out of it and shake free of the romance. *I have to tell Eddie in no uncertain terms that I'm not going and tell him tonight,* she thinks.

Sergio's tapas bar is crowded as usual but does not disappoint. The Gerbers stuff themselves on calamari, salted shrimp, and beer before returning to the apartment and settling in for the evening with a glass of sherry.

Eddie falls into the couch and begins paging through a sailing magazine. Camilla stops in the bathroom and then fetches her PC and begins reading her email sitting across the room from Eddie. She can tell from the pace at which he's turning pages that he's not reading, just paging and stopping occasionally to glance at an advertisement. She can sense that any minute he's going to start off on whatever it is that's on his mind.

Mmm. She begins to play a game with herself to see if she can guess what's coming. *Let's see; we just had tapas at Sergio's bar after the sailing club meeting. The tapas were a little dry, the table a little wobbly, service OK, crowded as usual. Earlier we were at the sailing club meeting and the new guy at the club. What did he say his name is?* she asks herself. *Oh, yeah . . . Helle.* She thinks through his attributes: ruggedly handsome, sailing experience, sexy. *Wouldn't mind a few days on a boat with him,* she chuckles and realizes that it's been a long a long time since she felt sexually attracted to anyone besides Eddie. She recalls how she had felt an unusual attraction toward him when she first spotted Helle in the back listening to the sailing club discussion. She dismisses the thought as Eddie tosses the magazine onto the coffee table.

"I like what that guy had to say at the meeting," he calls out.

Camilla thinks, *That in itself is a bit unusual . . . very unusual for Eddie to have anything but sarcasm about someone he'd just met.* She looks at Eddie with a questioning expression.

Eddie thinks for a moment and continues, "I mean about keeping the boat simple. It should be an easy crossing, the southern route at the end of August."

Camilla nods in agreement but thinks that there must be more coming from him after ten minutes of paging and staring at the magazine.

"I wonder how old he is," she says to encourage Eddie.

Of course Eddie isn't interested in his age, but Camilla's prompt works.

"That little tirade of his is supposed to impress us, I guess. He spoke pretty good English too. I mean, half the time my Castilian gets me there in conversations about sailing. I think he might be able to help us find the right boat. I mean, he might be familiar with the boatyards and suppliers."

Camilla thinks, *But why would he want to, and when will we see him again? In a month?*

Instead she keeps the conversation on course and says in a speculative tone, "He also could have lots of sailing experience, I mean as far as plotting the course and all."

"Well, I don't know about that," Eddie responds.

Camilla had anticipated that coming from Eddie, the great navigator he thinks he is.

"Hey, you know as well as I do, Camilla, that there's lots to do. Maybe it's time to think about some real help that can actively participate in making it work. In Hoboken we had plenty of help before we sailed. Jesus, what would I have done without Larry? And God knows you're not being as much help now as back then. You seem to be more interested in what's here on dry land and back in the office rather than setting sail."

"You know, Eddie, that's not fair!" she protests. But it is true; Camilla has her work on her mind but resents the unkindness of the comment after all they had been through in the initial crossing. Besides that, she is taken a little by surprise when, for the first time, Eddie admits that, without his old buddy Larry Frampton, they'd still be doing northeast sailings and getting ready to sail across the northern Atlantic. Larry had the time, love of sailing, experience, knowledge, and patience with Eddie to help prepare the boat and make several prep sailings with them along the eastern coast of the United States so that they'd be ready and excited about setting off on their first Atlantic crossing—a daunting task for most, to say the least.

Gritting her teeth, Camilla stays silent while feeling like whacking Eddie in the back of the head and cursing him out. But she holds back and lets him have the moment, wondering if the newcomer is somehow her lifeline and can save her from having to make the return crossing with Eddie. Thinking back on it, she hated the weeks it took to sail across. It was too long and tedious. Life with Eddie in such close quarters for such a long time was misery. His ranting, sarcasm, and narcissism became unbearable after several days. She thinks that she would have surely pushed him overboard or poisoned him or gotten rid of him any number of ways if she could have been sure of finishing the trip on her own.

It wasn't possible, so she had to put up with him and think about the splendor of living and touring Europe once they had completed their sail and sold the boat. Long before they arrived in Wales, she vowed to herself that she would not make the return sailing. Back in Hoboken, long before their departure, they had agreed that if either one wanted out of the return sailing, it would be up to the other to find a sailing partner for the return or they would both fly back to the States. So Camilla speculates if the newcomer at the meeting is her way out.

Somewhat playfully, yet in a resenting tone, she remarks, " And excuse me, Mr. Magellan. Have you forgotten who sailed here with you? I have been both supportive *and* accompanied you to the meetings. Let's not forget, OK?"

Sensing Camilla's annoyance, Eddie flashes back a smile, indicating his agreement, but does not apologize. He picks up the magazine again and, in a low voice, asks, "What did he say his name was?"

"Helle," Camilla quickly responds, "as in where you can go—to hell!" She gets up and exits toward the hallway, yanking the magazine from his hand and tossing it to the chair. Eddie is lucky to have not pissed her off too badly. Camilla is very capable of kicking his ass, having been a military brat and holding high ranks in various styles of martial arts—a remarkable women of intelligence, looks, physically fit, and more than most men are able to handle should she decide to inflict physical harm.

On her softer side, she is still as lovely now in her late

fifties as when she and Eddie Gerber met some twenty-plus years earlier, a shapely women, five feet eight inches in height, with blond hair at shoulder length, blue eyes, and a pretty smile. She and Eddie had met while working at Merrill Lynch, building derivatives management software. A couple of years later, they left Merrill to team up and develop hedge fund software as independent developers. It made them millions. Gerber's first marriage was failing, and soon after Merrill, he and Camilla fell in love and married once he became divorced.

Camilla's childhood, however, was not quite as rosy a picture. She grew up in a dysfunctional Swedish family on the continent and had moved between several foster homes while still in her teens before finally being adopted by her US Marine parents while they were stationed in Frankfurt, Germany. Soon after adopting her, they moved to an area near Fort Knox, Kentucky, where her parents became permanently stationed. Her natural mother, a drunk and prostitute, was dead; her father had vanished soon after her mother's death. She had one sibling, a twin sister, Lisbeth, who had rebelled and run off while in their teens and had not been seen or heard from in over thirty years.

Camilla's and Lisbeth's attitudes and outlooks on life were at opposite ends. While both very bright, Camilla's course through life was one of achievement, distinction, and success. Lisbeth was the rebel and exhibited little sign of interest in achieving success through any of the normal channels.

Camilla was amazed when Lisbeth actually ran, but understood her wanting to get away from their life as wards of the state, foster homes, and dysfunction. She respected and admired her sister for that, but felt hurt and betrayed by her sudden departure, lack of communication, and her leaving

Camilla to deal with the prospect of adoptive parents, the US Marines, and the eventual move to America. It was a lot to digest, but Camilla had embraced the changes and shined as a young adult in America. Citizenship followed, college, a successful career in management information systems, banking, and now the IPCC.

CHAPTER 4

Huelva

Eddie has been scouring the marinas along the coast, looking at sailing vessels and talking to the brokers he found listed in the sailing magazines. He began the search just days ago after the library sailing club meeting, looking in the Port Mazagón marina in Huelva, after which he and Camilla drove an hour west along the coast to the Isla Del Moral Canal marina to see several boats available for sale. They decided to spend the night in the adjacent island city of Isla Cristina and enjoy its reputation for fresh and delicious seafood and to look at a couple of boats the following day.

In the morning, Eddie receives a call from a broker in Seville who wants him to see a boat in the marina Chipiona, which lies at the mouth of the River Guadalquivir. It requires more than a two-hour drive from Huelva, going around the Donna National Park, through Seville to the east, and likely means spending the night in the town of Chipiona. Camilla is already fed up after the two-day search and wants to get back to Huelva to see more of Andalusia.

They arrive back at the apartment in Huelva when the broker calls and convinces Eddie that it's worth the drive to see the 2008, forty-six-foot Oyster, which he says is owned by a highly motivated seller. The boat has just come on the market and is part of an estate sale. It likely can be had for half its value, according to the broker, but "you must move fast" is the advice given.

"Gerber, I really don't think a forty-six footer makes sense. The thirty-two-foot Cape Dory cutter we sailed over was big enough."

"I have to at least take a look at it, Camy. It's at the marina along the Guadalquivir. You know, Columbus started his second voyage to America from Seville by sailing down that river. And look, look at this boat! It's magnificent."

The broker sent pictures and specifications: A late model 2008 G5 Oyster, forty-six with shoal draft keel, built to US specifications and set up for shorthanded and blue water cruising with modern safety, entertainment, and communications equipment. Its features include in-mast furling, electric winches, Yanmar inboard diesel with sail drive, bow thruster, twin-zone AC. Perhaps best of all, it has a modern maple interior with teak and holly soles and teak companionway steps for contrast.

Eddie is drooling, and Camilla loves it as well. "My god, Gerber, the main cabin is beautiful. Look at the size of the bed! And the cabinetry . . . a couch, too!"

"It's a piece of floating art!" he exclaims. "Look at the dining cabin, Camy."

"It is spectacular, Gerber, but can two sail it?"

"I doubt it's any more to handle than the Cape Dory once out at sea. It will take some getting used to in the marina, but otherwise, with the electric winches, mast furling, and other electronics, she's practically going to sail herself. Camy, just think of the places we'd go in a boat like this. It's amazing."

Just what Camilla didn't want to hear: more sailing. *What destination would be after this?* she wonders. *Jeez, the Pacific?*

"You go and look at it, Eddie. I'm going to stay in Huelva and see more of the city and the sights here tomorrow. Maybe I'll go see the museum, and the caravels too. They're near Palos"—meaning Palos de la Frontera—"just a few miles away on the other side of the river Tinto, near Sergio's."

Camilla has been itching to visit the museums in Huelva and see the replicas of the three caravel ships that Columbus sailed to America, and the fifteenth-century cultural center. She is also more than a little bit afraid of falling in love with the forty-six foot Oyster and being sucked back into the sailing adventure with Eddie.

"I'd ride to Seville with you, Gerby, but the temperature there is too much for me, already over a hundred the last few days with more tomorrow, and it's not even summer yet."

"Oh, so you rather do the Columbus trail than look at this floating masterpiece with me? Fine."

"Oh, come on, Eddie. I had enough boat shopping the last two days. Can't you wait a day or two? We wanted to see these sights. It's one of the reasons we decided to stay in Huelva."

But Gerber had made his mind up and was going in the morning. "I'm sorry, Camy, but if I wait a day or two, this deal will sail. I have to see it right away. I have an appointment at eleven so I'm leaving at eight in the morning to give myself enough time to get through Seville. There are a lot of berths there, anyway, so I'll see a few others as well."

The next morning Eddie is up at 7 am to shower and dress, reload his overnight bag, and be downstairs at 8 am to meet his waiting Uber. It's already another hot day at this morning hour as he finishes packing his bag and shouts out to Camilla, who is reading the news on her iPad in the kitchen.

"Last chance, Camy. I'm staying at a wonderful apartment on the beach, the Marina Luz."

Camilla is looking through the IPCC news online and barely pays Eddie any attention. "No, Eddie . . . sounds nice. I'm good here. I want to kick back and read the news awhile and then wander through Huelva to the museum and waste the day exploring the 'Columbus trail,' as you like to call it."

Eddie walks into the kitchen where Camilla is sitting. "OK, don't forget the sun block out there," he says and bends to give her a kiss. "I'll call you later this afternoon after I'm done."

"I guess you'll stop for some breakfast before you get on A49?"

Eddie has a chocolate cookie in his mouth and shakes his head yes to reply. She stands and they face each other to say goodbye.

"OK, goodbye Gerby. Love you." She kisses him on the cheek as they walk to the apartment door, his arm over her shoulder, hers wrapped around his waist.

He finishes the cookie and says, "Love you too, Camy," and gives her another kiss before he's out the door and down the stairs.

She waves to him from the terrace overlooking the busy morning street.

From Calle San Sebastian, 8, where the Gerber's apartment is, to the Museo de Huelva, located at Alameda Sundheim, 13, is about a fifteen-minute walk through the twisting streets of Huelva. Camilla spends the rest of the morning planning her day and decides to stop at a couple of the other historical sites on the way to the museum. After a salad for an early lunch, she packs a light backpack and exits to the street.

She takes out her cell phone and enters her first destination and waits while the map function loads and displays the route. With her head still down waiting for the map, her peripheral vision catches a glimpse of someone walking past her, just exiting her building. Suddenly, she hears a voice from the direction of the passerby, *"Hola, como estas?"*

Unsure if it is she who is being addressed, she looks up to see a man in his senior years standing in front of her looking at her. *Is that the guy who's just walked out of my apartment building?* she wonders. He's tall and slender, handsome, sharply dressed in light-colored casual clothes for the warm morning. He wears a multicolored plaid shirt, white slacks, and light brown loafers. *He looks like he belongs on the cover of GQ magazine,* she thinks.

"Ah, que no me recuerda, señora?" the man says to Camilla, asking if she remembers him.

Then it hits her; it's the guy from the library. Quick, she thinks, *What's his name? Don't want to look too stupid. Ah, his name is Helle.*

"Oh, sí, señor. Me has pillado por sorpresa. Estás Helle, correcto?"

"Oh, good. I was worried that I made a bad impression the other night at the library," Helle says, continuing in Spanish. *"Tu nombre es Camilla, verdad?"*

Make a bad impression? Camilla thinks. *He's too beautiful for that.* "No, not at all," Camilla says, changing to English. "Yes, it's Camilla. How nice to see you. What are you doing here?" she asks, laughing in nervous surprise. "Don't tell me you live here, too?"

"No," he chuckles. "But I am looking at an apartment here. Are you here?"

"Yes! Gerber—I mean, Eddie and I are renting here through the summer. The apartments are wonderful, and the central location is perfect."

"Yes, I'm thinking the same. My work situation has changed in Gibraltar, so I'm considering an office and apartment in Huelva. Are you looking for something or need directions?" Helle asks.

"No, I was just waiting for the map to load."

"Where are you going? I know Huelva pretty well."

"I'm basically on the Columbus trail today."

"Ah, OK! Can I suggest La Rabida, which is where you'll find great history and monuments? But it's several kilometers from here," Helle says.

"Yes, I know, which is why I was going to walk to the museum first and then Uber to the other side of the river."

"I guess you're going to see the caravels there too?"

She is laughing. "I know it sounds a little energetic, but the days are long, and . . . well, if you recall my husband, Eddie, and his plan to sail back to the US?" She looks at him with a questioning look, wondering if he remembers that from their library meeting.

He smiles and shakes his head, saying, "Ah, yes, Colombo's route. I remember."

Camilla continues, "He's looking at a boat . . . boats, in Chipiona. I want to see some of the sights here, so I didn't make the trip with him."

"I guess you have it planned out. The museum is just a fifteen-minute walk heading down San Sebastian. At the traffic circle, continue straight; it becomes Calle Pablo Rada. At the end, you'll see a Burger King on the left. There you go slightly left on Calle Palos de la Frontera, which becomes

Calle Fernando el Catolico." Helle hesitates a second before continuing. "I know, you want to ask why must we change street names all the time! *Es una locura*—crazy." They are both laughing as he continues with the directions. "Then a right on Calle San Salvador, left on Alonzo Pinzon, right on Alameda Sundheim, and you're there!" Helle opens his arms wide and takes a bow as she cracks up laughing. In summation, he jokes, "It's a good thing you have the GPS!"

Camilla is laughing and looking at him, thinking how cute he is. "Yes, a good thing," she says, waving the cell phone in her hand. But something has just happened to her inside. He's struck a chord, and she wishes that he wouldn't go away.

"Hey, listen, I don't want you to get lost, which is often the case here in these old Spanish towns."

"You can say that again," Camilla says, still laughing. "We were constantly lost walking in the old part of Granada."

"Seville is like that, too. I get lost walking there as well," Helle admits. "I'd be glad to walk with you to the museum. I've finished my business here and was just going to return home. There's no rush. Why don't I walk you to the museum?"

"Oh no, I couldn't impose on you. That's so nice of you to offer, but really, I'll be fine."

"No, please. It's a lovely day. I've nothing planned till the evening and I can be back home in twenty minutes. Come, it will be my pleasure." Helle extends his open arm in the direction they must walk.

"That's so nice of you. Thank you." Camilla accepts the offer, and they begin down Calle San Sebastian.

They walk on the shaded side of the street at an easy pace. Already the temperature is 89°F. A few awkward moments go by, but Camilla is glad that Helle is accompanying her; she likes his company.

"So, Helle, where is home and why are you looking at apartments here?"

"I have a place on the beach in Punta Umbria. It's an easy twenty-kilometer drive from here on Autovía Huelva-Punta Umbria, or as most people call it, A497."

"Oh, OK. We were on it recently when we went to Isla Cristina."

"You were in Isla Cristina?" Helle asks, sounding surprised.

"Yes, Eddie and I spent the night there two nights ago. We looked at a couple of boats in the marina there. Ahhh . . ." she says unable to remember the name of the marina.

"Isla Del Moral Canal?"

"Yes, that's it. We drove there the day before last after looking at a few boats here in Port Mazagon marina."

"You've been busy. Can't blame you for wanting to take some time to enjoy Andalusia. Did you see anything of interest in a boat?"

"Not really. But then, one of the broker firms Eddie is familiar with called him about a good deal on a forty-six-foot Oyster."

"Oh my god. Forty-six feet! That's wonderful!" Helle is excited for her.

"It's a two thousand eight. The pictures of it are just beautiful."

"Oh, wow. Two thousand eight! You're going to love sailing that boat."

To herself, Camilla says, *No, I'm not.* To Helle, she says, "And it's set up pretty nice for two-person blue water sailing."

"I can imagine! Electric winches, inboard diesel with a sail drive, a bow thruster—it will sail itself! Multi-zone AC. . . . A boat like that can be lived in."

"Not me! No, sir. I've about had enough sailing for one lifetime."

Helle is surprised at her remark as they stop and stand at the Cuesta de la Tres Caídas crosswalk. "Here is the Burger King I mentioned. We're going to go off to the left, just past it, onto Calle Palos de la Frontera."

As they cross and walk past the Burger King, Camilla walks over to look into the window and says, "The ones in the US are different."

"How so?" Helle asks.

"Bigger," she replies.

He looks over at her. "Everything is bigger in the US."

"No, I mean besides the size of the restaurant. The menu is bigger, the idea is bigger. Have it your way," she says, imitating the voice of the American advertisements for Burger King.

They continue toward Calle Palos de la Frontera.

"Do you eat there?" Helle asks her.

"No, do you?"

"No, I'm not a meat eater. I stick to the grains, nuts, fish."

"You are a healthy-looking man."

"Oh! Thank you, *señora*. You also! Oh, I meant, ah, you appear to be a healthy woman—healthy looking."

He's so cute, she thinks, and smiles listening to him stumble through his correction. "Oh, I'm sure I'm not as good as you, but I try, thank you. Living with Eddie means always being on guard against junk food, tapas, beer." They have a laugh. "Hey, don't get me wrong! I love my husband, but some things with him are not easy to get used to."

"Like every marriage, *señora*. I've been married several times myself. It's not always easy, but love and respect see us through the stormy seas. They are our lifesavers."

Camilla looks at him as they walk down Calle Palos de la Frontera. "Helle, that's beautiful, and you are right."

Feeling thirsty, Camilla stops in front of a small market convenience store advertising colas, bread, fruit, and vegetables. "Oh, did you have lunch?" she asks. "I had a salad before leaving the apartment. You probably haven't eaten lunch. Come, let's get something. I'm still a little hungry."

"You're right. I'll grab a piece of fruit and a bottle of water. What do you want?"

"No, it's on me. You're kind enough to walk me through the maze here. The least I can do is get something for you."

"No, *señora*, it's out of the question." He laughs and grabs a bag of Marcona almonds, a bottle of water, and a Coca-Cola and is at the register paying before Camilla can even get to her purse, which is inside the backpack.

"Helle!" She feigns being upset as she reaches into the purse and extends a fifty euro note toward the cashier.

"No, *señora*, I've already taken care of it. We can share the Marcona nuts as we walk." He pushes her arm and hand holding the money back toward the backpack as she laughs.

"You're too much." She playfully punches him in the arm as he snickers in delight at having won the battle.

They exit the store and continue toward the museum, munching on the delicious nuts.

"Have you had these before?" Helle asks referring to the nuts.

"Quite often. Gerber loves these when he drinks sherry, or when he's *not* drinking sherry."

"Ah, yes, they are a favorite with the sherry drinkers. Not my cup of tea, but the nuts are great."

Camilla lets out a breath, relaxed with Helle. She realizes that by referring to Eddie as Gerber, it is an indication of her level of comfort with the newcomer. She hopes the museum is not too close by, as she is enjoying the stroll with him.

They walk slow and quietly for a few minutes, munching the Marconas and looking in the store windows. Near the end of Av Martin Alonso Pinzon, they come to the Plaza del Punto and the Monument of the Virgin of Rocío.

"Helle, do you know about this monument?"

"It has to do with the Madonna of El Rocío or Our Lady of El Rocío in Almonte, which is about sixty kilometers from here. It is by the sculptor Elias Rodriguez, who also did the Monumento a Colón."

"Is it nearby?"

"It's in Plaza de las Monjas, a few minutes. We should go there if you haven't seen it yet."

Seeing the famous monument means walking back in the direction from which they came, but Helle doesn't care. He is beginning to feel that he doesn't want to get to the museum too quickly, either.

"It is the first stop on my itinerary! I'd like to see it!"

"It's just at the other end of Av Martin Alonso Pinzon, if you have the time."

"I have all day!" Camilla gestures with open arms.

"OK, let's go! Who's gonna stop us?" Helle bellows as he begins marching off in the direction from which they came.

Camilla stands watching him and laughing for a second, and then hurries to catch up. "Wait for me, Helle."

Still at marching pace, Helle says, "Ah, look at this plaza! Isn't it lovely? The flowers, the palm trees . . ."

"It is beautiful," she says. "I love the way the Spanish paint these old towns. The colors just sink in with Andalusia."

"Wait till you see the Plaza de las Monjas and the monument! The outdoor cafes, a beautiful fountain—you'll see."

Camilla is ecstatic, and in a few minutes, she makes out the statue at the end of the avenue, still several blocks away. "I think I see it."

"It's one of the most visited places here in Huelva. Some people say it's the prettiest place in town."

Soon they enter the plaza and are looking up at the statue.

"It is beautiful, Helle. The plaza, too."

"Let me take your picture in front of the fountain with the statue in the background." Camilla moves into position, and Helle takes the picture with her camera. "That's a good one. You can send it to *señor* later."

"Good idea," she shouts back to him with a big smile, and thinks about Eddie spending his day going through the marinas instead of being here with her. Or is she smiling for Helle, she wonders.

They wander around the plaza, window-shopping and reading the restaurant menus before ending back in front of the famous statue of Columbus.

"Just point me in the direction of the museum, Helle. I don't want to take more of your time. I can just follow the GPS on my phone."

"No, it's OK. I'm having too much fun and it's not far. Come on, we'll be there in ten minutes, and then you're on your own."

Camilla, too, is having fun. However, thinking about

Eddie shopping for a boat and the inevitable confrontation it will create, it takes some of the wind out of her sail. So as they leave the Plaza de las Monjas, Helle can sense she's changed. The walk back down along Av Martin Alonso Pinzon is subdued, but Helle is having too much fun to let the energy easily escape.

"Hey, come on, Camilla. I'll let you buy me a beer at that market. What do you say?"

It does the trick, as she flashes him a smile and lightly punches him in the shoulder. "Helle, you mentioned that you've had several wives—oh, ah, never mind, you shouldn't say anything. I'm just being nosy."

"No, it's OK. I don't mind. I've . . . outlived three wives, I'm sorry to say. The last one passed nearly twenty years ago. My first wife died too young of a cancer, the second in an automobile accident. I have children from the last two marriages."

"I'm sorry. I shouldn't have asked."

"No, it's OK. I've gotten on with my life in each case, and I've been successful in several careers. I have no regrets, but I miss them. The children are wonderful, but like their father, they live busy lives. We don't get together enough."

Camilla stops in front of the Hotel Eurostar. "Hey, how about that beer? Come on, I'm buying."

They walk through the entrance and enter the bar, which is called La Mirta.

"Now would you look at that," Camilla says, indicating the Alhambra taps on the bar. "*Camarero, podemos tener dos cervezas alhambra por favor?*" she calls out to the waiter and points to the Alhambra Especial tap. They sit at an empty table, and the waiter brings them each a glass of beer. "*Gracias, señor.*"

"*No es nada*," the waiter says as he turns to leave them.

"Ahhhh, that's gooood," Helle says with a big "ahhhh" as he takes a swig of the Alhambra. Camilla laughs at him. "So . . . when do you expect to sail back to the US? Colombo's route. You said earlier you had enough sailing for a lifetime, but *señor* is looking to buy a sailboat, and a rather large boat at that!"

Camilla is sipping her beer and looking down, not knowing quite how to answer. "Actually, Helle . . . I'm sort of dreading it, just the thought. I don't think I can do it, and Gerber is not paying attention to the agreement we made before we sailed from New York, which was that if either of us decided not to sail back, we'd fly back. Now he's on a mission."

"Haven't you said anything about your feelings?"

"I've been giving signals that I'm unsure, which honestly is how I've felt. But now he's on a mission . . . there's no stopping him. Next thing I'll know is that he's bought a boat. It makes me even more resistant to the idea. I mean, he's not even considering the possibility that I might not want to sail back. I'm freakin' annoyed at him about that," she says, sounding pissed off.

Helle takes his hair out of his ponytail and pulls it back and collects it before rewrapping it in a scrunchie. "Maybe you should just tell him."

"I have mixed feelings about it, and Gerber will make me feel guilty that I let him down. I just need to come to terms with it and work it out." She looks down again as if the glass of Alhambra holds the solution. She turns the glass inspecting its label design, a specially made glass for Alhambra pilsner.

Helle sits, looking at her and noticing her pretty face, smooth soft skin, and long blond hair. Sensing her sadness, he thinks, *The poor girl has this resting on her shoulders: she either submits to her husband and puts up with a few weeks of painful duty at sea, or she deals with the guilt trip he'd lay on her if she forces their return by air.*

"You know, Helle, I just would like to enjoy southern Spain before a joyful return to work and feel great about coming back from my sabbatical. But I know he's going to call about a boat he's found and bought." She looks up to Helle with a puzzled look as if he might hold the answer to her dilemma.

"Well, maybe it's not as bad as you think. Maybe you can convince him to sail the boat to the US at a later date, like the next time you take a vacation. The boat could stay at a marina and maybe be rented out. I have a friend in Málaga who could help with that."

Camilla ponders the idea, but doesn't think it will fly with Gerber. "He's not likely to postpone this. But maybe something else will develop to let me step away from it, and . . . thank you, my friend, for trying to help." She touches his hand in gratitude and swigs the rest of her beer.

Helle says, "Hey, I'm ready if you are."

"Aren't you going to finish your Alhambra?" she asks. He hasn't had any since the big gulp he first took.

"I've had enough. Let's go!" He stands and starts to go for his wallet, approaching the cashier.

"If you take your wallet out of your pocket, I'm going to break this empty beer glass over your head!" Camilla yells out to him.

Helle stops in his tracks, remembering she offered to buy him a beer, and slowly he turns toward her raising his empty hands. The waiter comes over and hands the bill to Helle. He passes it to Camilla, and she places a twenty-euro note in the billfold before giving it back to the waiter. They step back onto Av Martin Alonso Pinzon and head toward the museum. In five minutes they are standing in front of the sun-bleached white building that houses the museum.

"Helle, I really enjoyed walking and talking to you. It was very kind of you to escort me. I'd love it if you'd come over for dinner tonight so I can repay you."

"Thank you, but I can't. I have a yoga class this evening at seven, which I can't miss."

"Oh! Ah, that, ah . . . is too bad," Camilla says sadly. It runs through her head that she won't see him again. "Well, promise me you'll come for dinner another time . . . please?" She takes his hand.

"Hey, I have an idea," Helle says. "If you're not busy later, you should come to the yoga. It's at my home in Punta Umbria. It is just twenty minutes from your apartment."

"The yoga class is at your home?"

"Yes, I'm the instructor! It's on my beach! You should come. There's usually at least six or eight others who attend. Do you have something to wear?"

Camilla is excited and flashes a big smile. "I do. It sounds like fun! I love yoga but haven't done it much here in Europe."

"Here, let me give you my address and phone number." He takes a silver business card case from his pocket. "Do you have a pen? This is a business card with my phone, but I have to write the address on the back." Camilla hands him a pen from her backpack, and he writes the address on the back. "Here you go; come a little before seven—no, come at six thirty so I can give you the house tour."

"OK, thank you, Helle. You've made my day." She stretches to kiss his cheek.

"It's been my pleasure, *señora*, and I'm looking forward to seeing you later. I'm sure you'll find the museum well worth it. Their artifacts date back five thousand years and are very nicely displayed."

"Thanks again, Helle. I'll see you later. *Ciao.*"

"Adiós, nos vemos más tarde."

"Sí, adiós," she replies and watches him cross the street to a waiting Uber. She waves as the car pulls away and then gazes at the card seeing his Punta Umbría address. Flipping the card over and reading its printed side, she wonders, "Mmm . . . business services, Gibraltar?" as she puts it in her wallet while approaching the entrance of the museum.

Now on her own and feeling the loss of Helle's company, Camilla makes her way in lackluster fashion through Huelva's history as a mining, manufacturing, and trading center since the Phoenician era. She stops to watch a video and sees photos of ancient burial sites. Her mind slips back to earlier in the day, thinking of Helle, his handsome good looks and upbeat, good-natured, fun character. Upstairs, she wanders through a room full of paintings, the highlight of which is the work by Daniel Vázquez Díaz, a twentieth-century artist from nearby Nerva whose murals on the life of Christopher Columbus are at La Rábida Monastery just outside the city. She reads about Diaz's mural on her cell phone, and finally, she is reignited and decides that she must see the monastery and caravels.

The Uber is waiting in front of the museum and whisks her away toward the other side of the Rio Tinto where the Monasterio de La Rábida and Columbus's caravels are located. *What a great day it's turned into,* she thinks, reflecting on how much she loves Andalusia and meeting Helle earlier. *Can't wait to see him later,* she thinks, and slowly moves her hand under her blouse to touch her breasts. "Mmmm, Helle," she murmurs, recalling his soft hands, his mouth, and...and then tells herself to stop it before she gets carried away. *Save it for the shower, you silly girl,* she thinks, chuckling and smiling to herself.

Passing over the Rio Tinto along the N-442 Highway, she looks out in the direction of where the caravels are docked. They remind her of Gerber's search, and the dilemma she must resolve—and soon. She tells herself not to spoil the day and to forget about it and enjoy the sights. Again, she's uplifted as the Uber pulls into the circular courtyard of the monastery. Its sun-bleached white walls are like so many places in Andalusia she and Gerber have visited.

As she steps out of the car, she begins reading about the monastery from its webpage. The monastery has been a Franciscan property since the thirteenth century, chartered in 1261 by Pope Benedict XIII, allowing Friar Juan Rodríguez and his companions to establish a community on the coast of Andalusia. Christopher Columbus stayed at the friary two years before his famous first voyage, after learning that King Ferdinand and Queen Isabella had rejected his request for outfitting an expedition in search of the Indies. Then, with the intervention of the guardian of La Rábida and the confessor to Isabella, Francisco Jiménez de Cisneros, his proposal was accepted. The friary was declared a national monument in 1856.

Camilla winds her way through the church, cloisters, and reception room. It is in the reception room where the friars met with Columbus and debated theories and speculations about navigation. Camilla is impressed by the frescoes and paintings. She continues through the labyrinth of buildings that make up the monastery and exits to the garden entrance. Next to the entrance is a plaque made of painted Spanish tile work with the inscription:

"The Rábida is the first manifestation of the Hispano-American movement. This place, where the vision of a New World was conceived, is sacred to the hearts of people everywhere. Any Spaniard or American who reflects deeply and elevates his thoughts must ask, 'Won't you help us in our intention to spread love and peace, the forces that radiate from this humble monastery?' Christ, before whom Columbus, Friar Juan Perez, Friar Marchena, and the Pinzóns all prayed, opens his loving arms to men of all beliefs who harbor good will."

Such powerful words, Camilla thinks as she retrieves Helle's business card. "Ah," she says out loud to herself, "I thought so." Reading the printed side, she playfully says, "Helle Pinzón. What a co-inky-dink." She chuckles to herself while replacing the card in her wallet.

*   *   *

Helle is back home at his seaside villa in Punta Umbría, straightening the place so he can give Camilla "the tour." His phone rings.

"Hola, este es Helle," he answers. It is Gerber calling to ask Helle for his advice about the Oyster 46. "No, Señor Gerber, it is fine! I don't mind."

Eddie has just spoken with Camilla about the day's events, both his and hers.

"*Sí*, I'm glad she enjoyed the sites in Huelva . . . and it was no trouble," Helle responds to Eddie's account of his conversation with Camilla.

Eddie switches subjects to the Oyster. "It's an oh-eight, so it has some wear and tear, but its cabins have been refurbished and . . . she is a beauty." He continues on about its attributes for several minutes. "Fiberglass hull, hand-built, easy to handle—"

"I'm familiar with the boat, Señor Gerber. It's a fine one. You may want to refit it with new navigation equipment, depending on what's presently installed, check the engine, fuel tank, toilets . . . there's much to inspect. I know someone in Málaga I'll put you in touch with who can do this."

Eddie continues, bringing up the price he's discussing with the broker. "We're pretty close, and I think I can get it at my offering price."

Helle confirms the offering price is half the boat's value. "I'd be very careful getting it so cheap, Señor Gerber."

"Yeah, I hear ya. We're going to take her out tomorrow and sail up the Guadalquivir on the tide and then out into the gulf—can't wait. Listen, Helle, I'll get the information about your friend in Málaga when I return. Will you be in Huelva, or Camilla thought you may have business in Gibraltar to attend to, possibly?"

"No, I'll be here for a while before returning to Gibraltar. Did Camilla mention I'm looking at an apartment in your building?"

"She did! That's fantastic. When are you thinking of moving in?"

"I'm unsure. I still have loose ends in Gibraltar. Let's talk when you've returned."

"That sounds like a plan, and thank you, my friend."

"*No es nada! Adios,* Señor Gerber."

Helle hangs up and wonders if Camilla has worked things out with him. "Maybe she'll show up for the yoga session and have it all worked out."

He straightens a few items in his office and then walks out onto his patio to check that everything is in its place—the pool, chairs, umbrellas closed. He turns the fountain on, which starts a stream of water from the mouth of a seahorse at the opposite end of the pool. He steps down from the pool patio and onto the beach. A few steps and he enters his yoga den, which is under an open-air tent covering a thirty-foot square parquet floor. The tent walls are sheer curtains billowing in the light sea breeze. He ties back the sheers and lights a tray of incense, then several candles around the floor before returning to select music for the evening yoga session.

He turns to look out behind him to the west at the Gulf of Cádiz, speculating about the evening sunset, and smiles, noticing that a generous portion of high clouds are moving in. "*Ah, mira que hermoso cielo dios está pintando para mí . . . que sea un buen uno, Camilla se acerca.*"

His cell phone alerts him that someone is at his front door. He thinks, *Ah, Señora Camilla . . . temprano. She's arrived at six twenty. Bueno!* He accesses the front door camera from his cell phone. It is Camilla. "*Hola! Yo estaré allí en un minuto,*" he tells her.

"Hi, Helle. Take your time," she tells him as he watches her examine the array of beautiful flower plantings and the manicured landscaped surrounding the property.

Helle is at the door in under a minute. "Thank you for coming, señora. *Es bueno verte otra vez.*"

"It's great to see you again, too, Helle."

He takes her hands and they double-kiss each other on the cheeks. "The pleasure is mine, señora."

"Can you tell me, Helle, how you can grow all these beautiful flowers and lawn in this sandy soil?"

"One word, señora . . . irrigation."

"Ah, of course. That makes sense." She chuckles. "Oh, my . . . look at this place! What a beautiful place you have, Helle."

Indeed, Helle spared no expense, building his home once he succeeded in acquiring and tearing down the three properties his house now occupies. Standing in the front entrance, a large foyer flows straight back to a small sitting area overlooking the patio and pool area with the beach and Bay of Cádiz in the background. A grand stairway sweeps the eyes upward to the second floor, capturing the large crystal chandelier that illuminates the foyer.

"Come, I'll show you the place. Would you like a bottled water?" He leads her through the foyer and into the kitchen.

"Are the others here yet?"

"No, we have fifteen minutes before they arrive. They'll go out to the tent."

"Oh, this is beautiful, Helle," Camilla says as they walk into the kitchen. "I love the cabinetry."

"Oh, thank you, *señora*. I made the cabinets."

"You made these?"

"*Sí*, I once was in the furniture business."

"Beautiful! This work island is great. It must be fun cooking here."

"I love to cook, Camilla. I'll have you and Eddie here soon

for lunch. I make the best linguini and clam sauce, and I'll grill up some fresh fish for us."

Helle watches the slender Camilla, who is dressed in a boysenberry, open-knit, jacquard-patterned yoga tank top and matching floral leggings, as she continues to wander around, examining the kitchen. She opens a large floor-to-ceiling cabinet, revealing an oversized refrigerator, and continues past the double sink, ending up admiring the large circular table that looks out through sliding glass doors and onto the patio. "Oh, and the view! It's spectacular, Helle. You must really enjoy this place."

"Gracias, *señora*. I do, but it's too big for me, which is one of the reasons I'm looking in Huelva to buy an apartment."

"Oh, I see the tent now." She looks up at him, wondering about the tent.

"It's the yoga studio!" he says. "This way to the living room and dining room." He motions toward the archway adjacent to the table.

Before they are able to reach the rooms on the second floor, Helle notices that several participants have arrived for the yoga session and are taking their places on the parquet floor in the tent. He and Camilla exit the house and take up positions with the others. Helle is up front with the Bay of Cádiz behind him, Camilla in the back of the class. Helle removes the light white hoodie he is wearing, revealing a form-fitting Under Armour shirt that covers his slender, muscular physique. Camilla is impressed with his conditioning, thinking he's downright sexy.

The yoga session begins with everyone sitting in the lotus position as Eastern music lightly fills the tent along with the sounds of breaking surf. A light wind gust mixes with the incense and music to fill the senses and relax the mind.

The hour session passes quickly, and at the end, the group returns their yoga mats and props to their storage containers before wishing Helle thank you and good night. Camilla is exhausted from the session and her full day of sightseeing. She remains resting on her mat as Helle walks the others out, wishing them goodnight. He walks back to find that Camilla has moved herself to the front of the tent and now is lying on her side facing the sea and the sunset sky. He thinks she is resting from the yoga session, but in fact, she has again grown somber, thinking of her problem with Eddie.

Helle goes to his phone and starts some soft light music. Roy Orbinson's sad song "Crying" gently fills the tent. Camilla closes her eyes, letting the sweetness of the song fill her, relieving her anxiety.

"*Señora, estás dormido? Me concedes éste baile?*"

Helle holds his hand out as Camilla slowly opens her eyes and comes to a seated position. Looking up at him with sad eyes, she hesitates, then, after a few seconds, takes his hand.

He looks down at her and says, "Do you know what I say to this guy singing when I hear this song?"

Roy begins singing, "Crying over you, crying over you . . ."

Camilla, still with that sad look, shakes her head no.

Helle says abruptly, "Snap out of it!"

For a moment, they are both uneasy and quiet before smiling. He helps her to her feet, and they embrace in a slow dance to the Orbison tune. Camilla buries her head in his right shoulder, feeling a little embarrassed at not being able to control her feelings.

"Señora, I can tell you are still mulling over Señor Gerber," he says.

Camilla lifts her head to look at him while thinking how nice he smells and wonders what the fragrance is.

Helle goes on, "You only need to just tell him. It will work out," he stresses. "He'll find a shipmate or sail back at another time with you. . . . It's going to be OK."

Camilla thinks that she's unable to identify the fragrance. *I think it's . . . ah, the ocean. He smells like the beach, or the ocean.* And then she looks him in the eyes and slowly moves her face toward his and kisses him on the lips.

Helle is surprised, but he's been wanting to kiss her. They kiss for a few seconds, and then Camilla again rests her head in his warm shoulder, now back in the cover of his white hoodie as they continue their slow dance.

"You're probably right, Helle. I'm just going to tell him. Tomorrow he's going sailing and is probably going to make a deal for the Oyster." She raises her head, again looking into his eyes, and continues, "When he calls me about it, I'll tell him that I've made a decision, too, and that will be the end of it. He'll decide what to do and it will work out." She smiles at Helle, and he smiles back, not able to respond verbally; he is lost in her beauty.

Helle is no longer listening to what she's saying. Unable to stop himself, he moves his face closer to hers, and slowly she moves her face toward his and they kiss again. This time it is deeper, longer; holding nothing back, they soon are on fire. Helle reaches down and grabs the yoga mat near her feet and they move, arm in arm, from the tent deck to the beach where it has grown dark and shadowy under the cover of the tall reed grasses and dunes. They find a spot and lie on the mat as the soft filtered light from the tent strikes her breasts as she removes both their tops. They kiss and find each other's bodies, shifting positions on the small yoga mat.

He takes her hand and leads it to find his penis. She takes it and begins to stroke it and runs her thumb across the tip. She is soon straddling him and he is inside her. They continue in several positions before both are satisfied and exhausted, lying in the dunes, cuddling on the mat under a rising moon, kissing and talking about the day they enjoyed with each other.

"Helle, can you show me the rest of your house another time? I have to go. You've tired me out today."

"Only if you kiss me one more time before you leave."

They kiss long and deep.

Helle leads them through the tent and toward the driveway, stopping to embrace her in his arms again. "Hey, Camilla . . . if Señor Gerber does buy that boat, and if he asks me, I'm going to suggest to him that its new name be *Camilla's Kiss*. I'll just ask him, 'What is the sweetest thing you can think of?' He's sure to say your kisses, and I'll yell out, '*Camilla's Kiss*,' and it will be done."

"Don't you dare!" She chuckles at the idea and pushes him away in mock protest before walking toward her waiting car.

Helle laughs and waves from the front entry, calling out good night in several languages.

CHAPTER 5

The Pass

Within a few days, Eddie completes the purchase of the Oyster 46. With Helle's assistance, a plan quickly comes together to sail the boat to Málaga. But first, Eddie and Camilla spend several days sailing the local waters between Chipiona and Huelva to shake down the new boat before sailing it to Málaga. In Málaga, the Oyster will go into dry dock for painting and to update the navigation equipment and anything else they determine needs replacing or servicing. Helle's friend and owner of the marina and shipyard, Rocco, will personally oversee the work.

Eddie has already inspected the engine, electrical system, toilets, etc., and determined they will be fine with some minor servicing. The layover in Málaga is expected to be roughly ten to fourteen days, depending on weather, availability of parts, and specialists.

The evening before they leave the apartment in Huelva to sail to Málaga, Camilla receives a call from Dr. Reddy at the IPCC regarding her return. It's not a call of urgency, but a nudge that it's time for her to return to work. The call excites her desire to return as soon as possible and not to delay returning. It's eight pm in Huelva when Dr. Reddy calls; it's just before noon in Greeley, Colorado.

"Hi Camilla, it's Panalla Reddy! How have you been?"

Camilla falls back into the sofa cushion, elated. "Dr. Reddy, it's great to hear from you, just great. Our trip has been amazing. How are you?"

"Just fine. I meant to call so many times prior . . . earlier . . . So tell me about your sabbatical."

Camilla goes on for several minutes about their sailing and romp through Europe, but she is anxious to hear from Panalla about the IPCC and the work she'll be involved in once she returns. A feeling of being back before you're really there warms over her.

"So it's been really great. Is everything OK with you? I've connected a few times with Ron about his work."

"Just very busy, which is why I never got around to touching base with you. So, I was thinking about your return, and I suddenly got the urge . . . and just called this morning."

"Well I'm glad you did!" Camilla says, excited. "We must be tele-connected! I've been anxious lately to get back. What's going on?"

Panalla begins by telling her about the progress Ron Billings is making on the Living Environmental Theater (LET)—or sometimes called "LET It Be," which had become the unofficial name of the project.

"So!" Panalla says while letting out a deep exhale. "I think you'll be excited to return. Ron is in the final stages of completing the theater. It will be a big win once it's operational."

Ron Billings has been working for nearly three years with several universities to adapt and integrate recent advances in holography for the purpose of developing a climate change simulator for the IPCC. Working with a collaboration of scientists from the University of Waterloo's Institute of Quantum

Computing, the University of Maryland's Joint Quantum Institute, Boston University, and the National Institute of Standards and Technology in Maryland, they have designed and constructed a theater for the IPCC using new holographic capabilities based on neutron beams to create holograms of large solid objects.

Although yet to be live tested, LET will be a quantum leap in applied holographic science by effectively transporting an exact replica of the target area and its characteristics, along with real-time temperature, humidity, wind, movement, sound, g-forces, tides, sea levels, etc., using a plethora of monitoring devices both on the planet's surface and from orbiting satellites. The data recording capabilities of the LET facilitate before and after comparisons of the target environment, as well as replays and "what if" analysis.

The LET, project 05110, largely flies under the radar of the public and the press, like many IPCC projects. For the most part, just Ron and Panalla Reddy are intimate with the details. When other IPCC associates ask about its capabilities, Ron says little, maybe since he's a little unsure exactly what the final result will be, except he's certain his new LET will give the IPCC a dramatically new experience to demonstrate climate change. He's resolute that it will be awesome.

Camilla brims with excitement. "I'm looking forward to returning. I'm sure it will be awesome. Ron has made amazing progress since I left."

Dr. Reddy also informs her of the unusual tidal data and the possibility of a falling rather than rising sea level. "Well . . . Camilla, the sooner you can return the better. A new climate-related issue has surfaced, and I've suggested to Ron we use the LET in beta test mode to support the agency's response to the problem, if it makes sense. However, surprisingly, he's pushed back on that idea, citing resource availability issues and questioning whether it's a suitable initial application, the tidal change issue. I can understand, given his workload over the past year in bringing the LET to the state it is in. So I'd like you to come and take the lead in bringing the LET through beta, and support the agency's presentation to the public with some of the climate issues that have moved to the front burner, so to speak."

Camilla listens patiently as Reddy runs on a bit. She senses a note of concern as he continues.

"You're so graceful dealing with the PR this requires. . . . You know we've spent a lot of time and money on this project, so there will be a good deal of attention when we announce its capabilities. Other agencies will want to look at it—under the hood, I mean—and, of course, use its capabilities for their own purposes. So I need the testing and delivery to be top-notch."

A few seconds of quiet pass before Camilla chuckles and responds, "OK, I hear you Dr. Reddy. Believe me, I'm excited to get back. Like I said, I've been thinking about shortening my time away and not sailing back to the States, but fly back instead. That's a three-week difference."

"You'll be back in three weeks?"

"Possibly, but I only meant that I'll return about three weeks earlier than planned, but I have to finish some work here with my husband before leaving, which will be three or four weeks."

"Oh, that long?"

"I'll have a better idea in a couple of days. It could be less, but we're outfitting a new sailboat. In a few days, we'll have a better idea of the time required to do this. I also have to break it to my husband that I won't be sailing back with him. Possibly a friend will make the trip with him."

"Really? You haven't discussed this with him yet? Does your friend sail much?"

"I've been hinting. But, Dr. Reddy, what else can you tell me about the nature of the new climate issue you mentioned?"

"Well, I'm still examining the data. However, I can say it involves tidal data . . . and . . . sea level changes."

"Accelerated rising sea level data?"

"Falling. Reporting stations in the Atlantic—we're still validating and verifying the data and inspecting the equipment, which takes time. Camilla, I have to break off now. I enjoyed talking with you and happy to hear you're enjoying the sabbatical. So as soon as you know your return date, let me know . . . OK?

"OK, Dr. Reddy, I will. Thanks for calling."

They bid each other goodbye. Camilla stares at the phone in her hand for a few seconds, smiling and thinking about her call with Dr. Reddy, the LET, Ron Billings, and the accolades it will bring him and the IPCC.

Falling sea levels? she questions herself, wondering if the data will be validated. *Probably not,* she thinks. *The reporting stations are messed up—or, some program change affecting the reporting system.*

Sea levels had been rising for many years despite the many changes adopted around the world. "Well, maybe they're finally starting to work . . . yeah, right!" she says to herself and lets out a laugh.

"What's that, honey?" Eddie asks as he walks into the room.

"Oh, Gerber," Camilla gushes with enthusiasm. "You won't believe who I just got off the phone with."

"Well, let me guess . . . Paul McCartney?"

Camilla stands up, looking him in the face, still glowing with excitement despite disapproving of his joking around.

"No? Let me see," Eddie continues, still joking. "Was it that handsome devil on the cover of the *Yachting Times Magazine?* I saw you staring at him over coffee this morning."

"Very funny, you. . . . No, that was Dr. Reddy on the phone."

"Dr. Reddy? Was he calling to say he's ready? Ahahaha!"

"You idiot. Dr. Reddy from the IPCC—my boss!"

"I know, I'm just kidding with you, Camy. We met once—a nice guy. It was at one of those IPCC booze weekends in the mountains. I asked him, 'Are you ready, and if you are, what are you ready for?'"

"I hate it when you drink too much."

Eddie laughs. "Nice guy! Smart, lots of energy, *and* he has a sense of humor. I guess he wants you to come back to work."

"Yes!" Camilla was again excited, recalling the call from Panalla. "There's a lot going on. Ron's project is nearing beta test, and I'm going to bring it into production."

"That's wonderful, honey. I recall he was integrating several new technologies involving holographics. Sounded awesome on the drawing board."

"It is. Oh, Eddie, this is great news as my sabbatical draws to an end."

"What else is new out there in them there hills of Colorado?" That is how Eddie referred to the plains on the eastern front of the Rockies where Greeley is located.

"Oh yeah, there is something else! Dr. Reddy—I mean, the IPCC work groups—are investigating reports of falling tidal levels in the Atlantic. I'm wondering if we might tie this

issue in somehow as part of the beta test application data."
Camilla walked over and hugged Eddie and, with a smile
asked, "Isn't it terrific, Gerber? I mean, I was worried about
returning, not knowing what I'd be involved with, and now
this. Isn't it just great?"

"You have all the luck, Camilla. We'll need it tomorrow
on *The Kiss,* so let's get to bed early. I have something to show
you."

They kiss.

"What's that . . . that you want to show me?" she asks.

Eddie smiles and leads her by the hand toward the
bedroom.

Camilla is giggling. "You're being a dirty old man, aren't
you?"

"Horny, not dirty, my dear."

Standing in front of the bed, they hug and kiss again
before undressing each other.

She breaks away from his mouth, whispering in his ear,
"Is this what you wanted to show me?" She takes his penis in
her hand. Eddie's head drops back; a smile comes to his face
as she moves behind him while gently clutching his penis and
scrotum. Suddenly she pushes him onto the bed face down.

"Let's see it . . . what you want to show me, Gerber."

He rolls over, exposing himself. "What do you think?" he
asks.

"I've seen it before. It'll do."

They exhaust one another and sleep until the alarm wakes
them at 5 am. They eat a quick breakfast and are soon on the
water sailing southeasterly along the coast of Spain toward
their first port of call, Cádiz.

Camilla settles into a cushion near the bow, leaving Eddie

at the helm enjoying the new boat. It had been settled that they'd sail to Málaga with stops in Cádiz and Gibraltar. Helle is to meet them in Gibraltar, arriving earlier to conduct a couple of days of business before the Gerbers arrive. Together, the three of them will sail on to Málaga to meet Helle's friend, Rocco. The first leg of this multiday sailing to Málaga will take the Gerbers across the Gulf of Cádiz to the peninsula town of Cádiz.

Huelva to Cádiz is an all-day sail of roughly fifty nautical miles. It's a good distance, which the Gerbers can accomplish in full daylight while continuing to assess the boat's sailing habits and capability, its storage, comfort deficiencies, etc. They will continue to "shake down" the boat en route to Málaga, where they will make improvements, replace old, worn, and broken items, and give her new paint and her new name, *The Kiss*.

Near the end of the uneventful trip to Cádiz, Camilla opens her MacBook and begins a new entry into her journal. She writes about how much fuss had been made by Gerber and Helle of Gerber's selection of the new boat. She writes, "The two of them blew a lot of hot air; much ado about nothing, settling on the Oyster 46 cutter. Gerber is playing it smart and keeping it simple, as Helle suggests. By sticking to a relatively simple, single mast design like a cutter, it will make for easy handling, yet its two smaller headsails can be deployed for greater power as compared to a sloop."

During Eddie's search and rigging, Helle would stress to him to follow the K.I.S.S. method in all things about sailing. This meant to "Keep It Simple, Stupid." Eddie, soon after getting to know Helle, began to put stock in his knowledge of sailing and got on board with K.I.S.S., so much so that he is planning to have the boat renamed *The Kiss* once in Málaga.

As Eddie sails through the wide inlet toward the port of Cádiz, Camilla is reminded of how advanced Spain, and Europe in general, is in its use of alternative energy. There, in the distance on the coast, adjacent to the sprawling port of El Puerto de Santa María, are hundreds of windmills turning lazily in the light wind, as if waving hello to the Gerbers as they make their first port of call.

She makes another entry into her journal. The windmills make her think of getting back to the IPCC, and of the updates she had been getting from Ron Billings by email. She makes one final entry as Eddie calls to her that he is taking in the sails to go in under engine power. She writes, "It is time to go back to work ... becoming tired of sailing ... wish Helle was here in my place."

That torch had not yet been passed, but Camilla is determined to make it so before reaching Málaga. She has roughly four days to find the right time and words. She promised Helle that she'd tell Gerber during the shakedown sail to Málaga. "Keep it simple," Helle stressed to her. "You want to go back to work; it's as simple as that. You've sailed across the Atlantic, for heaven's sake, and you've been through a great deal of Europe with him. Don't be surprised when he says it's all right. He'll be OK with it. Don't be so hard on yourself. That's it, you know—you're feeling guilty but you shouldn't be."

Helle saw and explained it so simply. Camilla kidded him that he lived in the world of K.I.S.S., but he made her feel at ease, and she realized he was right. She'd handle it with Gerber, no problem. Even without Helle being there to support her, she'd take care of it, and so they agreed that she and

Gerber would sail to Málaga while Helle tied up his affairs, enabling him to sail to America with them.

"Hey, honey, do you see all those fucking windmills?" Eddie excitedly barked. "There must be a thousand of them. Some sight! Can you come and take the helm while I get the sail in?"

Camilla moves from the bow toward the stern, admiring the sight of *The Kiss*'s mast. She thought it to be massive compared to the mast of their thirty-two-foot cutter. Taking the helm, she feels good about reaching their first port and getting back on land. She breathes a breath of relief. *Everything had gone right,* she thinks as the Port of Cádiz becomes visible less than a mile off starboard. The cruise ships, municipal buildings, statues and domed cathedral are rising up from sea level, all shining in the late day sun. "It's beautiful," she yells to Eddie.

"Wow! Looks like a beautiful place to spend the night," Eddie says as he ties the sail and Camilla turns toward starboard, past the buoy and jetty marking the harbor. Then, passing the shipyards she heads for the harbormaster's dock.

"You're a natural, Camilla. Nice job." Eddie is glowing, having just completed his first solo sail of the soon-to-be-named *Kiss*.

"Well, I've had a lot of experience, you know . . . and good teachers."

Eddie returns to the helm to stand with her as they approach the dock. "You're gonna love this adventure, Camilla. The southern crossing—it's gonna be fucking great. Like how Columbus felt." He takes her around the waist and lands a big kiss on her lips.

Steering the forty-six-footer feels good to Camilla; she

likes it. She thinks how their first night in a new port is always a fun night filled with new foods, shops, wine, the local people, and their culture—and of course, celebratory sex. *It's going to be fucking terrific,* she thinks, *but* . . . Again, thoughts of the crossing creep back in. All those days, weeks at sea would be unbearable. Even with Helle, it still would just be the three of them, and she did not want to test her feelings for Helle in that way.

Eddie takes the helm and asks her to ready a rope to toss to the harbormaster as they approach the dock. "Hey, we made great time and have hours of daylight left! Let's get tied up and head into Cádiz."

Indeed, they had made the trip in under five hours, taking advantage of the strong easterlies, which at times gusted to twenty knots.

Camilla yells back, "Beautiful Cádiz," and tosses a rope to the waiting attendant.

"La bienvenida a Cádiz," the attendant calls to Camilla.

"Gracias," she replies.

"Su nada."

And just like that they are tied up. Simple. *Su nada.*

They grab a day bag and head into the center of Cádiz, a short walk from the dock. The colorful Plaza de San Juan de Dios greets them, filled with palm trees, fountains, and a beautiful statue of Segismundo Moret standing in front of the sun-bleached town hall building. Hundreds of tourists fill the plaza and dine outside at the many tapas bars and restaurants.

As they walk further into the plaza, near the entrance to town hall, a flamenco dancer attracts a large crowd of onlookers. Even with the shadows growing long, the temperature still reaches into the upper eighties. The dancer is in a long flowing dress, sleeveless blouse and scarf, and is working up quite a sweat for the euros placed in her hat. They watch her for several minutes, admiring her dancing skill, colorful dress, and resilience.

Placing a few euros in the dancer's hat, the Gerbers continue on, wandering through the narrow streets, past the gold-colored dome of the central cathedral, reaching the opposite side of the peninsula and the white sands of La Caleta beach where they are soon in their bathing suits, swimming and enjoying the late day sun on rented lounge chairs with a glass of sangria. Camilla dozes and Eddie gazes across the bay while spotting several nearby topless bathers.

All is good in Gerberdom, he quietly comments to himself.

But a storm is brewing in Camilla's head. She doesn't want to force her decision on Eddie. No, she feels it should be mutual. After all, he had agreed to the option before they left Hoboken. She can see in his face as they play in the water that he is glowing. Is the time right to break it to him? Or will he go off wildly and accuse her of being a "buzz killer," one of his favorite accusatorial expressions. *Not now,* she thinks. *Later, something to sleep on.*

"Camilla, are you awake?"

She turns her head toward him. "It's so beautiful here."

"I know, but it's getting on. Better put your top on and think about dinner and heading back."

She takes his hand and smiles. He kisses her and quickly they change and are walking through the center of Cádiz where they stop for some beer and tapas and shop in a small grocery, buying a bottle of Lustau Oloroso.

Back onboard, Eddie pours two glasses of the sherry and plates a portion of chips and olives stuffed with anchovies. He

picks up his phone and starts a song by the Rolling Stones—
"Tell Me (You're Coming Back)."

It was their unofficial wedding song, which Camilla soon
melts away into while sipping the sherry and munching an
olive and potato chip. Eddie lights up a joint and soon begins
to sway with the beat and sings along.

"Gerber, you look so sexy in your Speedo on the beach
today. Come here." Camilla holds her hand out.

He sings along with Mick and reaches toward her with the
joint, and she takes a hit. The bottle of Lustau flows, and soon
they taste the sherry on each other's lips.

As "Mother's Little Helper" begins, Eddie reaches into
a nearby desk draw for a little blue pill. Popping it into his
mouth, he gives instructions to Camilla, "If I'm not done in
four hours, call a physician."

Camilla bursts out laughing and lies back on the cushion.
"Aren't you a little late on that blue magic?"

"How did you know that is the name of this pot?"

Again she is laughing and can barely speak as she corrects
him. "It's called Blue Dream! Not Blue Magic. I'm talking
about the blue pill you take, you . . . if you're not done in ten
minutes, I'm going to alert the press!" Camilla says to him
while still giggling.

Eddie moves to her on the cushion. They kiss deeply as
he removes her panties, then crawls between and spreads her
legs, going down on her, saying how much he loves to eat
pussy. Camilla stops giggling. "I know . . . I . . . knowww,"
she moans.

An hour passes, and they begin to rouse and ready themselves for bed. With the late rising summer sun, it won't be
till 9 am before they get underway. A little more sherry and

they are soon drifting toward sleep, lying together, spooning. Eddie is again hard, but too tired to do anything. He wishes he were young again.

"Eddie?" Camilla whispers. He moans being awake. "I love you, Gerber."

"I love you too, Camilla," he replies.

"I can't do the crossing with you. I'm flying back."

After a few quiet seconds, "I know," he says.

Camilla lies still, eyes wide, not knowing how to respond. A silence falls within the cabin followed by a few gentle slaps on the hull as another boat's wake drifts across the marina. Then Eddie speaks again, saying, "Helle told me." He kisses her neck and rolls away from her, ready for sleep. "He and his fucking 'keep it simple,'" he chuckles and dozes off.

Camilla lays there stunned; near panic. *Is this a dream or did Gerber just say Helle told him?* she wonders. She lies there, calm, then frightened, but soon the sherry does its thing and she relaxes, then falls asleep dreaming of windmills, white sandy beaches, and flamenco dancers.

* * *

Eddie and Camilla push off the next morning from Cádiz, making way for Gibraltar where they will reunite with Helle before sailing to Málaga. It's a longer trip of over seventy-five nautical miles and will require a continuous sail through the next night, totaling twenty hours or more depending on the wind and currents. Eddie has volunteered to keep watch through the night, and not sleep until Camilla wakes in the early morning hours. His rest will be short, but enough to wake in time for entering the very busy port of Gibraltar.

Helle has arranged dockage for them at the Ocean Village Marina, which is close by to his office.

They plan to meet up with Helle after some shopping in downtown Gibraltar, and then come to his office at the end of the day before going out for dinner. The Gerbers arrive a little early, and Helle's meeting with his client has not quite ended.

"Just keep coming," Helle is telling Camilla on the phone as they walk in the direction of Helle's office. "In just another hundred meters, you will see a large sign with blue lettering for Mediterranean Computer Services. The entrance to my office is above that sign, and the stairway just to the left."

"Oh . . . Helle, I see the sign," Camilla replies.

"OK, the door is open and there's a comfortable waiting area. We'll be done soon. I'm just finishing up."

The Gerbers walk into the office, and after being offered something to drink by the receptionist, they sit together in a plush leather sofa. The offices are bright and airy, with colorful photographs of sailing themes, pictures of Helle with family and friends, several framed maps of significant value on the walls, and several coffee and end tables with the requisite number and selection of magazines. Eddie soon tosses the magazine he's selected back on to the coffee table and spots a more interesting piece on the wall, where he quickly moves to examining a map of the eastern Caribbean. It is old, but he's unable to tell its age. It soon annoys him that he is, in essence, unread in this area. He looks around to see if there are others and spots one across the reception area on the wall adjacent to the conference room where Helle is meeting with his client.

Camilla has meanwhile begun drifting through the pictures of Helle with friends and family. She recognizes some of the people in these photos from pictures Helle shared with them in Punta Umbria—his children, wives, business associates, and friends. Dating some of the clothing people are wearing in the pictures, she marvels at how remarkably well he's aged.

Helle pokes his head out of the conference room door to let them know they are finished and coming out momentarily. His client, they can see, is a smallish, slender, dark-haired woman in her fifties, dressed in motorcycle leathers. She is filling a leather satchel with the documents and statements she and Helle have just spent the last two hours reviewing. A motorcycle helmet rests on the table next to her. Her face is to the side as she finishes collecting her items. She throws the satchel strap over a shoulder, grabs the helmet, turns, and steps into the reception area to see Camilla waiting, arms extended and crying. Helle's client is Camilla's sister, Lisbeth, who she has not seen in more than thirty years.

Not seeing this, Eddie blurts out, "Helle, what is the date of this map?" Then finally he sees Camilla and more softly asks, "What's wrong, Camy?"

Helle's client stops in the doorway. Her jaw drops, and she stands stone faced. She isn't quite in touch with her feelings at first, but quickly places her items on a chair and embraces Camilla. They stand there for several minutes, crying and looking at each other and kissing each other's cheeks and hands, embracing over and over.

The two women separate and look toward the two men, who are unsure what to make of it. Camilla then explains, "Eddie, Helle . . . this is my sister. We haven't seen one another in over thirty years." She smiles broadly shaking her head from side to side and sweetly says her sister's name. "Lisbeth . . . I can't believe . . ."

Eddie and Helle go to the two women. Eddie extends his hand to Lisbeth as Camilla makes the introduction.

"Eddie, this. . . ." Camilla is smiling and crying at the same time. "This is my sister Lisbeth. We haven't seen each other in . . . it's . . . decades."

The two of them hug, cry, emotions, bursting like fireworks on the Fourth of July.

Finally, Lisbeth is able to speak. "Camilla, what are you doing here?"

"It's a long story," she begins as Helle offers the conference room to them.

"Please, take some time in the conference room. Can I bring you anything?"

They signal no and move back into the conference room.

"Eddie, the maps?" Helle gestures to Eddie and moves toward the reception area.

Camilla and Lisbeth sit across from each other, holding hands, sometimes crying, then laughing. Lisbeth explains that she feared their foster father. He had begun abusing her; she had to run. Camilla says she stayed for their foster mother's sake, but eventually the state moved her to another foster family. It was hard, until she was adopted and moved to America where, several years later, she met and married Eddie Gerber.

Eddie and Helle find it difficult to look through the items on display in Helle's office. The expressions and emotions on the two sisters' faces grasp their attention though the glass walls—horror, disgust, elation, fright. The two women laugh, cry, and hug each other repeatedly.

Lisbeth's life has not been easy by any measure. After running away from their foster parents at sixteen, she lived on the streets, homeless and destitute. After being arrested several times for prostitution and petty crimes, she entered a state program and remained a ward of the state. She discovered, through self-study, that she had an affinity for math and computer science, and developed this skill set to a very high level. Several years passed, and eventually she gained her freedom from the state, and using her math and computing skills, she made a fortune working as an independent programming consultant in the investment banking industry. A good deal of this money was of dubious origins, forcing her to squirrel it away somewhere where it would be hard to find. Gibraltar is such a place.

While she hid her wealth in Gibraltar, the money she made in several business schemes grew tenfold. Helle had taken control of managing Lisbeth's wealth after her initial manager became sick and died of cancer. It was he who had recommended Helle to Lisbeth eight years earlier. It was supposed to be a temporary solution until she could find a permanent replacement. However, Lisbeth found Helle's skills and personality as interesting and remarkable as the Gerbers have, and so the one-year contract which Helle and Lisbeth initially executed was repeatedly extended to the current period. But now, when Helle had mentioned to Lisbeth that he was planning to sail to America with the Gerbers, Lisbeth thought the timing was right for her to move the management of her wealth to a firm in Zug, Switzerland, where she now resided.

Helle was in no position to resist, nor did he want to. Lisbeth's success and generosity enabled Helle to make millions. He didn't need to worry about money even before they had met, and now he had made millions under their contract. He quickly warmed to the idea of sailing to America and enjoying life there for a while and exploring his relationship with

Camilla. The transitioning of Lisbeth's assets to new accounts in Zug went smoothly and had been completed with Lisbeth in firm control of the funds transfers and protocols using ocular scanning software verification.

Since early in the new millennium, ocular scanning had become the verification capability of choice for Lisbeth. While scanning an individual's iris was the commonly known feature of this security capability, the applied science technique, which Lisbeth favors, is in the mathematical pattern recognition techniques to images of the irises. Lisbeth's mathematical and programming skills enabled her to not only ensure the singularity of the ocular scan, but also to customize the mathematical pattern recognition equations, and customize and change those equations each time she wanted to transfer funds. Her adoption of this technique and ability to implement it herself was truly brilliant. Very few people on the planet had the programming skills and math needed to enable security to the degree Lisbeth had accomplished, making it virtually impossible for anyone to hack a transfer or to access any of her new accounts in Zug.

Eddie and Helle sit in the reception area across from a chart of Biscay off the coast of France. "Gerber, congratulations! You have a sister-in-law. Can't believe . . . it's so long, no contact whatsoever? You probably forgot her name. You knew she had a sister, right?"

"No, no . . . I did. But . . . it's been a long. . . many years since I last heard her name, and it was almost like registering for the first time that she has a sister, Lisbeth. You know what I mean? How long have you known her?"

"About eight years now. She was using the services of a friend and associate of mine when he became very ill with cancer and died six months later. I was the obvious choice to help his one client, your sister-in-law, Lisbeth."

"What can you tell me about her? She's so . . . so different-looking. I mean, she and Camilla don't look much alike for twins; fraternal no doubt."

"I don't know much about her private life. She doesn't spend much time here in Gibraltar, except to meet with me and review her accounts, mostly at year end."

Eddie sat back, the leather chair sounding like a whoopee cushion as he got comfortable, encouraging Helle to continue.

"Initially, it was to just extend a helping hand while she decided what to do, and, as is often the case in this business, the relationship changes, evolves, which with us, it's now been eight years . . . a very interesting and highly rewarding eight years. At the time my associate passed away and I *inherited* Lisbeth's accounts, there was a few million dollars. It's grown to much more. Lisbeth lives a *very* comfortable life, and she's made me a rich man as well . . . or richer I should say. She's had several private investment successes, but hit it pretty big a few years ago with an idea I thought would bomb. Are you familiar with the P-Nutter chain that's gone big across Europe?"

"Yeah, I had a beer in one in Paris a while ago . . . near the Sorbonne, I think."

"Probably. That's part of the magic. I mean, they open P-Nutters near college campuses." Helle shakes his head as in disbelief of what he just had said, still unable to get over the success of the P-Nutter chain of fast food restaurants Lisbeth had invested in. "Peanut butter, beer, and college students. I thought it was a crazy idea. She asked my opinion and I told her so. But that's not what my relationship with Lisbeth is about. I merely execute money transfers and keep her account records, pay her bills, and fund her expense accounts. But when she asked my opinion, I said I didn't think it would fly. But it did, and now she owns about thirty percent of the company. I'm not even sure how many shops there are."

Eddie is scratching his head and looking toward the women through the conference room glass. "I'm pretty sure there are as many P-Nutters as there are Starbucks in Europe, and there's a bunch of them—a very big bunch."

Helle chuckles and continues, "I think you're right. They grew like wildfire. There's one near to just about every campus in Europe, in some cases more than one. Anyhow, their last quarter operating income was . . . in dollars . . . *mmm.*" He gazes toward the ceiling, then to the conference room. Suddenly he blurts out, "About fifty million."

The two men sit and digest this number for a few moments before Helle realizes he maybe shouldn't be sharing this information with Lisbeth's newfound brother-in-law.

"Suffice it to say, she's doing very, very well. Her wealth is more than ten times what she had when I started, and"—he emphasizes the word "and"—"she spends a lot of money. Travels, owns quite a few luxury apartments in most major cities in Europe, some in South America, and has investments in other business partnerships."

The P-Nutter fast food business, which Lisbeth had invested in, was a piece of good luck for her and her co-investors who, six years earlier, opened several Starbucks lookalike fast food restaurants selling peanut butter and jelly sandwiches, coffee, and beer to the college crowd. The idea was simple, and apparently its time had come. Lisbeth and her partners thought that college students with little disposable income loved and ate peanut butter sandwiches and drank beer. So why not sell that following a Starbucks model: free Internet, smallish stores, busy locations, good coffee. In European fashion, beer on tap was included. And just like Starbucks, you could order your P-Nutter any number of ways: different breads, different jellies, peanut butter and butter, or select from an assortment of add-on spreads or items like banana, bacon, etc., to have it your way. And bingo! P-Nutter locations were popping up all over Europe. Some were corporate, some franchised, serving college-age types and yuppies. It was just what their customers wanted: a quick bite, a beer, and a place to sit and connect.

"Amazing." Eddie is shaking his head.

"Hey, they're coming out."

Helle stands as Camilla and Lisbeth emerge from the conference room. Forty minutes have passed. They appear to be elated, both smiling and wiping wet eyes, ready to celebrate and enjoy the night in Gibraltar, which they do into the early morning hours.

And then, just as suddenly as they came together, they part ways, Lisbeth to the airport for a morning flight to Zurich, and Camilla to *The Kiss* and onward to Málaga and back to the USA with a grand new supporter for the project she'll undertake with Ron Billings. Her new supporter, Lisbeth, had committed up to a million dollars to support the new IPCC environmental lab project.

Camilla is bursting with excitement. So much has happened in such short time, and she feels *The Kiss* has brought them good luck.

She shares this with Eddie, cuddling in bed as the sky begins to brighten a new day aboard *The Kiss*. A gentle rocking of *The Kiss* with a cool breeze is the potion for the end of this very long day. Camilla's hand is outstretched, falling across the night table, resting on a silk scarf she purchased in Cádiz.

Taking her hand, Eddie gently moves it to her side and whispers, "The touch of the velvet hand like a lizard on a windowpane. Sweetheart, have you changed your mind?" he asks.

But Camilla is quick to fall asleep and only able to think the answer without saying it before sleep takes over.

CHAPTER 6

Málaga, Spain

The summer air temperature in the Andalusia region of southern Spain can best be described as like a pizza oven, and this summer is no exception. Even along the coast the daily temperatures are typically above 90°F (32°C). Inland, in such places as Seville, Cordoba, etc., the daytime temperatures often hover above 100°F (38°C). Outdoor work becomes nearly impossible, particularly in places where the sun beats down and little shade is to be found. A boatyard is one such place.

Weeks have passed, and *The Kiss* is still blocked up in dry dock for painting of the hull, new navigation, and other electronic component installation. The temperature, both during and after daylight hours, is slowing progress and makes the work arduous at best. Progress is further impeded by a shortage of parts, delivery wait times, and the availability of mechanics specializing in components. Rocco had expected to be done more than a week earlier, and now, with the summer ocean sailing season coming to a crescendo and resources spread thin, the schedule has fallen at least twelve days behind. Rocco and Eddie are on edge with each other, but somehow Helle always smooths things over and defuses the situation.

"You know, Eddie, there are forty-five hundred sailors like us making a Caribbean trip every year at this time. It's the busy season for these guys." Helle reminds him of this on almost a daily basis to quiet and calm him down.

"I know . . . it's OK, we'll be on the water in a few days now. It just fucking pisses me off that every fucking week there's another holiday for this saint or that saint, and everything stops."

Helle laughs and hands him an ice-cold Alhambra.

Eddie continues his daily rant on the subject. "This country is gonna end up on its ass if it keeps going on with these old traditions. You remember all that shit that went down a decade or so ago? I thought they ironed out all that three-month holiday crap! A holy day every week. . . . They better get back to work like the rest of the world, or they'll be back to all that austerity again. Man, look again what's happening to the euro! They better shape up and cut all this time off bullshit."

Before retiring several years earlier, Eddie had worked hard and made a good deal of money back around the time of the new millennium, developing derivatives management software for hedge funds and trading with his own money in currencies. He hit it pretty big more than once betting on weakening currencies against the US dollar, at times doubling large sums of his own money in just a six-month period by holding large positions of leveraged currency options.

"I guess all that's important now is that we have a large position in ice-cold Alhambra," Helle chuckles.

"That, and a few delicious bottles of sherry. What else are you bringing for the trip? You do eat as well as sip Alhambra?" Eddie is wondering about Helle's diet, given the great shape he's in.

"I'm a very light sailor, my friend. Just berries, nuts, some grains. I'll catch and grill some fish for us. That's it for food, but I want to collect clothes, computer and other personal belongings from my apartment in Gibraltar. I'll drive back tonight and return in the morning. You're welcome to join me. If you do, we can go over the charts and discuss our route."

"I'll think about it. I'm already pretty comfortable here at Rocco's, and I've shored up my position in Alhambra and sherry." The two men laugh over Eddie's joke. "And I want to spend some time on the phone with Camilla, too."

It has been more than twenty days since Camilla boarded a flight from Málaga back to the United States, routing her trip through Switzerland to spend a couple of days with Lisbeth.

"You must miss her."

"I miss her *a lot*, despite phoning her every day, and I wish she had made the trip. But it's OK. She got homesick . . . and we'll be together again in just a few weeks. I'm sure she's loving it—I mean, getting back to work."

"Say hello for me too, Señor Gerber! A lovely lady, very pretty," Rocco calls out from the forward compartment, having overheard the conversation between the two men.

"I will, Rocco. She enjoyed meeting you as well."

Now, as the evening sun melts into the Mediterranean, the three men descend from the dry docked *Kiss*. Earlier in the day, Rocco spent several hours testing the navigation and communication systems, and then continued reviewing their operation with Eddie and Helle. In a few days, *The Kiss* would be afloat once again, and the final preparation for the crossing would continue. The men would be on their way within a week, perhaps in as few as five days.

They were interrupted a few times during the day by several deliveries and storing of dry goods. Rocco insisted that they be locked away and stored in his garage, rather than aboard *The Kiss.*

"It's not a good idea," he insisted, "to bring this on board now before we float *The Kiss.* Stuff happens in dry dock. Let's get her back in the water before loading."

The amount of cargo for a transatlantic crossing is significant, especially its first crossing when all the redundant equipment is included. Besides food, water, clothing, and toiletries, etc., a great deal of spare parts, backup, and safety equipment is initially brought on in case of failures, problems, and bad weather. Rocco is ensuring that *The Kiss* will be properly equipped in this regard and double-checking the rigging and safety equipment, spare blocks, turnbuckles, lines, sails, flares, fire extinguishers, life rafts, smoke alarms, starter motor, etc.

Provisioning for the crew, on the other hand, is left up to each of the guys. Eddie is mostly concerned with the "fun" stuff (i.e., beer, sherry, marijuana), and plenty of vacuum-sealed meat in the freezer. Helle is making sure they get off to a good start of apples, oranges, and pears. Rocco is seeing to it that it is stored safely in his temperature-controlled garage, which they return to at the end of the day to cool off in his air-conditioned office and have a cold beer.

"I'll lock up fellas. *Te veo mañana,*" Rocco says to Eddie and Helle, who are making the drive to Gibraltar and Helle's apartment.

"Hey, Señor Eddie! How about joining me here? The James Taylor sounds great, but . . ." Helle trails off, opening his arms in mock frustration and smiling at Eddie, who is in the adjacent living room. Eddie stops playing the guitar for a few seconds and peers into the dining room to see that Helle has gone back to organizing several charts of the waters around the Iberian Peninsula. Navigation charts are littering the dining room of Helle's apartment. Three or four lie across the dining room table, and several more are draped over a wire line spanning the far side interior wall hiding a self-portrait and two other portraits Helle has painted in oil.

Eddie peers again into the dining room. "How about those portraits?"

"I moved them from the house in Punta Umbria. They make me feel more, you know . . . at home. I have quite a collection of them in Punta Umbria. If I ever move here and sell the house, I don't know what I'm going to do with them all."

Eddie still fingers the guitar, feigning interest in Helle's painting.

"Hey, you know, Eddie, Rocco told me last night that *The Kiss* will be ready next week. I think we need to work out the navigation details. We've been busy with everything else but done very little course planning, except talking in general terms."

Eddie lightly picks a few chords on the Martin D-45 in adagio style.

Now expressing some annoyance, Helle continues, "You're lucky to have me on this trip with you." He pauses and listens. The chord picks continue. "Many people take weeks, months, or a year to plan and prepare a trip like this. You're lucky I've done it so often or you'd never have gotten it done so quickly."

Eddie stops playing the Martin, lays it on the couch, and walks into the dining room to join Helle. "What are you doing with these charts?" he says. "They aren't needed; I think I'd like to use the iPad nav."

"We'll do better if we enter specific coordinates," replies

Helle. "Let's look closer at these charts and start the coordinates entry into the iPad then." He stands up and pages through several charts until he finds what he's looking for. "Take a look at this chart."

Eddie sidles up to where Helle is standing and looking at a chart suspended on the wire line. Together, they look at a chart of Andalusia, spanning the Gulf of Cádiz as far north as Huelva, west to Málaga, and as far south as Gran Canaria. This is where their adventure will start. Either they will start from Huelva or Cádiz, and sail to Gran Canaria, just as Columbus did in 1492.

"Is there any reason to put in at Rabat or any of these?" Eddie asks as he points to the western coast of Morocco. "How far is it to Gran Canaria?"

Helle quickly charts this on Google Earth and says, "Seven hundred sixty-four nautical miles."

Eddie looks up as he does the math in his head. "Let's figure, by making four knots, that's about eight days. I think it's a little long for our first ocean sail. We don't know the boat that well. We don't know what we don't know."

"True, but if we go straight along the coast of Morocco, we can stay close to land just in case . . . and let's hope we make better than four."

Taking a minute to look again at the Google Earth display, Helle asks, "Have you been to Madeira?"

Eddie is again self-absorbed with the guitar and barely paying Helle any attention. Helle begins searching through the maps as Eddie gets up to answer the doorbell.

Helle is shouting, "It's pretty straight forward, but we have to make entries to the new software before setting out! And it's still a pretty long sail . . . Five hundred seventy-two nautical miles from Cádiz . . . six days." Helle is hoping to convince Eddie to sail from Cádiz, or Gibraltar, rather than go all the way north to Huelva, which is where Columbus's first trip began. Eddie's heart is set on departing from there. Helle reminds him on a daily basis that Huelva is very different from that era and is no longer much of a port, due to the 1755 earthquake that significantly reshaped its geography.

Eddie can be heard ranting as he answers the bell and opens the door expecting the bottle of sherry he ordered. Helle stops and listens to Eddie curse out the delivery drone. "Eddie, you sound like Donald Duck! You're quacking . . . *como un pato.*"

"You piece of shit!" (Inaudible quacking.) "Put the fucking bottle down . . . and leave!" Eddie is cursing the drone as it hovers near the door with its propellers spinning and throwing off rain into Eddie's face. Thunder echoes in the background as a shower passes.

Eddie returns, wiping the rain from his face with a towel from the bathroom in one hand and a bottle of Sandeman in the other.

"What's in Madeira? No, Helle, I've never been there."

"I'm guessing that you'll want to pick up a couple of bottles of their Madeira wine. It's similar to the Spanish sherry you like so much. It's also a fortified wine like the sherry but a Portuguese formula, different from the Spanish sherries."

"Well that's not much reason to sail there . . . but it is shorter than sailing to Gran Canaria."

"I can pick up some Marcona almonds there, too."

"Are those different as well?"

With a smile of gastronomic pleasure, Helle describes the

almonds. "They are the queen of almonds. Usually I eat the Spanish ones, but they also grow them in Madeira. They're sweeter, and hard to find in Andalusia."

"I've never had those. But I've eaten almonds with sherry. They're delicious. Did you every try them with a glass?"

Helle was laughing. "Hey, you know me! I can't even finish one beer and it affects me." The truth is that Helle really doesn't drink at all. He continues about the sail. "Anyway, then from Madeira to Gran Canaria, it's about two hundred fifty nautical miles, directly to the south." He pauses, looking at the chart as Eddie opens the bottle of sherry.

"You know . . . I know you want to follow Columbus's route, but we could just make for the Caribbean from Madeira. We'd save two days, maybe . . . it's practically—"

Eddie cuts him short. "No way . . . don't fuck with me on this, Helle. I'm not cutting the Gran Canaria out of this for some fucking sherry and almonds."

"OK, OK." A broad smile crosses Helle's face. "I'm just teasing. Caniçal (Madeira) is a good deep-water port . . . cruise ships come in there. We'll set course for it and spend a day or two depending what we find out about the blue water sailing of *The Kiss* as we make our way . . . I expect we'll find nothing out of the ordinary."

Eddie is smiling now too. *So that's how it's going to be?* he thinks. *This old man of the sea pulling my leg all the way across the Atlantic. That's OK; it'll be great, a once in a lifetime sail.*

The two huddle around the dining room table moving from the Google Earth application to the charts and plotting a course from Gibraltar to the port city of Caniçal on the island of Madeira, and entering the coordinates into the navigation system on the iPad. It all seems to be at peace as the rain shower activity picks up again, and Eddie walks over to close the balcony door.

All is set. They'll depart in about a week once everything is loaded onboard *The Kiss*. Once underway, they'll plot a course from Madeira to the Gran Canaria. Helle relaxes on the couch now that their initial course is set. Eddie picks up the Martin, and Helle asks him to play "Fire and Rain" as everything begins to shake. A few small tremors. Eddie starts the song as a quiet calm sets in, followed by more gentle tremors lasting two minutes uninterrupted. Again it stops and becomes calm.

A few minutes later, Eddie finishes singing and reaches to refill his glass.

Helle applauds. *"Bravo ... bellisimo, bravo.* That was nice. I hope you plan on bringing that guitar on our voyage."

"Of course! Now it's your turn to sing something. I know you sing; I've heard you ... come on."

Helle is laughing now as he stands and starts up. *"Che bella cosa, na jurnata 'e sole."*

"Wait a sec." Eddie takes a few seconds to find the key and figure out the chord pattern on the guitar.

Neither of them wants to say anything and spoil the moment; however, since Eddie's performance of "Fire and Rain" ended, a light rumbling has started once again and continues unabated.

Earthquakes are common to the Iberian peninsula, which the town of Huelva, Columbus's home while waiting for Ferdinand and Isabella in 1491–1492, unfortunately found to be the case when it was nearly wiped off the face of the Earth in 1755. The high occurrence of earthquakes in the region is largely due to the number of faults and plate boundaries surrounding what is known as the African Plate.

On its west, south, and east sides the African Plate is surrounded by spreading centers, and on the north side, the plate forms a convergent boundary with the Eurasian Plate in the central and eastern Mediterranean Sea. At the extreme northwestern boundary of the plate lies the Azores Triple Junction, where the Mid-Atlantic Ridge meets the right-lateral strike-slip Azores-Gibraltar Transform Fault, which is an east-west trending structure that continues toward the Strait of Gibraltar as the Gloria Fault.

Helle jumps from his seat with a burst—"That's it!"—just as the shaking strengthens.

It is 10:35 pm now as everything again begins to shake, very violently, and continues for nearly ninety seconds. The next day the media reports that the earthquake, with its epicenter in the Atlantic Ocean, off the coasts of Portugal and Morocco, is a magnitude 6.3. The shock occurred at a plate boundary where a number of large, very large and great earthquakes are known to have taken place as far back as the eighteenth century. Fortunately no serious injuries or significant damage is reported.

The Kiss, however, will require three to five additional days to repair damages to her hull, torn cable riggings and cleats, and, a complete inspection of everything below the waterline. She had slipped her blockings in the middle of a line of five boats in dry dock. Fortunate for Eddie and Helle, she is not on the end of the line of dominos.

CHAPTER 7

The Living Environmental Theater (LET)

Camilla returns from Europe ending her sixteenth-month sabbatical and rejoins the IPCC staff in Greeley, Colorado. She and Ron Billings meet to discuss the LET architecture, testing, and implementation. Although testing has been mired with numerous issues, Ron and his team have moved to the final testing phase. Implementation of the beta LET product is unofficially reported as "being within sight."

"Ron, hey, . . . again, I'm very impressed and can't wait to see the theater. It's just brilliant what you've achieved. I mean . . . this following so soon after your achievements in transportation."

Up until now Camilla has been reading papers written by Ron about the LET project. Soon she will participate in a scheduled test run.

Since returning from Europe and rejoining the IPCC group, Panalla Reddy has officially assigned her responsibility to implement the theater into production. In essence, it is planned that Ron will turn the product over to Camilla once testing is complete. She will market and implement its use across the IPCC and its participating member nations.

Ron will continue to support the theater maintenance

and engineering, build additional theaters assuming this first one is well received and successful, and continue to develop enhancements. The meeting today is Camilla and Ron's first of many steps toward a smooth handoff—and, at least for the present, it gives Camilla full authority as product manager for the theater and places her in complete charge of Ron and his staff. Ron now reports to her, which he's happy about since the last thing he wants is to have to take the theater into the real world. Like most engineers, his focus and commitment is to the design, build, and test. He has no aspiration to "live" in Camilla's "public" world. Camilla, on the other hand, has neither the engineering, training, nor skill to live in his world.

"Again . . . Camilla, you've been so complementary. It's my job; I love building stuff . . . but thank you. And I'm very glad to move this out with you." Ron emphasizes the word "very" and eases back into the large leather recliner he is seated in. They are in his Greeley office, a large expansive twenty-by-twenty-foot space with a west view of the eastern front of the Rockies. Last year's snow still covers the mountain peaks on this sun-drenched, late summer day.

"You know not everyone at the IPCC is so nice to work with as you, Camilla. There are quite a few in similar positions as yours who are on ego trips. I can tell you love the work and see its importance across the sciences. *And* I love that our skill sets blend so well together. I simply can't do what you do; you'll take this theater and bring it out across the agencies. They will recognize its importance in understanding what's going on with climate change."

"So what's the plan, Ron; how are you going to transfer this to me? I have some thoughts but really need some direction from you in terms of what would be the most efficient way for me to internalize the product."

"Well, tomorrow we're going to continue a broad-based implementation test that intends to bring several of the Earth's monitoring satellites into the presence of the theater. I think you'll find this especially interesting as it focuses on oceanographic data." He pauses, and Camilla wonders what that really means as she watches the border collie he's doggy sitting rub its nose into Ron's left hand, which is resting on the side of his chair. He swivels the chair to a small cabinet behind him and opens the lower drawer to retrieve a treat for the dog. The collie crunches it up.

He looks back toward Camilla and breaks into a wide smile, ear to ear. It is one of his best features. "I can tell . . . you don't know what the fuck I'm getting at. I'll explain. I can't expect you to know the details of the test plan."

"I understand where you are on the test plan, but please explain so I know what to look for tomorrow. Do you want me to review oceanographic data or the theater readings . . ."

"No, don't look for anything in particular tomorrow. My team will be measuring the functions of the LET to insure it's working according to plan. I'd just like you to experience the test tomorrow and begin to think of your agency audiences once we move further into implementation."

Ron isn't being as straightforward as he can. Camilla is possibly the best staffer in the IPCC to experience what he is planning to conduct the next day in the LET. In her absence he would have had to bring in several NOAA consultants to participate, and, in fact, he likely will have to do just that further down the road. But, for now, Camilla's deep sailing experience will suffice. So he doesn't want to give her too much information about tomorrow's test run. He wants to observe her reactions without her anticipating what is going to happen. He wants her to have little expectation about the experience, as she is as much a part of the test run as the theater components themselves. He considers monitoring her physiology, but that might change her expectations. He decides for now to just video record the session to observe her reactions in the theater.

Camilla asks, "Are you still planning to integrate the satellite ocean monitors?"

"Absolutely—those and every other oceanographic monitoring component we have available online."

"Great. I'll read through the test plan tonight and be a little smarter tomorrow."

Shit, Ron thinks, *I'd rather she didn't,* but he can't do anything about that . . . or maybe he can. "Well, Camilla, it's not a bad idea, but if you don't, it's no biggie. Remember we're meeting at the Marriott over in Fort Collins tonight for some dinner and karaoke. You know it's Panalla's birthday."

"No, I didn't forget, but I feel that I've been away from the IPCC for so long I need to get on top of the LET project material. I'm going to skip the party. Panalla will understand."

"Hey, it's just one night. Don't sweat it. It will be lots of fun—some dancing . . . karaoke."

Camilla chuckles. "Karaoke, huh?" They're both quite for a few seconds. Camilla asks, "Are you going to sing?"

Now Ron is the one chuckling. "Oh, yeah, I'll be up there."

"Really? . . . Well if you're singing I better be there to make sure Panalla doesn't fire you."

Now they are both laughing.

"So you'll come?"

"Yeah, OK. I want to see this!"

"OK!"

They're both smiling.

Camilla wants to review the plan for tomorrow. "So let's take a look through the plan for tomorrow now. Did you have anything else on the agenda for our meeting this morning?"

"No, but I have a staff meeting at ten thirty to review the latest sensor readings. I have to be there. It's the last thing we need to confirm before tomorrow. If the sensor and monitor integrations are not functioning properly, tomorrow's session will bust. I don't anticipate any trouble, but as you know, there are a lot of failure points, particularly with the oceanographic portion of the LET."

"Well, let's spend the rest of this meeting reviewing these and the probable integration failure points," Camilla says. "You know I've spent a few hours at sea the last few years. I may be able to help if I understand how this portion of the LET works. How many points are we talking about?"

"Let's go over to the conference table, and I can bring the design plans up and a list of the points we're concerned with." Ron looks down and sees the collie standing beside his chair again. "You're gonna get too fat to run."

Camilla thinks at first that Ron is addressing her, then smiles seeing the dog. Ron motions toward the conference table. They both get up and head across the office to the table. The collie whines and follows, still hoping for a treat.

"Pepe belongs to a friend of mine here in Greeley. He's away a few days, so I'm taking care of the old guy. Come on, Pepe . . . go on out back for a while." He lets the dog out, and Camilla sits at the conference table, seeing the LET specs.

"See you later, Pepe," Camilla says and then to Ron, "That's a sweet dog. OK, let's get started."

The LET was several years in the making and draws upon Ron's best skill set, which is the integration of many information technologies, both old and new, to deliver a new and unique product value significantly beyond the original singular components. Systems integration had become an important evolution of the information technology boom since the late 1980s as mainframe, mini, and personal computers grew in presence and number. Seamless integration became an exigency.

Ron Billings took integration a step further inasmuch as he aspired to develop only major system products, which, when realized, delivered exponential result to achieve great social impact. Using this model, the LET followed Ron's development of the AVE (Automated Vehicular Enabler), now in its eighth year of production.

The AVE system automated vehicular use and traffic around the globe, and completely supported all other vehicle-related functions like licensing and registration, maintenance, replacement, etc. All powered passenger road vehicles, both new and old, were now required to be equipped with the technology as of several years earlier. Very few vehicles or class of vehicle were permitted to opt out. The AVE (commonly pronounced *ah-vey*, as in Ava Maria, which was how several cultures spoke of it due to the many lives it saved—traffic-related deaths were largely a thing of the past), integrated thousands of older automotive and vehicle registration systems and technologies like radar, voice recognition, GPS, etc., along with new onboard computerized steering, braking, and power systems. A central registration component also managed all maintenance and scheduling functions.

At the core of the AVE, IBM's Arthur AI serves as the backbone integration enabler. Now in its third iteration of the forerunner Watson class, Arthur AI (named for the third son of IBM's early president Thomas J. Watson whom the Watson IBM computer was named) enables the AVE's global data integration and communication capability.

At the time of its development, the AVE also benefitted from a plethora of vehicle longevity-extending devices and materials, as well as supporting enhanced recycling and reuse of parts and components. Flat tires, dead batteries, and most other common twentieth-century breakdown issues were long gone along with most internal combustion engines. Developments in solar power, hardened materials, adhesives, and achievements in electronics and software were the enablers of a new revolution of vehicles in the twenty-first century.

In conjunction and support of these changes, all interstate and state roadways, as well as many local roadways in the Western world use Global Grid System (GGS) sensor and monitoring equipment. Not that vehicles require GGS to operate and drive themselves automatically without human interaction, but particularly in busy metropolitan areas, GGS supports and achieves unprecedented traffic flow, relieving congestion and speeding everyone safely to their target destination. Onboard voice-activated subsystems also interact with the vehicle operator to accomplish personal preference tasks like parking.

All human interaction with the vehicle's controls are voice activated and enable the user to interface with the many onboard systems, whether necessary or optional. Besides parking, for instance, the owner/user has options concerning maintenance scheduling and location, maximum highway speeds, destination routes, and many others.

The AVE system also supports local operator licensing, where operators receive access to additional control functions of their AVE-supported vehicles. Presently this is limited to basic functions like giving GPS coordinate directions to override vehicle routing or to request a specific destination.

AVE-equipped vehicles automatically sense GGS signals and are automatically monitored and controlled as if part of a large electrical grid.

The IBM-led rollout of the AVE product was completed in the developed Western world in three years and the rest of the world a few years later. The United Nations, who cosponsored the development and implementation throughout the world, estimate that more than 92 percent of global vehicular movement is automated. Vehicles no longer are operated by humans, and in most countries, a special permit is required to own and operate non-AVE vehicles like off-road, heavy equipment, and other specialty vehicles. Most of the AVE implementation was paid for by government, insurance, and automobile company funding. AVE was the brainchild of Ron Billings, and for it, he was awarded several prizes, including the Nobel Peace Prize for its expectation of saving a great number of lives; *Time* magazine's Man of the Year; and, the Automobile Association of America's Medal of Distinction.

Now, in similar fashion to the AVE, Ron utilizes IBM's Arthur AI to enable the integration of advances in presentation and holographic-display technologies, global monitoring atmosphere, weather, oceanographic, seismic, volcanic, etc., the data from which the LET is able to create a real-time simulation of a targeted environment anywhere on the planet.

Camilla is excited to be part of the product rollout and amazed by the sheer size of data engineering that the LET accomplishes. "I've gone through much of the integration design, at least through levels zero and level one. It's an amazing piece of work, Ron." Camilla is referring to the level of design that shows at the highest level, level zero, the major integration points, and one level lower containing such entities as tidal datum monitors and data warehouses maintained by NOAA's Center for Operational Oceanographic Products and Services, also known as CO-OPS.

The breadth of data available to the LET approaches that of being limitless. Just the CO-OPS data warehouse alone contains 200 years of US coastal tidal data. Six additional data warehouses contain geodetic data, nautical charts, and a plethora of planetary data like GPS, orbital, aerial imagery, gravity monitoring sites, monitoring geographically dependent changes to gravity over time, and much, much more.

"Thank you, Camilla. The data is the easy part. I mean . . . if there is anything easy about the LET."

"I guess the real magic is in the presentation functions," she says, tempting Ron to continue on the subject, which he does.

"Yes, and that is the tricky part, having the holographic energizer interpret the integrated data and produce the presentation correctly, again executing a plethora of technologies to engage the senses with holograms, sound, displays, movement, mechanics . . . best to go through the specs."

Camilla opens and begins to go through the table of contents, which describes the various functions that Ron is alluding to. "This is huge, Ron," she says. "How many people are working on the code?"

"Roughly twenty-six hundred around the globe. It's a killer app . . . and it may kill me before it's done."

Ron and Camilla have a laugh over Ron's statement.

"Where did the idea for this come from? It's so different from anything I've ever seen or heard about . . . or could have imagined."

"In a way I think of it as an extension of the AVE application, except it engages the user a different way. Actually the end *user* itself is a different entity. What I mean by that is that the AVE end user is a device (that is, a vehicle) most of the time, not withstanding the registration, maintenance, and similar people-related functions. The LET is *all* about people—their senses."

"So do you use anything as a model for the LET; where does this brainstorm of yours come from? You didn't just wake up one morning and say, 'I've got an idea for a brilliant new way of presenting climate change,' and begin building the LET!"

Ron is laughing as Camilla waves her arms in animated excitement.

"The basic idea came about as I repeatedly heard Panalla and others in the IPCC vent their frustrations at not being able to convince the general public of the seriousness around climate change and how they wished there was a way to transport people to places being affected to give them a firsthand live climate change experience . . . they wanted to give people a kick in the seat of the pants. It just came to me one day that the idea of transporting people, a la *Star Trek*, was not feasible, but perhaps the technology was there to effectually transport a virtual environment."

Camilla was riveted. "Ron, that's bizarre; I mean it's brilliant, but bizarre to think something like that . . . wow."

Ron inches up toward Camilla, sitting across the conference

table from him and in a soft, quiet voice, as if to tell her a secret says, "I was kind of thinking of back in the late seventies . . . early eighties, about my first trip to Disney's Epcot center in Orlando, and the large presentation theaters they built. From that experience many, many years ago, I began to imagine a similar, larger, more environment-producing capability using all the planetary monitoring sources available today, and the exceptional presentation capabilities, those both existing and those we and our partners have built and customized, integrated with new technologies to produce the kind of lifelike experience that is equivalent to being . . . ah . . . transported."

Ron is looking right at Camilla, and without realizing it, his tongue is pushing his cheek outward. He's waiting for a response from Camilla, but she's caught off guard, mesmerized like the proverbial deer frozen in the car's headlights.

He waits another second and continues, "But the environment is effectively transported, not the audience. New capabilities in holographic and display technologies make this new level of experience possible."

"And I guess some of the older stuff at places like Epcot are also employed?" Camilla guesses, snapping out of her momentary brain-freeze.

Ron sits back, smiling. "Yes, of course. Those, however, are on steroids compared to the presentation technologies that existed and were employed in the seventies and eighties. Take a look at the section describing the latest Sony presentation equipment they've built for us and the specs for integrating it with the plethora of monitoring devices it relies on. They've done amazing work."

Ron contacts the conference room where his 10:30 staff

meeting is underway and instructs them to review the latest sensor readings without him in order that he and Camilla continue their review of the LET design specs. At half past noon Ron orders lunch for himself and Camilla, which is delivered, and they continue their discussion of the LET and generalize about how and when to announce it to the public.

Camilla is excited about the test run they are planning and moves the lunch conversation in that direction. "Ron, I'd like to review the test plan after lunch."

"Sure, I think that's a good idea. It will also give you a more detailed look at the monitoring devices available to the LET within the target area we select."

"Have you selected a target area in the test plan?"

"No, that part of the plan is open since we have to verify and validate the data that the test is going to rely on. There's no sense in targeting an area if the monitoring devices are unavailable, which may be due to any number of things both planned and unplanned; however, the test levels we are working on are uncomplicated, so I expect we will not experience problems."

"*Not complicated*—what does that mean?"

"Well, you'll see after lunch as we get into the test plan that what we are testing for at this stage is to re-create a simple environment in the LET. For example, a location where change is relatively slow but ongoing, like a shoreline, or perhaps twenty miles out at sea. The test plan at this early stage will validate simple and easy to verify locations like these, and then progress to more and more complex environments as the test plan is executed."

"What is an example of a complex environment?"

"Well, think about those many days you spent sailing the ocean. What's happening as you experience that environment on an ordinary day?"

Camilla rubs her chin, giving the question some thought. "*Mmm*, actually not much, in terms of the environment. The boat is sailing at wind speed, the sea is rolling at eight-foot swells more or less, and there's constantly changing amounts of sun and clouds, a few wind gusts . . . but not much is happening from the perspective of those sailing in terms of the environment."

"Exactly. You pretty much covered it. The environmental experience on the surface of the sea is a simple one in terms of the LET re-creating it. At the other end of the spectrum, a complex environment might be a location on the Amazon River where the jungle exists on its shores and animals lie on its banks and the environment changes relatively quick as one travels down the river, and the speed and conditions on the river can change rapidly as it widens, narrows, changes directions, encounters rapids, etc."

Camilla returns to the test plan. "Got it—just as with a traditional application, the test plan starts with testing small components and moves to test higher levels of functionality as the smaller components are integrated until the system level test is performed at the highest level. Testing the re-creation of environments takes the same approach."

"Yes, it's the same approach."

"Got it. Let's go through it some more. I'm really curious to see the LET re-create being on the water off the coast of Spain."

"That's a good idea . . . off the coast of Spain, which you recently sailed."

Camilla is nodding in agreement while thinking Eddie is still in those waters.

Ron gets up and walks over to the door to tend to Pepe. He then walks to the opposite side of the room where a console controlling a wall-size display is located. Using voice commands, the glass window on the western wall darkens, and the Rockies disappear as the wall-size display on the opposite wall illuminates, and he navigates to a listing of all planetary-monitoring devices. He selects the oceanic subset and returns to the conference table where he and Camilla will continue their review of the test plan.

"Let's see what we have in the European Atlantic off the coast of Spain."

Camilla is pounding with excitement thinking that Eddie and Helle are still in those same waters. *Wow*, she thinks, *I might be on that sail after all*." She chuckles to herself. "So, Ron, I know I'm skipping ahead, but what exactly should I expect when we run the test . . . I mean how does one experience the LET?"

"Fair question, since we haven't at all discussed or reviewed the mechanics of the LET. For this first version of the LET we've built a platform vehicle structure with seating for twenty. The platform, from the attendee's perspective, is a car or ship. In this version of the LET you're either on land or on water."

"To what extent can the LET mechanics produce the real-time environment? I mean . . ." Camilla stopped for a second, not quite sure how to ask the question. "Well, when we sailed to Europe, the North Sea got pretty rough on one occasion. For example . . . terrible downpours of rain, cold temperatures, fog, thirty-foot seas pitching and swamping us . . . we were like a cork floating out there for hours without any control, battened down just waiting it out. Will the LET produce that kind of experience?"

"Yes, the LET can produce those effects and can be downright scary. Wind, rain, movement, speed—it accommodates all this. The housing containing the LET is the largest structure of its kind. Its floor space is over three million square feet, it measures over four hundred feet from floor to ceiling. Madison Square Garden could fit inside many times over. At first we thought the retired aircraft hanger there at the Air Force Academy would fit the bill, but that quickly was seen as being puny. We tore it down and built the existing LET housing, utilizing some of the plumbing and electrical services there from the hanger."

"Plumbing to manage the rainwater, I suppose?" Camilla was laughing thinking this all sounded too incredulous to be for real. But Ron was serious. He and his team, largely from the IPCC, had designed and overseen the building of the massive structure that housed the LET, along with an equally impressive basket of huge presentation display and holographic equipment and devices like nothing ever before seen.

"And all of this 'hardware,' including the LET vehicle is integrated with the plethora of planetary monitoring and satellite imagery to produce a real life experience in real time for the location selected."

"Ron, is the operator in the vehicle able to navigate?"

"Yes, the vehicle was built by a specialty vehicle company in the United Kingdom of Lentheric, Green Leaf Transportation."

"How does that work? I mean, despite its great size, you can only navigate so far before hitting a wall!"

"Actually, as with all simulators, the LUV itself doesn't

move, or navigate I should say, as much as you think. But it does, in fact, move throughout the theater in addition to it pitching and rolling, moving left, right, up, down, etc., much like an aircraft or NASA simulator, to give its passengers the experience one would have if in the actual environment under actual conditions. And then further enhancing the movement of the LUV is the presentation display and holographic components within the theater."

"The love?" Camilla asks with a perplexed look. "Is that the vehicle's name?"

"Yes—it stands for the largely unmoving vehicle. I like to say when going aboard that I'm going to *feel the love.*" Ron is smiling, and Camilla is laughing while thinking, *That's so fucking corny.*

"Well, I'm looking forward to reading the specs on the LUV. And I'm specially looking forward to . . ." Camilla drops her voice and does her best Luther Vandross, "Feeling the love . . . baby." She lets out a big laugh. "Amazing stuff, Ron. You outdid yourself with this."

Ron is smiling, but isn't sure he sees the humor. "Yeah, OK, maybe it's little corny, but I'm pretty sure you'll have to change your underwear after the test."

"Oh, come on, Ron! I think it's great. I can't wait for us to run the test. What are you gonna do, start to test it in the middle of the ocean in a hurricane?"

"No, I suppose not . . . we'll follow the test plan and find a very simple calm environment to test the LET . . . and feel the LUV. We'll initially be examining the integration of datasets between the monitors and imagery systems and the LUV, and see how Arthur AI interprets and stores the information for later use. I mean, the beauty of Arthur is its ability to learn and develop its own intelligence. This version of Arthur includes organic processors and memory stores, and learns much in the way we humans do."

"Well, it's been a long time coming," Camilla says. "I remember first hearing of IBM experimenting with this technology around Y2K."

"Hey, time is flying. Let's get back to the test plan."

Ron walks to Camilla's side of the table and sits next to her as the table display opens to the test plan. He smells her perfume and thinks about his badly timed remark about her dirtying her underwear in the LET test. She doesn't seem to be offended. He's glad.

"So, now that the component testing has been completed, we'll test and examine how the path of data from the monitoring stations is handled by the integration programs and interpreted by the presentation equipment, and then the Arthur AI processors. The test staff will check these lists of data values and evaluate the integration points for timely interpretation by the presentation devices."

They continue to 3:15 pm when Ron excuses himself to meet the test staff at UNC on the other side of Greeley. Camilla stays in his office and continues her review of the LET specs and test plan.

CHAPTER 8

Sketch for Losing *The Kiss*

onths have passed since Dr. Reddy and Ron Billings's breakfast meeting to discuss the anomalies concerning falling tides and sea levels along the European Atlantic coast. Since then, Ron has confirmed the data, and Dr. Reddy has involved and assembled several engineers and scientists at the IPCC in Greeley, Colorado, to discuss the data and propose causes and solutions. The primary members of this team are gathering here in a state-of-the-art conference room, equipped with the latest integrated display technologies, which will enable the participants to illustrate and share ideas, maps, data, etc., from a myriad of data sources from around the globe.

The conference room is a marvel of technology, having numerous display components embedded within the walls, as well as at each chair position and a singular gigantic oval-shaped display at the center of the conference table. The output of the center display is partially controlled by AI watching and listening devices. The room is also equipped with video recording, speakers, microphones, etc., in order to share everything with remotely located participants and to record meeting sessions. Virtually all of the equipment, by design, is concealed, camouflaged, unseen. This installation design feature makes the room appealing as a simple and comfy place to meet, should it be used for social gatherings. However, once empowered, everything comes alive and the world is engaged.

Typically an AV engineer attends to support the equipment needs of the participants. However, in this case, Dr. Reddy has not brought in such a resource due to Ron Billings being part of the group. Also included on this newly formed team is an old friend and part-time associate of the IPCC, Dr. Suresh Veerabhadran from the Scripps Institute of Oceanography in San Diego, California. Now in his eighties, Dr. V, as he is often called, was born and educated in India, only coming to the United States later to work on his PhD on planetary atmospheres. Widely considered the foremost authority on atmospheric conditions of the oceans and how the ocean's atmospheres affect climate change, his work has earned him numerous awards, including NASA's highest scientific honor—the NASA Exceptional Scientific Achievement Medal. He is also highly regarded among oceanographers and well connected with the top oceanographic institutes.

Dr. Reddy has also drafted a geophysicist and expert in seismic activity, Dr. Jordon Cooper. Dr. Cooper is also with the IPCC and resides in Berkley, California. He has been evaluating the recent seismic activity in the area of the Iberian Peninsula, and working with Ron Billings on the LET as subject matter expert concerning his field and the hundred or so monitoring stations and satellites reporting geophysics and seismic related data into the LET.

Dr. Cooper's resume is significant. Several years earlier, he was awarded the coveted Inge Lehmann Medal for "outstanding contributions to the understanding of the structure, composition, and dynamics of the Earth's mantle and core."

Since completing his PhD at the University of Rochester and post doctorate at the Geophysical Laboratory of the Carnegie Institution of Washington before joining the IPCC Geophysical Laboratory in Greeley, Colorado, Dr. Cooper has over the past decade redefined solid Earth geophysics, demonstrating that the mantle and core are accessible in the laboratory through direct study of their components at high pressures and temperatures. Through diverse, ingenious experimentation, his journey to the center of the planet has revealed the many dramatic ways that Earth materials transform under extreme conditions. He has also established a materials-based understanding of the deep interior. In short, no other person on the planet is more capable of understanding what the recent seismic activity is signaling and if it has relevance concerning the sea level and tidal changes.

Dr. Reddy is about to start the meeting and begins striking his pen against his coffee cup when a young Asian woman looks into the conference room, smiles, and signals to Dr. Cooper. Everyone has taken a seat at the conference table when Dr. Cooper stands up to greet the young woman. "Good morning, Dr. Lin. Dr. Reddy, this is Dr. Lin. She's a member of my team and member of the Geochemical Society. I asked her to join us this morning; her knowledge of crustal thickness anomalies in the North Atlantic Ocean basin may help us understand what is happening."

"Good morning, everybody." She quickly walks toward Dr. Cooper's end of the conference room.

Dr. Tingting Lin works at the Institute of Theoretical and Applied Geophysics, School of Earth and Space Sciences of Peking University in Beijing, China. Her work with two associate geophysicists has developed methodologies enabling extensive studies about the different crustal thickness of the Earth.

"I'm glad to be with you this morning," she says and moves around the table, shaking hands before taking a seat next to Dr. Cooper.

Dr. Reddy makes the remaining introductions, that being Dr. Veerabhadran, Camilla, Ron, and himself. Concluding that formality, he begins the meeting by saying that their purpose today is exploratory in nature with the intention to share information and find common ground to proceed. He refers to the session as "a brainstorming session, if you will . . . At the end of our session this morning, if we can agree there is a problem that no existing work group is working on or should be, we can begin to organize one or continue to evaluate and study the information as it comes, with a follow-up meeting or meetings at a later date. Each of us will come away from this meeting with an agreed fundamental understanding of the problem, its degree of severity, a principal method of how we will proceed, task or tasks to accomplish, and next steps this group will take within a defined timetable."

Dr. Reddy is nothing if not organized. Without saying it, it is also understood that if any member of this group is unable to commit to what the group would recognize and recommend in the meeting that morning, they are free to say so and depart from the group. The IPCC is very deep in resources, having at its calling the power of the United Nations and a worldwide plethora of brainpower.

Dr. Reddy continues to lay out this operating method, which is that if they determine that there is a problem to be solved, it will be confronted and not pushed aside by politics, money, or lack of manpower. His work ethic is highly organized and he is tireless, working sixty or more hours a week. He does not screw around, and he lets everyone know it from the start.

"I believe you all received the agenda for this morning, so I'd like to start." He is pumped, excited. He reads the copy in front of him on the conference table. "Problem Definition: I'll begin by stating the fundamental problem as it is currently known to exist, and ask each of you to comment on the statement and support your statements with information available. We'll refine this statement as we move through the information as it becomes available to us—i.e., we will refine our definition of the problem as our understanding of it grows and changes."

Dr. Reddy pauses and looks up for reactions. They are all sitting quietly, looking at him, iPads open, ready to take notes. With the exception of Ron and Camilla, the others are all new to working directly with Dr. Reddy.

Looking across the table at the group, he continues, "Several weeks ago, as we began integrating global-monitoring facilities and satellite-monitoring capabilities to a new IPCC product being built here in Colorado, tidal water levels were repeatedly observed and recorded as more than three standard deviations from beta along the European Atlantic coast, and, inconsistent with records dating back to nineteen ninety, these observations and measurements have never recorded falling levels."

"Dr. Reddy, where specifically were the observations made?" Dr. Lin asks, jumping ahead.

"Yes, before I get to locations, it's important to understand the data collected, which is from NOAA base elevation datum. It's used as a reference from which heights and or depths are reckoned. Tidal datum is a standard elevation defined by a certain phase of the tide and are used as references to measure local water levels."

The group makes a few quick notes and few shift about in their seats. They all appear excited as if seated in a movie theater with the main feature about to begin.

Dr. Lin again stops him. "Dr. Reddy, what does NOAA say in general about interpreting the data?"

"A good question, Dr. Lin, but NOAA only says that it should not be extended into areas having differing oceanographic characteristics without substantiating measurements. This is important, but let me continue explaining the nature of the observations."

Using his tablet, Dr. Reddy brings down the lighting in the conference room and initiates the displays on the conference table. "I realize that some of you are unfamiliar with such measurements, so suffice it to say that NOAA is responsible for reporting water level observation datum values from water level stations. The two commonly used tidal ranges are the Mean Tidal Range and the Diurnal Tidal Range."

He pauses as a pair of maps populates the displays. "The two maps in front of you, I'm using to show how sea levels are changing along the European Atlantic. On the left, 'V,' you will likely recognize this . . . it is showing trends in relative sea levels at the tide gauge stations in Europe from nineteen seventy to twenty twenty-one. The vast number of these show significant evidence of rising tides and sea level."

The map clearly shows colored arrows of varying degrees of yellow, orange, and red, indicating rising sea levels and tides all along the European Atlantic coast from as far north as Norway, all the way south to Gibraltar and North Africa.

Dr. Reddy continues, "The tidal data mapping on the right uses a different data set to show recent tidal changes recorded over the past six months from these same stations along the European Atlantic coast. These negative deltas from normal are expressed here in standard deviations and represent MHW; that is, mean high water tides; DTL, the Diurnal Tide Level, which is the arithmetic mean of mean higher high water and mean lower low water; MLW, Mean Low Water, which is the average of all the low water heights observed. These and other available but not included here are as of Saturday . . . two days ago."

"Dr. Reddy?" Dr. Veerabhadran has a question.

"Yes, Suresh . . . Dr. Veerabhadran."

"Please, Panalla . . . Suresh, or V is fine." Panalla shakes his head in agreement as Dr. Veerabhadran continues, "I would have expected to see the Mean Range of Tide expressed here as one of the attributes." Dr. Veerabhadran is referring to the measure of the difference in height between mean high water and mean low water.

"Yes, it and several other attributes are available in the project dataset. It is equally upsetting and especially complementary of the pictures recently taken, which I'm now bringing to your attention."

"Dr. Reddy, are we looking at high tide in these?" Camilla asks.

"Yes, I know, they're amazing, aren't they? Camilla, you have quite a lot of sailing experience and recently sailed these waters. Did you come across anything like this?"

"Actually we completed our sailing across the Atlantic over sixteen months ago; and, as you know I recently flew back to the States, so, no. I *can* tell you about our sailing into the

Bay of Fundy at low tide though. That was a little more than nerve-racking seeing many boats lying on their sides and acres of exposed sandbars along the coast. These pictures remind me of sailing in there . . . but I believe it was a normal low tide."

Dr. Reddy starts a display series of pictures of marinas, fishing villages, and seacoasts where half the boats had already been relocated, and the remaining are only able to float at high tide. In some cases, small fishing villages had been abandoned and boats relocated further out on sand bars away from the village. Many of the pictures look as Camilla described . . . boats on their sides waiting for the tide.

Dr. Reddy continues, "Yes. Well, it is common for NOAA to observe tidal ranges and sea levels in those places with large tidal ranges. However, the data is clear that such a falling sea level as that observed, if unchecked, points to significant severe and dire climate change consequences."

He clicks the display off and the room glows again with normal lighting.

"So what causes sea levels to fall? From where does it emanate? Can the source of the problem be pinpointed? What are the consequences in the near, mid, and long terms? What are the timeframes, and what actions, solutions are necessary to restore the norm?"

The room is quite for a moment before he continues.

"This is the reported and observed problem that we are dealing with, and I can tell you there is no more important event or work group on the agenda of the IPCC. We must quickly confirm or explain away that which is being reported and observed. If the recorded trends we've seen here today are confirmed as accurate and continue unabated, it's clear that in a relatively short time our planet will experience climate change like nothing we've dealt with before. Suresh, you are the only atmospheric climatologist here. What are your thoughts on how climate can be affected by this trend?"

"Well, without doubt, should this trend continue unabated, the planet is at great risk of dying." Looking briefly around the room for reactions, Dr. V continues, "I'm sure you all realize that most of the oxygen in our atmosphere comes from the oceans." Heads are shaking in agreement around the room. "Also, the ocean dynamics strongly affect climate and weather patterns, transferring heat from the equator to the poles and moderating carbon dioxide levels in the atmosphere. The consequences, if this trend continues, are dire to say the least."

Dr. V looks over to Dr. Reddy, indicating he is done speaking.

"Thank you, V . . . in short, a climate calamity is possibly at hand. I'd like to ask you to extrapolate the data we have to develop timeframes we are dealing with. The dataset available to the project is available to you and your staff. Of course you have access to everything in any case, but let me know . . ."

Dr. Reddy trails off knowing that V has all the resources and manpower he'd need to develop timetables from everything to rising air temperatures and air quality, to changes in growing seasons, fish migrations, etc.

"Panalla, I will have my staff at Scripps work with the data and develop this, but I think I can help by offering other services as well."

Dr. Reddy, smiling, says, "Which is the real reason I asked you to join us today. I know where you're going with this."

"That's right; we'll have to move fast once we're ready, and more than likely whatever is going on with the falling sea levels, is going on at unfathomable depths. But also I'd like to add a calming word here; that is, whatever is going on may run its course and . . . for all we know right now it has ended."

Dr. Reddy asks, "So what we are observing now may be the result of an event that has already abated, but we are just now observing it?"

"Yes, Panalla, that is correct. We should be careful about what we report. It's one thing to read seismic activity in a volcanic range and warn nearby towns to be ready to evacuate; something very different to report that a tectonic plate shift recently occurred out in the deep Atlantic permanently altering the tidal activity from Le Havre to Santander."

"Dr. Cooper?" Panalla is addressing the geophysicist. "I realize we are just getting underway, but would you and/or Dr. Lin like to add to the discussion from a geographical perspective at this point?"

"Dr. Reddy, Dr. Lin and I are suspicious about whether the crustal thickness anomalies in the North Atlantic Ocean basin are somehow related to the falling sea level. Also, recently there's been quite a lot of seismic activity in the Iberian Peninsula. Dr. Lin has suggested we use her methodologies to examine crustal thickness of the Earth in additional ocean basins of the European Atlantic."

"What do you suspect?"

Dr. Lin answers with a question, "Dr. Reddy, has it been cited anywhere that sea levels or tides are rising in other parts of the world in an offsetting fashion?"

"No, that's not been cited anywhere."

"Exactly . . . so where is the seawater going? I mean, there hasn't been a sudden tidal shift where now tides and sea levels are notably higher—or a tsunami, which is often the result of a plate shift . . . an earthquake. Where's the seawater going?

Has it rolled over to another part of the planet? Is it evaporating?" Answering her own question she continues, "No. Is it somehow, somewhere escaping through the Earth's crust? And more important, to Dr. V's point, is it ongoing or has it abated entirely . . . partially?"

Dr. Reddy looks toward Dr. Cooper and asks, "Dr. Cooper, your studies of the Earth's mantle and core leads you in this direction as well?"

"Well, yes. Historically, we've recorded the movement and relocation of rivers and mountains by changes in the Earth's crust. So I feel strongly that we have to consider the possibility that something seismic has occurred and is at work here, especially given both the recent activity and history associated with the tectonic plates in the area of the Iberian Peninsula."

Dr. Reddy has another question. "I never would have imagined such a thing. You're suggesting that there could be a . . ." He trails off, searching for a scientific phrase or word. "A hole? In the bottom of the ocean where all the seawater is rushing, or rather draining?"

Dr. Cooper picks up on the idea. "*And into what?* is the rest of the question."

The room is quiet for a moment as they digest the idea and update their notepads.

Dr. Cooper continues, "It's a hypothesis—and the reason why I need to get into the geo-lab and run several experiments, using materials and conditions that may exist in the Earth's deep interior."

"Thank you, Dr. Cooper, Dr. Lin. If you could provide the project folder with summary detail pertaining to the activities you'll be performing, the IPCC and this work group will be in a position to support your work."

The two geologists indicate they are in agreement.

"OK! Let's continue," Dr. Reddy says in a spirited fashion. "But before we dive into other activities and tasks, I'd like to see if we are able to reach an agreement on a problem definition statement."

The group spends the rest of the meeting developing the problem statement and working out action work plans, deliverables, and short-term objectives and calendar dates. They will be in regular contact, sharing information electronically, via global project file access, and will meet again in one week.

The work group breaks up and the meeting concludes. It's nearly noon when they leave the conference room. Dr. Reddy stays behind on the phone. Camilla and Ron confirm their post-lunch meeting to continue reviewing the LET test plan. The next morning, they are planning to drive to Colorado Springs where the LET is located within the US Air Force Academy campus. Ron heads to his office as Camilla catches up with Drs. Cooper and Lin near the front entrance.

"Dr. Cooper, Dr. Lin!" she calls out to them. "Hi . . . I was wondering if you like to grab a bite for lunch."

They are standing in the large glass lobby entrance of the building, once the headquarters of the Montfort Beef Company, and now occupied by the IPCC. Its entrance is a large thirty-foot high glass A-frame containing a twenty-five hundred square-foot entrance hall, which looks directly west toward the front range of the eastern Rockies. On a clear day, the view is majestic, breathtakingly beautiful, made so by the twenty-five miles distance between the town of Greeley and the mountains.

Dr. Cooper is headed to his lab at the Geophysical Laboratory of the Carnegie Institution in Washington, D.C.

"I'm afraid I'm taking the Uber to DIA for a flight to Washington, but Dr. Lin may have time before her flight."

"I'd love to, with one condition." Dr. Lin giggles and smiles. "Please call me Tingting."

Camilla agrees. "Sure. Such a pretty name, Tingting."

"But does anyone want to go out in this?" Tingting motions toward the parking lot outside where a fierce windstorm is whipping up a red dust with such intensity and thickness, the cars in the lot just sixty feet away are not visible.

"It seems to have started in the short time it took us to walk from the conference room. It was clear as a bell outside when we left that room," Camilla says.

"Well, that was about ten minutes ago," Cooper says. "I'm going to stop in the men's room, and then I'm hoping it blows through. Even the AVE needs to see the road. Tinting, I'll see you in the lab tomorrow—what time is your flight?"

"It's at five seventeen pm, on United."

Dr. Cooper turns to Camilla to shake hands and say goodbye. "I wish I could join you. I'd like to hear more about the LET project. Ron and I have only discussed the monitoring stations. I'd like to understand more about how it actually works."

"I think you'll soon have a chance to experience the LET. Ron and I will be in Colorado Springs tomorrow to continue testing. I hope you both will be there with us very soon."

"OK, sounds good . . . I better run. I'm catching the three thirty-three. Goodbye!" Cooper turns and walks away in the direction of the restrooms located in the rear of the lobby.

"See you soon and have a safe trip!" Camilla calls out.

"Do you have an idea for lunch, Camilla?"

Camilla turns toward the glass, straining to see the cars through the dust still blowing across the parking lot. "I was looking forward to the huevos rancheros at a place called The Egg & I—about ten minutes away out in west Greeley on west twenty-seventh. But . . ." She motions toward the parking lot and the dust storm.

"I tell you what, let's make a stop in the ladies room. When we come out, if it's clear, we'll go. Otherwise, we'll go to the cafeteria here."

Twenty minutes and several phone calls later, the two women emerge from the ladies lounge to find that the windstorm has subsided and once again a beautiful sun-filled afternoon sky shrouds the Rockies in an azure hue.

The cars in the parking lot look somewhat less perfect as the windstorm has covered them in a fresh coat of red dust, which soon is blown off as the Ubers make their way to West 27th.

"Yes, we're ready," Camilla tells the waitress. "We'll both have the huevos rancheros please. A dark roast coffee for me. Tingting, coffee?"

"Hot tea, please. Thank you."

"What time will you get in tonight? It will be late?" Camilla asks.

"I think my flight lands around ten thirty. I'll be lucky to be in bed by midnight. But I'll sleep in tomorrow and get into the lab around nine thirty. There's some lead time anyway in what Dr. Cooper has to prepare so it's not a problem."

"I know a little about Dr. Cooper's work. It's really amazing that he is able to draw accurate conclusions pertaining to the Earth's core based on materials extracted from the Earth's mantle."

"His work is nothing short of genius," Tingting adds.

"Can you tell me what you think his hypothesis is about?"

Tingting describes the general theory she and Cooper

plan to explore. "Well, given that the falling sea level and tide changes are confirmed, our thinking is that it is not a plate shifting like that which we've seen in modern time, but something associated and significantly more dramatic."

Camilla looks perplexed. "Can you explain what that might be?"

"I think a good way to look at it is more as a series of events, rather than a single event. For example, the shifting of tectonic plates is an event. That event causes another event, an earthquake, which is manifested by collapsing mountainsides, redirecting of rivers, etc. The quake may lead to a volcanic eruption under certain circumstances, etc."

"OK, I follow—and the final event could be something new?" Camilla asks. "So, you and Dr. Cooper are suggesting that a new event that we haven't seen in modern times may have occurred."

"Possibly, and furthermore, it may be ongoing!"

Camilla doesn't like the way that sounds. It scares her.

Their huevos rancheros, coffee, and tea come to the table.

Tingting tastes the huevos rancheros. "Delicious. I don't eat much Mexican food; this is very good."

"I'm glad you like it. I love Mexican food."

The two women enjoy their lunch quietly for a few minutes, thinking to themselves.

"Tingting, I'm basically an IT person. I have to tell you that a lot of what I read, hear, and see about climate change . . . the changes our planet is undergoing . . . well, it really frightens me."

"In a way, I think that's a good thing, Camilla. Most people are out of touch, unaffected, uninformed, and misinformed. Ignorance is bliss . . . that's not a good thing."

"Does your work sometimes frighten you?" Camilla asks.

"That's an interesting question. I'm sort of lost in the science, too deep in the study to be frightened. Which is why it's important for people like you, Ron, and his team to be successful. It's important that the IPCC and Dr. Reddy do all they can to convince the nations of the world that climate change events affect their lives . . . make it real before there is a cataclysmic event from which there's no way back."

Again, a sinking feeling overcomes Camilla. Tingting is scaring her. She wants to ask another question but is afraid of the answer. She asks it anyway. "Don't you expect that this is likely to be some sort of shifting in the Earth's crust, like an earthquake where tectonic plates shift? Forgive me, but isn't this likely a normal sort of event just located far away, deep in the ocean? What's the worst case you and Dr. Cooper are talking about . . . a worst-case scenario?"

"We're not talking about worst case scenarios just yet. The tidal data is incomplete. But we have discussed several possibilities should the data continue to be consistent with that we've observed to date."

"Well, forgetting about the worst-case scenario—is there something less than doomsday you can share with me? I'll take it in complete confidence."

Tingting finishes her egg dish and signals the waitress to remove her plate as she sips her tea while watching the time. She still has an hour drive time to DIA. "Camilla, I'll paint a broad picture of where Dr. Cooper and I are going with this. Much will be dependent upon the tidal data; however, given recent seismic activity in the Iberian region and the thin crust of the Earth's mantle in several area of the Atlantic I've studied, I'm speculating something has occurred to dramatically change the profile of the planet as we know it. The first question is what is that new profile? Has a large portion of the Atlantic deep seabed collapsed?

"You mean like someone stepping in a mud puddle, altering the bottom of the puddle so that the resulting area around the perimeter of the puddle and the puddle itself is smaller?"

"Yes, that's one way we're thinking of it—except, in this case, the stepping action is something like volcanic activity or tectonic movement."

"If that were the case, the retreating sea level would plateau and cease to fall, right?"

"And that would seem to be the end of the event," Tingting says. "But there are other possibilities more deadly."

"Such as?"

"Well, your scenario is somewhat benign. On the other end of the scale, modify your mud puddle experiment such that when the floor of the puddle is stepped on, it cracks and caves in, like a sinkhole might. So now a portion of the supporting layer of the puddle is gone and the puddle does not just sink to a lower level, but finds a much lower support level, and possibly drains till it empties the surface puddle."

Camilla asks, "How much could escape? Where would the ocean water flow? Wouldn't it just find a lower ground and settle to a new lower level, like the first example?"

"And again, the event would end. We would hope so. But if we find that the end of the event has not occurred and sea levels are continuing to fall, this would suggest that ocean water is escaping to a deeper structural layer, perhaps from the Earth's crust to the mantle or into the Earth's core."

Camilla is stunned by Tingting's explanation.

"Camilla, when you were in Europe, did you spend any-time exploring the great caves of Europe?"

Now caught off guard, she is flustered and answers slowly. "What . . . no. Why?"

"Those caves are indicative of the fact that much of the European continent contains ribbons of a vast karst topography. It's sort of a big Swiss cheese. Excuse the pun, but if we get far enough into this, Dr. Cooper's work will be key in understanding whether events involving oceans and karst topography are possible scenarios. Camilla, I'm sorry, but I have to cut this short and catch my flight. Do you mind if I run? We'll take this up again next time when there's more data."

Camilla, still in a sort of daze, not expecting what Ting-ting is implying, shakes her head in agreement. "Of course; don't miss your flight. Thank you for joining me. I'm very glad we could have lunch."

"See you next week, Camilla—and, thanks for lunch."

"You're welcome. See you next week. Bye, Tingting."

Camilla signals the waitress for the check, pays the bill, and drives back to her room at the Fort Collins Marriott where she picks up her review of the LET documents.

After twenty minutes she's unable to keep from thinking about her conversation with Dr. Lin. "A karst," she wonders. "I've never heard of a karst . . . is it different from a cave . . . what are the implications?"

Putting the LET specs aside, Camilla dives into every-thing she can find online about karst topography and the caves of Europe. A couple of hours go by and she dozes off on the couch, waking to the vibration of her phone. It's Eddie calling from aboard *The Kiss*.

CHAPTER 9

The Call

The sea level data continues to worsen as the tidal monitoring sites are confirmed by the IPCC and new data continues to indicate that tide and sea levels are falling unabated all along the western European Atlantic, Mediterranean, and North African seacoasts. In the context of the IPCC's mission statement and Dr. Reddy's work group, the matter is escalating beyond a "normal" climate change study issue and is beginning to look more like the beginning of a planetary crisis, the latter of which they have little experience.

Dr. Cooper's geophysics group, led by himself and Dr. Lin, run numerous experiments using materials found deep within the mantle of the planet to better understand the potential for ocean water to escape and flood the deep mantle of the Earth's crust and the inner core. Dr. Reddy can't believe what he is hearing from Dr. Cooper and his team. They believe there are likely numerous channels for ocean water to escape and flow through once the crust is fractured. They hypothesize that it is possible that a network of large and deep karsts are enabling the flow of seawater through a massive breach in the oceanic crust. Dr. Lin's work confirms the oceanic crust to be as little as just three miles in some of the ocean basins near where recent seismic activity has occurred in that part of the Atlantic off the Iberian Peninsula.

Dr. Cooper's team is ready to present results of experiments on various materials thought to exist in the oceanic crust, supporting the idea that these materials could extend much deeper into the Earth's mantle before reaching the thicker crust commonly known to make up the continental crust—i.e., granite. The team likens this to a weakened artery wall, which if ruptured in an ocean basin, can flood the crust via a karst. The team presents a high probability that such a formation could exist. Dr. Lin's associates suggest that man-made karsts are further promoting the possibility, given the millions of barrels of liquid man has pumped from the crust over the decades.

Dr. Reddy can't believe his ears as Dr. Lin adds this man-made karst idea near the end of there video conference.

"Dr. Lin, you believe the oil industry may have contributed?"

"Dr. Reddy, what I've presented here is based on what we've tested and results in the lab . . . hypothetically, yes, but it's besides the point. A tremendous amount of seawater is going somewhere. It's not escaping into the atmosphere. One of Dr. V's teams confirmed atmospheric gases are currently within normal ranges. We cannot confirm any event on the land surface of the planet where the ocean is flowing inland. All that is left is the probability of seawater flowing into the Earth's crust. The closest indication of that is studying the geology of karsts. Now, we've taken that knowledge and expanded it in the lab using material and formations under similar pressure and found that once such a structure is void of the material and liquid, what is left presents very positive for a karst to form should a massive water flow occur. Seismic activity may have introduced the water flow."

It sinks in as Dr. Reddy stares upward thinking of the possible long term affects on the climate.

Dr. Cooper picks up where Dr. Lin leaves off. "Dr. Reddy, you should understand that what we're proposing here is a hypothesis, one which we are unlikely to prove 100 percent. But given what we know has recently occurred and is ongoing in the region, its history, and what we've recently learned in the lab discovering basalt deeper than expected in the Earth's mantle, we are roughly eighty percent plus confident of the theory."

Cooper is referring to that there are two different types of crust: thin oceanic crust, three to thirty miles thin, made of basalt, that underlies the ocean basins, and thicker continental crust, twenty to thirty miles thin, made of granite, that underlies the continents. What Cooper had proved in his lab was the probability of the existence of basalt much, much deeper into the core of the planet, raising the probability that water could flow and spread through the crust at a deeper level, thereby allowing the possibility of a sea or ocean existing deep below the surface of the Earth's crust.

"Dr. Cooper, how is it that this is happening now?"

"Well, in that part of the planet, Western Europe, great geological events have been causing havoc throughout recorded history. The Earth's crust is very unstable all along Western Europe. Recent seismic activity, once again in the Iberian peninsula is a likely suspect."

"Dr. Cooper, what would move that eighty percent probability higher, say to ninety-five percent?"

"That's easy. Find the breech in the ocean floor. Assuming we could get close enough to take deep samples of the materials in that part of the Earth's crust, we would raise, or lower, the probability of our hypothesis. But, Dr. Reddy, if we find the breech, I would assume we'd dismiss the hypothesis as rhetorical and focus on developing a solution to close the breech."

"No doubt. My god . . . what might that require?"

"That depends on its size and characteristics. Given the amount of water flow . . . it's hard to say."

Also participating on the video conference call are Dr. Suresh Veerabhadran and members of his team in Woods Hole.

Dr. Reddy consults his old friend. "V, what are your thoughts about finding this monster?"

"Panalla, I anticipated that we'd have to move fast, so there are a couple of activities I've added to our work plan. We've already started to look for the monster. But again, I want to caution everyone that whatever is going on, it may have run its course and has ended as abruptly as it started leaving us to observe lagging effects."

"V, can you be more specific about how you're searching for the monster?"

"Sure . . . please, I shouldn't have referred to this as a monster, and I'd like to suggest we refrain from the term before it ends up in the press. But, yes . . . we have begun looking at atmospheric conditions that might point to such an oceanographic disturbance. More than likely, the anomaly is leaving a mark on the atmosphere."

"V, Dr. Cooper is suggesting a breech in an ocean basin." Looking at Dr. Cooper for agreement Dr. Reddy continues, "Likely deep in a basin floor I believe. So what might you find by examining the atmosphere?"

"Dr. Reddy, just to clarify . . . of course the depth of the basin is likely relevant; however, this may be occurring at a relatively shallow depth as well as in a deep ocean canyon or somewhere in between," Dr. Cooper adds.

Dr. Veerabhadran continues, "Let's hope it's not the latter or it's very unlikely we'll ever find it. Of course our best hope is that one tremor started it and another ended it and we're witnessing the lagging result. However, we're proceeding as if it's ongoing. To answer your question, Panalla, there's a likelihood, depending on the depth of the breech, that the flow of water extends to the surface, causing moisture in the atmosphere above this area to be present and can be identified using satellite observation."

"V, how will you identify it by satellite?" Dr. Reddy asks.

"How many of you have been to Victoria Falls, or Niagara Falls?" Dr. Veerabhadran asks. Heads are nodding positive. "Or at the beach when the surf is up; what do you see? In a calm state, the ocean is giving off oxygen but as the ocean water is stirred up, moisture is captured by the atmosphere through movement of air, wind, water, and temperature. So much so that under certain conditions, clouds are formed and carried into the atmosphere. In essence, we might start to look for evidence of the disturbance by looking closely at the ocean atmosphere."

"Can I suggest you begin examining that part of the Atlantic off the Iberian Peninsula?" Dr. Cooper suggests.

"Thank you, Dr. Cooper. Exactly. We've started this analysis in several quadrants of that part of the Atlantic."

"What are the perimeters of your search area?" Dr. Reddy asked.

Dr. Veerabhadran brings up a satellite image display of that part of the planet outlining an area from the mouth of the Strait of Gibraltar extending hundreds of miles west into the Atlantic, south to the Tropic of Cancer, and north to the northern most part of Spain. "As you see here, we're starting with this large area outlined from twenty-three degrees north to forty-five degrees north, six degrees west to the twentieth parallel."

Camilla is also observing the video session from her room at the Fort Collins Marriott. She begins pacing the room, unable to watch the conference. She tells herself to calm down . . . there's no reason to get excited . . . it's just one area of a very large ocean, which they may or may not find anything . . . there is no threat to Eddie and Helle onboard *The Kiss*. She pours herself a glass of water and picks up her phone to check the time. She wants to call Eddie. She sits again at her desk and continues observing the conference; however, she cannot shake the scare Dr. Veerabhadran has just put into her.

Dr. Veerabhadran finishes explaining the methodology, which is to examine the imagery for signs of large amounts of moisture appearing to be fixed to an area of the ocean surface. This he likens to a large stationary fog or cloud. "I believe such a static unchanging condition over an extended period of time could be the telltale sign we're looking for."

"What would be the next step if you find something?"

"A drone device, or more likely, a submersible device to examine and confirm. The latter would give us a better idea of what we're dealing with both on and below the surface."

Dr. Veerabhadran has already been thinking of the capabilities that the Nereid's joint venture could lend to addressing the problem. The Scripps and Woods Hole Oceanographic Institutes had teamed up and developed a new class of underwater vehicle, capable of reaching and surviving the greatest depths of the ocean for an indefinite period of time. The

Nereid submersibles are three times the size of the earlier generation of submersibles, nuclear powered, capable of fully untethered remote operation from anyplace on the planet, which is enabled by a floating communication pod. The motorized communication pod is in constant contact with the submersed vehicle, sending and receiving signals between the remote operator and the vehicle through satellite communications. The surface pod automatically changes its position relative to the submersed device and has an inexhaustible nuclear fuel supply. New materials developed a decade earlier using the mineral unobtainium had enabled a generation of new communication capabilities, resulting in the ability to carry higher frequencies and speed communication signals over a great distance and through dense structures.

Veerabhadran is glowing.

CHAPTER 10

A Day at Sea

Eddie and Helle complete their first full day of sailing with a successful run from Málaga to Gibraltar, about sixty-two nautical miles. *The Kiss* performs well as the two men busy themselves making final checks of mechanical, electric, and electronic systems onboard the forty-six-foot Oyster. They go through virtually everything they can get to above the waterline in order to identify anything that requires replacing once they reach Gibraltar. Everything checks out in good order: spinnaker, mainsail, genoa furling, storm jib operations, and all the riggings.

They use the oven and kitchen components and inspect the deep freezer and refrigerator operation; the electric windlass and anchors are checked, all the covers are examined, the toilets, pressurized water systems, hot-water heater, the several showers onboard, etc. Even the davits from which they've rigged a pair of Sunfish sailboats are double-checked.

With everything looking good, they depart the following morning at sunrise from Gibraltar, heading west toward the strait and the island of Madeira, a trip of more than 600 nautical miles. Except for some light summer fog, the morning tide, wind, and weather is in their favor for passing through the tricky Strait of Gibraltar. Helle is well aware of the challenges that sailing the strait can present even the avid sailor. Its flow

of winds, along with periodic calmed winds and dense summer fog, have long challenged sailors since the early Roman
Empire.

The strait is the portal between the Atlantic Ocean and
Mediterranean Sea, formed by the Baetic Cordillera mountain range of Spain, and the Atlas mountain range of North
Africa. In this position, the strength of the wind flow through
the strait is mostly influenced by the change in air pressure.
Often winds of light or moderate force in the eastern strait
can quickly turn up to a gale as the wind funnels westward
through the narrowest portion and into the Bay of Cádiz. Of
course besides the prevailing wind, the easterly current from
the Atlantic into the Mediterranean along with the tidal flow
is of paramount importance when passing through the strait.

Eddie and Helle have done a good job of planning. It pays
off, and with luck on their side, they pass easily through the
Strait of Gibraltar, making way in the Atlantic for the island
of Madeira. Eddie has also relented on his earlier insisting that
they return to Huelva and start from that point as Columbus had on his first trip to America. But Helle convinces him
that it's really a waste of time to add 200 miles to sail in the
opposite direction given they had already lost a week after
The Kiss had slipped her blocks in dry dock. On top of that,
Eddie's adventure had indeed begun from Huelva where he
and Camilla had been staying.

The intense westward blowing wind known as the Gibraltar levanter finally quits as the sun sinks below the horizon and
a full orange moon begins to rise from the southeast, painting
its golden path across the becalming ocean water, climbing
to its snowy white zenith in the southwestern sky where it
will then slowly sink and disappear in a few hours into the

western horizon. *The Kiss* is nearly 100 miles west of the Strait of Gibraltar, and Eddie and Helle are relaxing on deck after their long triumphant day.

"Man, what a beautiful evening. Have you every been at sea on a night like this, Helle?"

"Many . . . many nights."

"A hundred miles from land . . . hard to believe we're so far off shore . . . and so calm now after today's sail through the strait."

Eddie is in the mood to talk. A sense of complete relaxation has taken over any sense of concern at being, as he liked to put it, at "deep" sea.

"You know, . . . I was thinking that we've been so busy getting ready for this trip, preparing and stocking *The Kiss* . . . we really haven't had much time to kick back before taking out from Málaga. I'm glad you and Camilla hit it off. I never thanked you for showing her around Huelva and inviting us over to your beautiful house."

"Es nada, Señor Gerber."

"Well, I'm glad we're sailing . . . I've been looking forward to this time together and . . ." He trails off and smiles across at Helle, realizing he was running off a bit. Helle just sits there listening and looking out across the ocean as the moon paints itself across the gentle heaving water.

It's quiet as Eddie begins thinking that he's not really sure how he feels about Helle—or, more particularly, how he feels about Helle and Camilla spending time together while he was searching for a boat. He has been so consumed with readying *The Kiss* and preparing for the trip, he's now for the first time feeling guilty and maybe even jealous of Helle. Taking another sip of beer, he wonders if he's taken Camilla for granted and turned her toward Helle for the attention that is only his, Eddie's, to give.

This motherfucker! Why isn't he saying anything? he thinks.

"It's funny how things work out . . . it's fate I guess. Do you believe in fate, Eddie?"

"To an extent, but I think we have great deal of control over our lives as well."

"What about God?"

"That's way too complicated a subject . . . but I'll tell you one thing, Helle . . . look out there . . . out across this ocean . . . such a beautiful night. It's impossible to deny the existence of God."

Eddie regains control over his feelings of guilt and jealousy. He begins to recall that Helle has been a godsend and that, without having met him, he'd still be rumbling through marinas and shipyards and attending the local sailing club meetings. *Is that fate,* he asks himself and rests his head back against the mast, feeling tired and telling himself that he, Helle, is a sweet guy, great sailor, and probably the best person he could have hoped for. He chuckles as he thinks about how Helle is a huge plus if he compares him to Camilla. Helle loves sailing and is an excellent sailor; Camilla, she's tired of sailing. Of course there is the sex, which he is missing, but Helle covers so many more aspects of *this* particular trip. He wonders if that makes up for the lost sex.

Like other kinds of sex, boat sex with Camilla was no longer "virgin" territory. They had made sure to "do it" under many, many conditions: on deck in full moonlight, sunset, break of daylight. These were the first to be crossed off the list, followed by having sex during varying degrees of rough seas on deck, stormy weather, select positions for weather conditions, and then repeating the same below deck, to be followed by variations on and below deck; in the water, various tarpaulin strappings, on and on. So while Eddie is surely missing it, it isn't any longer quite like the first dozen or two times they had done it at sea. But then again, he tells himself smiling, *Isn't it kind of like golf; inasmuch as every time you address the ball and take the shot it's different than any other time before.* He grins with this idea and then snaps out of his daydream and opens his eyes to the beautiful evening sea . . . *Such a calm ocean,* he thinks.

He doesn't care that there is barely a breeze, or that they are nearly stopped. He speculates that they had made better than eight knots for most of the day. Now the evening is falling with a bright moon and calm seas. Time to relax a bit. His mind wanders back to recall the first time he and Camilla had a night like this; the hours romping nude on deck, moonlight swims and sex, pot, wine, more sex. *Yeah, pretty fucking great,* he thinks. But he could tell weeks ago that Camilla wasn't into this trip and that well before she left for home, her mind was back at work.

The reality of it, however, is that Camilla was unable to tolerate even the *idea* of being at sea with Eddie again, especially once she had recognized Helle as a possible "savior."

Again, the jealous side of Eddie begins eating at him. "Many, many nights," Eddie repeats, sounding a suspicious tone.

Again, another long quiet pause as Helle is dozing off in reverie.

"I guess living your whole life in this part of the world, you had early and frequent access to the sea. How many times this crossing—what did you say . . . five, six times?"

"No, no, many more." Helle snaps out of his daydream.

Eddie opens a small backpack and is feeling for his stash of marijuana. He locates an envelop with a quantity of the drug and begins rolling joints. "Well, that's good; . . . so I guess it's pretty safe if we smoke one of these." He lights one and says, "Many, many nights, huh? I know you've more than once or twice; how many . . . really . . . what number do ya figure?"

He passes the joint over toward Helle. He waves it off, and Eddie withdraws it. For a minute, they both gaze up to the cloud-draped moonlit sky and out across the ocean.

"Oh . . . I don't know. It's probably . . . sixty . . . maybe eighty or a hundred."

Eddie is into a deep hit off the joint when the last number crunches through his brain. He exhales with a nasty, raspy sounding cough. "What?" he coughs out to Helle. "How could you do that many?" Eddie chuckles. "Were you sailing across the oceans in diapers?" Then lowering his voice, Eddie asks, "Are you Captain Nappy?" They both chuckle. "How old are you anyhow? It's not your birthday, is it? I didn't bring a cake. Although we might be able to bake one in that oven below."

Helle is laughing. "Actually my birthday is coming soon— September 11th. I usually forget. When I was married, my wife would remember and remind me. I never remembered it."

"Well, I guess I have that role now. Nine-eleven—a date hard to forget. So what will you be this year? Let me guess . . . sixty-four! Don't worry. I'll still need ya, I'll still feed ya." Eddie recalls the Beatles tune, and sings out, "When I'm Sixty-Four."

The pot is having its effect as Eddie continues. "There's a guy I worked with a few years ago . . . great shape at seventy and still skied like a thirty-year-old, cycled and hiked the

Green Mountains of Vermont, ice skated like an Olympian. Damn, I couldn't keep up with him on a bicycle . . . or with him on skates either. You know, you look to be in that sort of shape."

"Eddie, you are too kind. Thank you . . . I have quite a few years . . . many more than most."

"How many years, Helle?"

"More than a century."

"What are you talking, man?"

"I've met maybe forty like me." Helle slides closer to where Eddie sits, glaring into his eyes and lowering his voice as if telling a secret. "I know they've been living and working among us in vast quantities all over the world, and . . . well, you're talking to one right now."

Eddie is trying not to laugh in his face, thinking this is pretty bizarre coming from Helle. Or, he wonders, is he hearing things through stoned ears? Unsure what to make of it he says, "Wow, that's something, but it's not exactly real believable. You know what I mean?"

"We are people just like you, but more highly evolved. We're not political—no leaders. Each of us is a leader. I mean, each man because of this evolution is able to feed, clothe, and transport oneself—"

Eddie cuts him short. "Well, it sounds like a crackpot idea. How about that?" Eddie is laughing out loud. "A crackpot idea!" He pauses a few seconds in the still ocean breeze before continuing. "I mean, if you all are so evolved and smart, why don't you just reveal yourselves and get it over with?" He chuckles again.

Waving his head back and forth, Helle says, "Why don't we just reveal ourselves? Well, . . . if we did it would cause a general panic . . . I mean it's clear to me that it would cause a shock to this antiquated way of life. What about today's leaders? They surely would repress this information."

A rouge wave tilts the boat unexpectedly and then settles back to calm.

"Now, the result is that we've contacted people in all walks of life, *all* walks of life . . ." Helle continues after chuckling to himself, "Yeah, it would be a devastating blow to human systems. So now we're mating with people in all walks of life, and in an advisory capacity, so for once man will have a guideline control over his own destiny. He will have a chance to transcend and to evolve with some equality for all."

"No shit." Eddie again offers the joint to Helle. Again Helle waves it off, and Eddie flips it overboard thinking he's pretty high, tired, and hoping to get first crack at sleeping. "What else sustains this longevity?"

"I've been lucky, Eddie . . . never sick. I've lived a healthy lifestyle since very young, although I did almost die once from food poisoning. I was fifteen years old. My family had traveled to Seville to celebrate the feast of Semana Santa with friends and family. Food was all around us with many street vendors in the Alameda."

"I've been there," Eddie says. "I think they call it Alameda de Hercules."

"That's it! Back when I was young, it was festive like today, but more like New York's Times Square in the sixties and seventies . . . prostitutes, muggings, street food that could make you sick."

"So you ate some pussy and got sick?"

"Not quite. The feast is several days of celebrating and the partying starts in the afternoon and continues into the night.

You eat, drink, screw, and the next day, you don't know what you ate, what you drank, or who you screwed. And I paid the price—big time. I was deathly sick for three or four weeks. I nearly died from dehydration. I wasn't well again for two months. I couldn't eat anything for days. I just drank beer as an elixir until my insides cleared up. Since then it's just nuts, seeds, fruits, and vegetables that I clean and prepare myself . . . fish I catch. That's it. I've been eating the same since then."

"That's it!?" Eddie asks surprised. "And the Alhambra."

"Not really. I'll have a few sips from the bottle and let most of it turn warm and then I pour it out."

"Yeah, I've noticed you do that. No tolerance for alcohol?"

"That, and, I consume very little food . . . especially at sea. When I was young and sailed with my uncle's shipping company, I'd get seasick a lot. But I loved the travel and being on the water, and just dealt with the seasickness. It was much easier if I ate less and stayed away from alcohol. I never cared for alcohol anyway, and . . . you know, I don't need it!"

Helle is one of those people with a natural high; always busy, enjoying himself and when out with friends, he is always having a good time. He speaks several languages, loves to dance, sing, and trade jokes. Women love him, and he loves them back. There aren't too many who are more fun to be with than Helle.

Eddie is smiling and laughing now. "Yeah . . . I can say, that seems to be the case with you. You're fun to be with."

"As are you, my friend. Hey, salute!" He takes a swig of Eddie's beer. *"Che bella cosa!"* he shouts and slams the bottle to the deck. Its golden suds come bursting from the top of the bottle as he begins singing the classic Italian love song, *"O Sole Mio."*

"Na jurnata 'e sole, n'aria serena doppo na tempesta."

"Where did you learn to sing like that, Helle? I've heard you several times now . . . it's a classical voice."

"I studied opera and learned to sing when I was young . . . in my early twenties. Come and sing the refrain with me."

Eddie joined in and the two sailors belt out the famous Neapolitan refrain: *"O sole mio, sta 'nfronte a te, 'o sole mio, sta 'nfronte a te!"*

As they laugh, Eddie swigs the Alhambra and shouts, applauding and encouraging Helle to continue. Now standing, Helle extends his arm toward his singular member of the audience, and with the voice of an accomplished tenor, he continues the verse, *"Ma n'atu sole, cchiu' bello, oi ne', o sole mio, sta 'nfronte a te."*

"Beautiful, Helle. You're amazing."

Helle continues on, *"O sole, o sole mio, sta 'nfronte a te."* And then with great enthusiasm, he sings the final, *"Sta 'nfronte a te!"* slamming his foot on the teak decking.

"Yeah! . . . bravo, bravo, Helle!" Eddie is standing and applauding now. "Amazing pipes, Helle."

"Multi bene, multi bene," he says while taking a bow.

"You must have been something else back in your twenties. Did you perform?"

"Yes . . . actually I did quite a bit back in my early days, but it's very hard to make a living unless you're at the top. In those days, very few could survive in the European market for opera singers . . . even decent tenors. Let me ask you, how many European Caruso's have you heard of? None, right? Maybe Beniamino Gigli, and you've probably never heard of him, right?"

Eddie shook his head no. "But you're so good, Helle!"

"Thank you, Eddie, but I sang even before Gigli's day. Opera was young; theaters were tiny and failing. Sometimes an opera opened in the writer's home . . . most opened and closed quickly and sometimes suddenly."

A fish splashes in the water off the port side of *The Kiss*. The men look over the side, and in the clear water and moonlight they see a school of dolphins chasing bunker. Simultaneously they look up at the sail to see that the wind has died. They shrug it off, unconcerned and content to enjoy the calm moonlit evening.

"So you couldn't make it in Europe?," Eddie asks.

"It's not like today where you have many established opera houses around the world. I know . . . it's still tough today, I'm sure. Still lots of competition . . . probably more."

Eddie gets up to go below to exchange his empty for a fresh Alhambra. "No doubt! But I guess the houses are in better shape . . . I mean, larger, better financed, etcetera."

"Oh yeah . . . and in better shape physically!," Helle shouts so Eddie can hear him below deck. "I once opened a new production of *Les Contes d'Hoffmann* in Paris and after the second performance a fire destroyed the opera house."

Eddie returns on deck. "No shit! What fucking bad luck. Were you able to perform the opera somewhere else? I mean after all the hard work you and the rest of the production company went through, didn't the producers find another theater?"

"Sort of, but it took five years."

"Five years?!" Eddie is shocked and then laughs at Helle's misfortune. "Jesus, what the fuck took so long?"

"I don't recall exactly. It is a long time ago. And there wasn't much work for me while it was being investigated. You know, a gas explosion, fire . . . it is a mess. A big investigation took place, looking into the cause of the gas explosion, which I'm pretty sure was intentional."

"Holy shit! Just like in the opera!"

They are both laughing now.

"Right! As in many operas . . . lots of nasty goings-on. Lots."

Eddie stands up again, this time announcing he is going below to "tap the keg"; meaning it is time for him to pee. Indeed, his belly looks like a keg after eating his way through most of France, Germany, and Northern Italy over the past year. The latest weigh-in has him gaining almost fifteen pounds. He swore to himself and Camilla that he would take it all off on the sail back home. It is going to be a tough battle though, at least until the Alhambra and sherry run out.

Helle gazes out across the reflection of the moonlight on the water, feeling a calm come over him as he sits back against a cushion recalling the fire that destroyed the Opéra-Comique in Paris. "Eddie, can you check on our heading and position while you're down there?" he calls out. Helle thinks that *The Kiss* is doing nicely, cutting through the water with very good speed despite a nonexistent wind.

"Yeah, in a minute . . . I'll get it," Eddie replies as Helle pushes deeper into the cushion, daydreaming about the fire in Paris. . . .

* * *

"Hey!" the inspector called out to Helle. "Nobody is supposed to be in here; this is a crime scene. Who are you and what business have you here?"

"I'm a member of the opera company. I've come to collect my things from my dressing room."

"I'm afraid that is out of the question. You'll have to leave here immediately," the young inspector Bourgeois of the Paris Prefecture ordered the twenty-six-year-old Helle.

"But as you see, the dressing rooms were spared the fire," he said, and glanced toward the center isle of the theater and the orchestra pit. "It consumed the orchestra pit."

The inspector signaled to one of his men standing ten yards down the isle. The captain rushed from his men to join the inspector.

"Captain, please collect this gentleman's information and see him out."

"But, inspector, I'll—"

The inspector cut Helle short. "Young man! As I've said, this is a crime scene. You will have to leave at once."

Dumbfounded Helle said, "What crime scene? There was a fire!"

"Captain!" The inspector signaled the captain that it was time for Helle to go.

The captain firmly took Helle by the elbow and turned him toward the exit. "Sir, if you'd just step to the exit, we'll clear this up."

The young inspector and future chief of police, Monsieur Bourgeois, headed back down the isle to join the investigation team.

"Captain, I'm just collecting—" Again Helle was cut short.

"I'm afraid it will have to wait. You see, the explosion and fire last night not only burned the theater . . . several also perished. We have to treat this as a possible homicide. I'm sure you can understand."

"Oh, Santa Maria," Helle muttered making the sign of the cross. "I didn't know. Yes, yes, of course. Can I be of help?"

"Let's start with your name and address please."

"Helle Alonso Pinzon, Avenue de Saint-Cloud One twenty-four."

The captain took out a notebook and began writing. "Thank you, Messier Pinzon; now, can you tell me your affiliation with the theater?"

"I'm a member of the opera company."

"In what capacity?"

"I'm a tenor."

"Were you scheduled to perform last night?"

"Yes."

"What time did you arrive at the theater for last night's performance?"

"Let's see. I had a baguette on Rue Marivanta and then . . . I'd say . . . I was in my dressing room around five thirty-five or five forty."

"Were you in your dressing room until the curtain called?"

"No, sir. I have to go out into the alley to warm up . . . not my voice so much as my body."

The captain's interest stirred as he looked up and stopped writing. He expected to hear that the tenor would be warming his voice in the dressing room, not in the alley.

"Can you explain please, monsieur?"

"Yes . . . yes. You see the role of Hoffmann is very demanding, not just vocally but also physically, especially in the first act. So to combat my anxiety of first going out onstage, and to be physically ready for the role, I exercise for fifteen, twenty, sometimes thirty minutes in the side alley as I perform my vocal exercises as well."

"Is anyone with you during this time ... other performers, perhaps a coach, your fans ... anyone?"

"No, everyone else is pretty much busy getting ready inside. Normally the stage director comes for me, but once I heard the explosion and opened the door to the smoke and flames inside, I took my leave out the alley and returned to the front where the audience was making its way out in a rush as you can imagine."

"Yes, I'm sure it is not an experience you'll look forward to again. What time would you say you heard the explosion?"

"Six forty or six forty-five."

"The stage director's name, monsieur?"

"Monsieur Vizentini."

* * *

Still daydreaming onboard *The Kiss*, Helle has a sinking feeling as he recalls leaving out a small but important detail about the night of the fire. Vizentini never came for him that night, despite its being time for him to do so. Helle always felt Vizentini might have had something to do with the explosion. Few people knew that Vizentini had associates in the nearby competing Italian opera house. Helle did, but was afraid of possibly implicating him in the disaster. Many people died in the fire, and for a long time, it haunted Helle, so much so that he decided to leave the opera and find another occupation.

Helle's reverie suddenly deepens as he drifts into a more dreamlike state. He is standing on the stage of the Opéra-Comique in Paris, in the role of Hoffmann. A small but well-built man at age twenty-six, he is dressed in a wide-lapelled, double-breasted overcoat with a ruffled white shirt extending up under his chin and across the lapels. It is the opening tavern scene, and he is singing his beloved "Va Pour Kleinzach."

He wakes on *The Kiss* recalling how he never got the call that night from the stage manager although it was due. It's haunted him all these years.

"Who or what is a Kleinzach?" Eddie is asking as he stands looking down at the waking Helle. Eddie is holding a pair of ice-cold Alhambras. He places one down next to Helle and begins walking around the deck and checking that all is secure. He is ready for a rest and to give Helle first watch.

Helle rubs the salt from his eyes. "I was dozing . . . Kleinzach is the subject of an aria in *Les Contes d'Hoffmann*— or, I should say, *The Tales of Hoffmann.*" He laughs at himself.

"Helle, the current here is pretty aggressive. We've made a solid eight, maybe ten knots average since underway. I think *The Kiss* is clipping along pretty good in this light wind, but she's drifted a little west so I've corrected course."

"OK, looks like we're still doing four or five in this light wind . . . it's a good current. Eddie, how far did we sail today?"

"Hundred twenty or so from Gibraltar. Hey, Helle, I'm going to crash. Can you take the watch for three or four hours?"

"Sure. I had a little snooze just now. I'll sing you a lullaby. Any requests?"

"Your choice, buddy. I'll be fast asleep before you finish the first verse."

"Are you familiar with the opera *Les Contes d'Hoffmann?*"

"I saw it performed once . . . it's been a while though."

Now on his feet, Helle begins animating and singing the prologue "Va Pour Kleinzach" from *Les Contes d'Hoffmann. "Vaaaa, Poouur, Klein-zach! Il était une fois à la cour d'Eisenach!*

Un petit avorton qui se nommait Kleinzach! Il était coiffé d'un colbac, Et ses jambes faisaient clic clac!"

"Hey, Eddie, I was just thinking that the last time I sailed to Madeira, it was with Sergio Garcia. Do you remember him?"

"Yes, of course . . . I attended a PGA golf tournament he won . . . many years ago."

"No . . . Sergio Garcia, the physician from Huelva." Helle is laughing out loud. "He's my doctor! I suspect you met him in a sailing club meeting."

Eddie disappears below and is asleep before Helle sings out the second verse sound of Kleinzach's head ringing *cric-crac, cric-crac.*

CHAPTER 11

The Delivery

The C-530 Super Galaxy takes off for Seville a day after Dr. Veerabhadran tells Dr. Reddy that more than likely it will be a submersible. What he isn't ready to tell Dr. Reddy is that his team has also identified several positions between the southern part of the Bay of Biscay to south of the Strait of Gibraltar, where atmospheric conditions are exhibiting what they are looking for. In a few hours, he expects to tell Dr. Reddy they have high confidence in a single location.

Not wasting any time, *The Nereid* with its component cargo from the United States is quickly transferred at Morón Air Base near Seville from the American C-530 to a Spanish C-5 cargo jet. It is ready to go as the final site coordinates are communicated by Dr. Veerabhadran and his team. The twenty-plus-year-old C-5 will deliver the submersible in under two hours to any quadrant in the area being examined.

It parachutes *The Nereid* submersible and its communication pod at N35 degrees, W11 degrees, just south of where *The Kiss* is making way, still struggling to stay on course for the island of Madeira. The C-5 makes numerous passes, collecting and relaying surface-level data to Falmouth, where Dr. Veerabhadran and his team are managing the effort and operating *The Nereid.*

Dr. Veerabhadran's team earlier identified this area using

satellite weather and atmospheric imagery. Soon after the coordinates are given, he departs Colorado for a flight to Boston and on to Falmouth, Massachusetts. The press catches wind of his team leading a significant environmental effort sanctioned and supported by the IPCC, and he is met by a group of reporters at Logan International Airport in Boston.

He waits onboard the arriving flight as it empties its passengers, having been updated during the flight by an assistant to "expect reporters." As it is, he is the victim of bad timing, with Dr. Reddy having given a statement earlier in the day. Dr. V decides it's best to make a brief statement and move as quickly as possible to the waiting helicopter once he receives word the helicopter is ready to go. He gets the call and proceeds through the Jetway and into the terminal where a half dozen news crews are waiting.

"I'll make a brief statement." Reading from what he's scribbled ten minutes earlier, he continues, "The events described by Dr. Reddy at the IPCC, you heard earlier. The Institute has decided further examination is warranted. We are here to conduct this. As you know, we're looking further into falling tides and sea level. It's unclear what the cause is or whether there is a risk to the environment. We expect to know more in a few days once we gather additional data."

Dr. Veerabhadran then quickly moves toward the main corridor and to his right, where the helicopter staff attendant is motioning him.

"Dr. V, from where and how are you collecting data?" a reporter from *The Globe* asks.

He continues the short walk to the end of the terminal. "There are several possible areas along the European Atlantic."

A reporter from *The Herald* asks, "There's been speculation that recent seismic activity has opened the planet's mantle and ocean water is flowing into it—is that correct?"

"That's pretty wild, but if seismic activity is responsible, keep in mind that all seismic activity, once begun lasts a long time and . . . ." Dr. Veerabhadran is interrupted.

"You mean that the break in the mantle is still going on? Is it stretching further?"

Dr. Veerabhadran replied, sounding a little annoyed, "No, I only meant that what may have caused the initial change may have subsequently initiated a countering change . . . that is, if seismic activity is found to be at work."

And with that, Dr. Veerabhadran walks down a secure ramp toward his short helicopter ride, leaving the news crews looking perplexed and frustrated.

Earlier that day, Dr. Veerabhadran and his team examined and tracked new satellite imagery and data revealing a stationary cloud covering a thousand square mile section in the Atlantic, despite surface winds at times gusting above twenty-five miles an hour. The shape of the cloud swirls like the eye of a hurricane, yet the cloud does not move from the quadrant. Finally, they observe that the ocean current surface speed around the eye is in excess of forty miles per hour, while wind speed at 3,000 feet altitude is under twenty miles per hour. At the far edge of the cloud, the ocean water surface speed falls off to six to ten miles per hour until it blends in with the southward moving current.

It's peculiar—a surface level hurricane with such slow wind speed, is Dr. Veerabhadran's thought when observing the imagery and data. He doesn't like what he sees; maybe Drs. Cooper and Lin were right and there is a hole in the ocean. His last thought before falling asleep on the flight to Boston is, *How do you fix a hole in the ocean?* Then chuckling, he says to himself, *I'll have to listen to the song.*

Finding it uneasy to sleep, he drifts off with the help of a Bloody Mary.

Earlier, sleep for Dr. Reddy came less easy. His day started with a relatively calm press briefing in Greeley, Colorado; however, as the media speculated and escalated the story, it became necessary for him to hold a day-ending session with the press and several disaster groups that were attempting to determine where humanitarian efforts might be needed. They left nothing to guess about, inasmuch as they examined the information available and made their own assessment about what would need to be done. For the time being, they concluded that their initial focus should be continued support for those requiring aid related to the earlier seismic activity in the Iberian Peninsula.

CHAPTER 12

That Big Sucking Sound

Aboard *The Kiss,* it's daybreak of the third morning since leaving Gibraltar. Helle comes up on deck from his bunk. "Good morning, Señor Gerber. Wow, we've added quite a lot of cloud cover. What's NOAA reporting?"

"Hey, good morning to you, Helle. It seems that we may not see much sun today, but still a dry day."

Helle goes below and pours a glass of water and throws a few almonds with sunflower seeds into his mouth.

Eddie calls out to him. "Helle, I was just noticing our speed this morning is more than nine knots despite a reported wind speed of just seven. From what I've read of these waters, the currents here are pretty tame. What do you make of it?"

Helle falls back into the galley table cushion, finishes chewing, and sips some water while thinking about the question. "We may have caught the equatorial current. That's good news if it's the case. The South Atlantic gyre feeds into it and is essentially what is going to take us to the Canaries and then America. How about our position?" He gets up, opens the refrigerator, and pours some milk into his cup before walking over to the charting table where he grabs the Garmin GPS. "Let's see . . . thirty-four north, fifty minutes, twenty-eight; longitude, eleven, nineteen, nine . . . still fighting whatever it is that wants us to go west."

Back at the galley kitchen, Helle opens a bag of sunflower seeds before continuing, "And as you said, our speed is a bit faster than expected. I guess all we can do is continue to adjust course . . . but we'll make Madeira on time. I think we'll hit that equatorial current soon and shoot south."

Eddie comes below and adjusts course in the autopilot. "OK, but I'm annoyed the fucking Raymarine isn't taking care of this. Why do you suppose that is? Rocco checked this out before installing it. We didn't have any problem from Málaga through Gibraltar and the rest."

"I'll have it checked out in Madeira, I promise. I'll call Rocco too."

Eddie is finishing a big yawn.

Helle asks, "Do you feel like sleeping?"

"I wouldn't mind a few winks. Thought I'd give Camilla a call first before it gets too late for her."

"Go for it . . . and give her my regards."

"I will." Eddie grabs his cell phone and disappears, closing the compartment door behind him as he enters the owner's bedroom suite. He sits down at his computer and navigates through the European AccuWeather website to browse the weather report and radar while placing his call to Camilla.

"Hey, Camy, sweetheart."

Whenever the Gerbers are away from one another for any period of time, they call each other by their "pet" nicknames.

"It's Captain Kiss. How are you, darling?"

It's late at night in Fort Collins. Camilla had fallen asleep reading about karst topography and the caves of Europe. Along with hearing Eddie's voice, she recognizes the sound of the sea as he sails *The Kiss* in open blue water, still hundreds of miles from Madeira. She feels anxious and uneasy.

"Gerby, I miss you. Is everything all right? How is Helle? I'm glad you called . . . I have something I need to bring you up to date on."

"We're fine. But I'm off to my bunk soon and so much missing you rocking there next to me. I wanted to hear your voice before I kick back. It's getting late there, isn't it?"

"Almost midnight. I fell asleep reading, but I'm glad you called." She reaches for a glass of water on the couch table and takes a big gulp to help her regain her senses and come more awake.

"Oh, I'm sorry, Camilla. I lost track of the time, and you know how I miss talking to you before sleeping. Call me in the morning, sweetheart."

"No, it's OK . . . I wanted to call you earlier, but I unexpectedly dozed with the computer on my lap." Camilla was coming around now. "The sessions with Dr. Reddy and this new work group are very interesting. Gerber, he's brought in several world-class scientists on this. They're not really saying much yet since the data is still being validated, but I get the sense based on the level of people involved that this anomaly concerning tides and sea level is pretty serious."

Eddie is listening intently, but sleep is coming soon. "Who else?" he asked.

"Are you familiar with a Dr. Suresh Veerabhadran?"

Eddie runs his hand through his thinning hair. "*Mmm* . . . he's from Woods Hole?"

"Close, Scripps Institute in San Diego."

"Likely he's well connected with Woods Hole. Who else?"

"Geologists from the IPCC Geophysical Laboratory, Drs. Jordan Cooper and Tingting Lin. She's from Beijing. Eddie, are you there?"

"Yes, I hear you, Camy."

"It appears they are focusing on geophysical properties of the Earth's crust on the floor of the ocean. Gerber, do you know what a *karst* is?"

"Yes, sweetie. Before we met, I spent sometime working in Nashville and took every occasion to visit the caves in Kentucky."

"Mammoth cave—so you know about karst topography."

"Well, Camy, I wouldn't say that, but . . ."

"Gerber, I've been reading about this. It's new to me—the term *karst topography.*"

"Where is Lin going with it?"

"It's still unclear. But from what I've been reading about karst topography in Europe, I get the sense they suspect some event has occurred linking the changing tide and sea levels."

"What do you think about it, Camy?"

"I don't know what to think at this point. I only feel uneasy about it."

"That's just feeling uneasy about the unknown, honey."

"I know, Gerby. It's OK. I just have a lot to think about right now with the LET tomorrow and the project today."

"Tell me what you found out about the karst, and then I'm off to bed."

"There's a lot. You've been to one of the largest examples, Mammoth Caves in Kentucky so you have the basics. The thing is, the fundamental topography can be very scary in that it's hard to say where the hydrology ends . . . like at Mammoth, they keep finding more and more miles of cave. A relatively small crevice could lead to a huge space like a sinkhole and gradually enlarge unseen until the roof of an underground cavern suddenly collapses swallowing homes . . . or whatever else.

Gerber, did you know that a cavern sinkhole swallowed part of the collection of the National Corvette Museum! What the fuck . . . that's scary!"

"I was just thinking about that as you were talking, Camilla. It was scary hearing about it. I think it was a while ago . . . two thousand twelve, thirteen, or so. They don't think seawater is flowing through a karst do they? Sounds pretty extraordinary. Where would it go?"

"Gerber, I can only guess at that. It's too soon for them to say. All I can tell you is what they're looking at as they try to solve the problem. One of the geologists also said that the drilling and pumping of oil in that part of the world —"

Eddie's reaction is incredulous as he cuts her off. "How the fuck could that be related? Man! Climatologists! Maybe Reddy should hand this off to the geologists. I mean, is this a climate change issue? It's starting to sound like it's not. I mean, well, they're supposed to study climate change, right? Is it in their charter to solve issues brought on by geophysical properties and events related to earthquakes and changing sea levels?"

"Well, Eddie, if this continues, it will trigger the greatest climate change event ever—and one that will likely result in great change to life on this planet. I don't think any related field of study should be excluded from the effort."

Several quiet seconds go by as sleep is getting the better of them.

"Well . . . anyway . . . I'm too tired to think about it right now, honey, and this boat is rocking me to sleep."

What Eddie really wants to say but holds back telling Camilla is that he is tired and that the problem autopilot, unexplained speed, and lack of sunshine is nagging at him.

He decides not to open that can of worms without a clear head and with both of them needing sleep.

She lets out a deep breath. "Yeah, me too. It was a long day, and tomorrow will be another. I have to meet Ron at eight. We're driving down to Colorado Springs ... about two hours south."

"Good night, Camy. I'll say hi to Helle for you when I wake up in a few hours."

"OK, don't forget. Sweet dreams, Gerby. Talk again tomorrow. *Ciao, bello.*"

"*Ciao, bella.*"

They both smile, disconnect, and go to sleep.

Eddie wakes six hours later, just after noon, and notices an unusual sound like the droning of a herd of cattle upon the Colorado prairie, and, at the same time perceives that the chopping character of the ocean beneath *The Kiss* has changed with the westward current. He calls out to Helle.

"Hi, Helle—are you playing something meditative?"

Still rubbing the salty sleep from his eyes, Eddie checks the clock and realizes it is almost half past noon and that the little bit of sun coming through the cloud cover is off to his left, indicating they're moving in a southwest direction. He charges to the helm and insists that they adjust course to the south. But Helle has already done so without *The Kiss* responding as he would have expected. The westward current would continue several more hours more before shifting their course south, and then back to the east, then north, again to the west, south, east, north, and so on.

Unknown to Eddie and Helle, but soon to be realized by Dr. Veerabhadran's team controlling *The Nereid*, the same current affecting *The Kiss* will soon acquire a monstrous velocity and threaten the submersible. Within ninety minutes of the operation, *The Nereid* is swept by its fury as Dr. Veerabhadran's team unknowingly guides the submersible toward the center of the vortex. Here the waters, seamed and scarred into a thousand conflicting channels and gyrating in gigantic and innumerable vortices, whirl and plunge in a precipitous descent to the bottom of sea.

Still far away and unseen to Eddie and Helle, but visible by satellite imagery to Veerabhadran and his team, is the mark of a thousand channels of water generating streaks of foam spreading out over a great distance and rising upward to create the demarcating cloud. Hidden from all, a distinct and definite circle, hundreds of yards in diameter, is the mouth of the terrific funnel, whose interior appears as a smooth, shining, jet-black wall of water, inclined to the horizon at a forty-five degree angle, speeding round and round, creating an appalling roar, exponentially greater than Niagara's.

Communication with *The Nereid* is suddenly lost, but not before transmitting terabytes of data to the surface pod and Falmouth. Everything is collected, transmitted, and examined by Dr. Reddy's team at the IPCC and by Dr. Veerabhadran's and Dr. Cooper's teams. It is clear to them upon examination of *The Nereid* data that a significant change has occurred to the ocean basin floor and the Madeira sea basin has collapsed, raising the likelihood of seawater flowing deep into the Earth's mantle, finding its way to new places within the planet's core as never imagined possible before.

CHAPTER 13

Last Call on *The Kiss*

Eddie is sleeping while Helle has the watch. The two men have become more relaxed as their heading comes to the south, on course for Madeira.

Helle is below at the navigation table going though quadrant maps of the area and looking at his notes about ocean currents in these waters, which he's sailed many times over the years. He's concerned but closes his notebook, chalking up their course problems to unusual currents. He reminds himself to check their position, course and speed every thirty minutes and enter it into their log. Earlier in their trip, they had been making entries at the end of each watch, every six hours or so.

He picks up the paperback Eddie is reading, opens a bottle of Saint-Géron mineral water, and sits at the chart table with the top open. *Ah, just right,* he thinks, smiling, making himself comfortable for an hour or so to do some reading. He looks through the table of contents. It's *The Complete Short Stories of Edgar Allen Poe.*

"Oh . . . perfect," he says facetiously. Eddie is in the middle of reading Poe's 1843 story, "The Tell-Tale Heart." Helle is smiling and chuckles, "Oh god . . . that's depressing," and turns the pages to open to the 1841 story "A Descent into the Maelstrom."

"Ah, this sounds interesting and just thirteen pages long."

He begins to read quietly out loud Poe's preface to the story taken from words by Joseph Glanville: "The ways of God in Nature, as in Providence, are not as our ways; nor are the models that we frame any way commensurate to the vastness, profundity, and unsearchableness of His works, which have a depth in them greater than the well of Democritus."

Helle stops reading and looks up to think about the statement Poe brings to the reader at the start. Again he says the words, "Nor are the models that we frame . . . commensurate . . ." He trails off, and lowers his head, feeling sorry for the smallness of humankind and the meaninglessness of this trip for him. "A favor to friends, a pleasure trip," he says.

He goes back to Poe's "A Descent into the Maelstrom," which is the tale of a man recounting how he survived a shipwreck and a whirlpool. Helle is fascinated by the story and soon is lost in the old man's character, who reveals that he only appears to be old. "You suppose me a *very* old man," he says, "but I am not. It took less than a single day to change these hairs from a jetty black to white, to weaken my limbs, and to unstring my nerves."

Helle wonders about his own age and when old age will come to him—if it will ever come. He looks out through the opened top above the nav station, wondering when they will be clear of the cloud and fog they've sailed in for days, and the "models we frame." He says these words, thinking of destiny and returns to Poe's story of the terror of being killed in a maelstrom.

With a smile on his face, he finishes the story and stands to stretch while thinking of the description of the whirlpool and Poe's brilliant writing of the old man's terror. He looks out again at the foggy night and moves to check the radar, their position, course, and speed. It's fifteen knots heading two-fourteen—; it's too much to the south. Poe's maelstrom comes to mind, and in a flurry, it strikes terror in Helle for an instant. He shakes it off.

"Damn it." Annoyed at the autopilot he sees they've slipped from their heading of two-forty. He stands, looking at the autopilot charting and is perplexed also about their speed of fifteen knots. Wind speed is just half that. *It's the current,* he tells himself.

Earlier in the day, the current dragged them off course to the west. Now it is dragging them south and off course again. Helle hears Eddie stirring in his cabin in the stern from which he comes, half awake and unsteady on his feet. He stops and sees Helle standing over the nav table, the paperback just aside.

With a Cheshire cat grin, Eddie says, "I can tell by the look on your face, you read it."

Helle just looks at him, thinking he's still asleep. "What?"

"Poe," Eddie points to the book of Poe stories. "By the look on your face, you just read his story about the sea. It was one of the first short stories I read while sailing from Málaga."

Eddie makes his way to the refrigerator where he takes a bottle of the Saint-Géron. Helle turns back to the chart.

"Are we making up any time?" Eddie asks. "I can't believe we've had a turn of luck with the wind. I can tell we're making good speed, and good thing that fucking autopilot has us on course."

Helle is a little caught off guard by Eddie's reminding him of the Poe story. "Yeah, I did read Poe's story earlier while you were sleeping."

"Well I have to tell you something." Eddie sits, and with a

serious tone in his best pirate voice, he says, "Don't you think for a second any of that is going to happen . . . we're way out at sea for those forces to affect us."

"Really?" Helle replies with a questioning look. He grabs and opens the paperback and reads the preface aloud in his best stage voice, "The ways of God in Nature, as in Providence, are not as our ways . . ."

Eddie joins in the recitation, "Nor are the models that we frame any way commensurate to the vastness, profundity, and unsearchableness of His works . . ."

"Amen!" Eddie shouts.

The two men stand in laughter.

Helle finishes the preface. "Hey, don't forget the well of Democratus."

"Oh right . . . Democratus . . . let's have a sherry and toast him and his fucking well later, and you can have a half bottle of beer."

"Good idea, Ollie," Helle says, imitating Stan Laurel.

"Listen, Eddie . . . I have to tell you that we're still having some issues with the autopilot staying on course."

"Mother fucker, are we on course?"

"Yes, but I've had to adjust. It's getting to the point that we should steer manually. We're making good speed, so twenty or thirty minutes off course becomes a large adjustment to get back. We're adding too much time by wandering the way we are now at fifteen knots."

"Fifteen knots?" Eddie looks at him, questioning the speed.

"Yeah—really nice speed with this current and wind. But we have to stay on course heading two-forty."

Helle sets the autopilot to *off.* The two will steer *The Kiss* to Madeira themselves.

"Here," Helle is motioning him to take the helm. "You've done this before. I know, I've seen you."

Eddie sits, resting his hand on the wheel. Helle falls back into the cushions, looking like it's his turn to sleep. "Listen, Helle. Earlier, before I slept, I spoke to Camilla. She says hello."

"How is she?"

"Just fine, but she was telling me about an alert being issued by the IPCC to all marine vessels in this part of the Atlantic."

Helle perks up, Poe still stirring in his head. "We haven't received any yet. What's it about?"

"Something related to the earthquake activity we experienced in Gibraltar while prepping *The Kiss* in Málaga. They're still examining the data from a deep-sea submersible. It could be the cause of the unusual currents and speed we're experiencing . . . it may be from shifting plates."

"Do they think this area will have a giant wave or an onshore tidal wave? Unusual tides were being reported before we sailed . . . you remember seeing those stories."

"They're still looking at the data. Hey, you look tired. I'll keep us on course. Get some sleep."

Helle was tired and wasn't going to fight it. "That sounds like a good idea. Keep on course and in a few watches we'll be in Madeira." Helle walks toward his cabin.

Eddie wants Helle to get as much sleep as possible, knowing their situation could turn for the worse within the next several hours. He waits for Helle to fall asleep and switches the autopilot back to *on* so he can study their movement history, prevailing wind, the current, and the charts.

Good thing he's so exhausted, Eddie thinks, *or this*

ever-increasing roar coming from the sea might keep him from getting to sleep . . . or perhaps it's more like a sleep-enabling white noise.

The distant roar is becoming more present as each hour goes by, as *The Kiss* is drawn to the Poe-like whirlpool of giant, deadly size, capable of swallowing any vessel on the planet once caught in its grasp.

* * *

The Kiss is one such vessel in its grasp, which Eddie has learned about from Camilla and retired Navy lieutenant Dennis Peary of the Woods Hole Institute. After sixty minutes of discussion about what can be done to save Eddie and Helle, Peary was losing his patience.

Peary had presented and discussed several proposals; however, Eddie Gerber refused to listen to any of the solutions he presented. It became clear to Peary that it would require an order from the Coast Guard if *The Kiss* is to be abandoned.

"Mr. Gerber, I'll tell you something; we think that in about eight hours *The Kiss* will be lost to a giant whirlpool and sucked down like a thirsty eight-year-old sucking a milkshake through a straw on a hot summer day."

Peary makes a sucking sound, like when one takes that final slurp from the bottom of the cup with a straw.

"Do you really think our best course of action is to abandon ship?" Gerber asked.

"Look, we're trying to buy some time while a SAR helicopter is routed out to you."

CHAPTER 14

Let's Get This Party Started

Hours earlier, Lieutenant Peary had walked into Dr. V's conference room at Woods Hole. Often described as a "long drink a water from Texas," being six feet, five inches tall and from Dallas, that was the least of his distinguishing character traits, having Clark Gable good looks and a distinguished career as a US Navy SEAL. Several people owed their lives to his courage, can-do attitude, quick thinking, and affinity for risk taking. Having retired as a lieutenant from the Navy several years earlier, he subsequently finished his doctorate in ocean climatology at MIT and now runs the Special Operations division at the Woods Hole Institute.

Mr. Peary's being an IPCC affiliate and interface with NOAA and all other government agencies for the Woods Hole Institute, Dr. Veerabhadran was not surprised to see Peary when he cowboy-walked his way into the Special Events lab as if arriving to enjoy a day at the rodeo.

Having never lost that cowboy strut or his affection for western wear, Peary was truly a fish out of water since leaving the Navy and landing in Cape Cod.

"Mr. Peary!" Dr. Veerabhadran calls out as Peary comes through the door.

"Dr. V." The two men shake hands. "I hope you're having a good day," Peary says, still with a hint of Texas drawl in his voice despite not having lived there in almost twenty years.

Dr. Veerabhadran looks back toward the graphical display and changes the perspective of its shape. "Dennis, I just want to thank you for bringing the resources together in such short notice."

Looking toward the several oversized displays in the lab, Dennis greets the other participants joining in remotely.

"Hey, Dr. Reddy, it's good to see you."

Panalla Reddy and Camilla are in Greeley, Colorado, while Drs. Cooper and Lin are in the lab in Washington, D.C.

"And, Camilla, I was glad to hear about your return to the IPCC. I want to hear all about your sabbatical."

"Hi, Dennis. It's a nice surprise to see you. We'll have to catch up later. I want to hear all about your civilian life."

Several years earlier, Peary and Camilla had met when he joined WHOI. He had just retired from the Navy and had been designated as one of the Woods Hole Institute interfaces to the IPCC. Camilla also was new with the IPCC staff and given the task of integrating external capabilities into the IPCC work groups and the organization structure in general. Their time working together was short lived, but Dennis felt something between them and having a new life outside the Navy gave him ideas of settling down. Camilla appeared to be someone he might take to the rodeo, or at least go sailing with.

However, Camilla dismissed any idea of having anything but a working relationship with him. Besides, she had already fallen in love with Eddie Gerber, and Dennis Peary was not her type. The cowboy swagger, the drawl in a speech pattern too slow for her likes, coupled with his towering frame—it all added up to a big "No, thank you, sir." She didn't care that otherwise he was a big, beautiful man with dreamy blue eyes, neatly cut thick dark hair, a chiseled face with a Kirk Douglas–like dimpled chin, and olive complexion.

"Pretty easy on the eyes," she used to describe him to Eddie back in New York.

Eddie was of course driven crazy by such talk to the point where he'd tease her by asking if she wanted to fuck him, and then start talking dirty to her. This all led to monumental sex on the weekend when Camilla would return to Hoboken, and a heightened love between them culminating seven months later in marriage.

Camilla let Dennis Peary down gently. She made it clear that their relationship would be strictly business, and after a few weeks time, they parted as fond friends and had no contact until just before Camilla and Eddie left to sail to Europe. When Dennis learned she was taking a sailing sabbatical, he called her and wished her luck and to call on him as a resource anytime, given his significant time at sea.

"Dr. V, I'm guessing this is Dr. Cooper and Dr. Lin?"

"Oh, yes. Excuse me," Dr. Veerabhadran says and makes the introductions.

Dennis sounding a bit rodeo says, "Well, let me just say that I'm very impressed by your work but praying each and every night that you are wrong about the capability of the mantle to absorb sea-size portions of our oceans' water."

"Mr. Peary, we are all hoping and praying that isn't the case," Dr. Cooper says while playing with the wedding ring on his finger and wearing an anxious look on his face. "However—"

Dr. Veerabhadran interrupts, "Dr. Cooper, if I may?"

"Of course."

"Dennis, we were just discussing new events and data as you walked in."

Peary moves to an unoccupied chair at the conference table. "I'm sorry to interrupt. I just wanted to check the status of resources and equipment delivered."

"I'm glad you joined us and appreciate what you've done. New information makes it necessary I . . . I mean the IPCC that is, to make additional requests."

Looking at the display containing Panalla Reddy's image, Peary sees Reddy nodding in agreement. Peary thinks that the situation has somehow worsened. He turns back toward Dr. Veerabhadran. "How can I be of service, Dr. Veerabhadran?"

Dr. Veerabhadran stops examining the object on his display and turns his full attention toward Peary. "The submersible was delivered to the target quadrant off the coast of Spain. I'm afraid it may be lost."

Dennis Peary is a very cool-headed individual if nothing else. He is surprised to hear that the submersible is possibly already lost, and so early in the operation. He sits virtually expressionless, quiet, wanting to hear more, despite the negative report.

Dr. Veerabhadran continues, "I should clarify that we've lost communications with *The Nereid* . . . perhaps we will recover this."

"How long has it been silent?" Peary asks.

"Just ten minutes or so. However, as Dr. Cooper just alluded, the picture is not favorable. We operated *The Nereid* for nearly two hours before losing comm. The data collected in this period shows a collapse of the sea basin floor in the

Madeira Basin and the existence of a submarine canyon reaching all the way beneath the continental shelf. During the data collection period, *The Nereid* encountered currents forming a cyclical cone from the surface to the sea basin floor exceeding sixty plus miles per hour. The display here is a 3-D graph of the size, shape, and speed bands going cool blue to red purple."

The six-foot displays show bands at the surface reaching seventy-five to ninety miles from the core containing speeds of forty-plus miles per hour and the outer bands of fifteen miles per hours before falling to normal ocean currents for that part of the Atlantic.

The other graphical dimensions illustrate a funnel-like shape from the surface to the floor of the basin, with an irregular-shaped hole at the basin floor spanning nearly half mile at its widest point and running roughly eight miles in length. As Dr. Veerabhadran moves the position of the shape left, right, and from different observation points, Dennis Peary utters what everyone else is afraid to say.

"A whirlpool…Jesus…a *giant* whirlpool extending from the ocean surface clear to the abyssal plain floor. That opening along the floor and extending into the canyon must be at a depth of over four thousand feet!"

A silence fills the room as Dr. Veerabhadran moves the display orientation of the giant whirlpool, exploring the velocity bands at various depths, zooming in at the ribbonlike tentacles extending from the center of the vortex and outward for several miles, moving the surface seawater for miles at speeds greater than twenty miles per hour.

At the depth of a thousand feet, the structure of the vortex begins to shift in a bending fashion, not unlike that of a tornado. As it shifts and rotates in a funnel-like pattern, smaller whirlpools are seen breaking and then reattaching to the main vortex at other points, their riverlike ribbons extending miles from the center and reaching upward to suck in the seawater above and join in the main surface funnel.

Along the base of the great vortex where the graphical display gives the impression of it being attached, a large number of riverlike ribbons can be seen terminating into the seafloor along cracks running for miles mostly in a north-south direction—and, off to the east, a trenchlike opening more than a quarter-mile in diameter opens the abyssal plain floor where it meets the continental shelf, and the base of the great vortex quenches its thirst for deep blue ocean water.

"Dr. Veerabhadran, can you zoom in on that trench?" Peary can't believe what he is seeing as Dr. V zooms in. In his typical Texas drawl, he says, "Well, how about that! I'll tell you something . . . that's a lot of seawater moving through that canyon."

The display indicates that water is moving through the canyon trench in excess of fifty miles an hour.

"Dr. Cooper, Dr. Lin, it appears you may be on to something, and I can tell you from a climatological point of view this is pretty bad. Do you agree, Dr. Veerabhadran?"

It was a rhetorical question. He didn't wait for a reply and continued, "The climatology aside . . . Dr. V, I'm going to alert NOAA and the US Navy about this, assuming I have agreement from everyone."

Peary didn't have to ask them given the threat to ocean going vessels; however, he looked around the displays to find heads moving up and down.

Panalla Reddy, however, watching from the Greeley lab, felt it was time to slow things down. "Dennis, V?"

"Yes, Panalla," Dr. Veerabhadran responds.

"Dennis, I'd like to have Drs. Cooper and Lin add their perspective here before you go. Given the data from *The Nereid* and what we're looking at, we should be clear on their assessment and expectations for a solution. Dr. Cooper?"

"Regarding the latter, Dr. Reddy, we should think about buying time. Is it possible we can keep this quite while we continue to examine this data and expand our knowledge about this part of the mantle and formulate solutions?"

"Yes, I believe we can fulfill our responsibility by alerting the necessary agencies and the IPCC. We can leave the news media out for now, but what are your thoughts on this?"

"I'll ask Dr. Lin to comment given her study of crustal thickness of the oceans, but I think it's safe to say that formulating a solution will take some time. Dr. Lin?"

Dr. Lin stops her typing, sips water from a coffee mug, and looks up to address the group.

"It's unfortunate, but it appears that the event that caused this change in the abyssal plain left it as we've seen illustrated here. I was hoping that a subsequent event would have remedied this . . . not the case currently . . . it may yet; however, we are not in a position to do nothing."

Dr. Lin explains the structure and attributes of the Madeira Abyssal Plain and how seismic activity earlier in the year was the likely catalyst, opening the floor of a wide trench along a hot spot in the African Plate and revealing access to a massive submarine canyon where the seawater is able to flow deeper into the continental shelf and the Earth's mantle.

"The canyon appears to be a steep-sided valley cut into the seafloor of the continental slope, extending well onto the continental shelf and having relief comparable to even the largest of land canyons. It's fairly large, but not unlike structures on the surface of the planet. However, unlike similar structures on the surface, this opening is very difficult to explore and understand. Until we devise a way to measure its characteristics, we will be guessing at a solution."

"Yes, since we think the submersible *Nereid* has been lost, monitoring the trench opening will be difficult," Dr. Veerabhadran adds.

"Dr. Lin?" Panalla Reddy has a question. "Is it possible that the space where the water is flowing will fill up and the problem will be solved?"

"Yes, and furthermore, this may have already occurred."

"If that were the case, wouldn't the whirlpool we are seeing stop?"

"Well, keep in mind that we are not looking at live data from *The Nereid* any longer, but besides that, we have no idea where the seawater is going. It's possible that the flow of water may be terminating in or flowing to something like, for example, the Caspian Sea. In essence then, it's like a river."

"If that were the case, the falling sea levels and tides would abate."

"Yes, Dr. Reddy, which is why it's key that the IPCC continue to monitor changes. There are many scenarios."

Dr. Reddy pushes back in his chair. "From what we've seen here today, what are your expectations, Dr. Lin?"

"Well, I wouldn't count on the flow of this water to just stop without there first being some measured indication that it has slowed. That's currently not the case. This canyon trench is in an area of the abyssal plain where the oceanic and continental faults transform and where lithospheric slabs of the two different plates meet and the denser, older slab descends back into the mantle. At the edge of the plate, the oceanic lithosphere can thermally contract and become quite dense. I believe that is what has happened and that it has sunk under its own weight in the process of subduction."

"So the subduction process has provided access deep into the mantle?" Dr. Reddy asks Dr. Lin.

"Apparently, but describing the water flow once it passes from the collapsed trench floor is very speculative."

"What should we pray for—another Iberian earthquake, Dr. Lin?"

"Perhaps. This part of the Atlantic has a long history of dramatic change. Sediment samples from below the deep seafloor of the Mediterranean Sea show that about six million years ago, the Strait of Gibraltar closed tight, and the Mediterranean Sea desiccated. Perhaps something as dramatic as that is occurring now, just four thousand feet below the surface."

"Dr. Reddy, Dr. Veerabhadran?" Dennis Peary stands indicating he's "ready to ride." "If you'll excuse me then. I should make sure shipping lanes are secured from these waters. I'll return within an hour to report on vessels at risk and discuss additional resource requirements."

Dr. Reddy picks up and begins making an entry into his iPad while turning to Camilla. "Camilla, I'd like you to put a team together with Ron Billings to expand our climate change monitoring capabilities associated with this event. Dennis also might have an idea on atmospheric measurement." Dr. Reddy wants to ensure that they stay on top of the associated climate change effect and not allow the subject to take a backseat to devising a solution to the geological problem. "The climate has not yet been impacted, but for sure, over time, if things don't change, there will likely be serious consequences. The world will expect us to be able to answer questions concerning air quality, temperature, and so on."

Peary turns toward the display containing Camilla's image. "OK . . . Camilla, I'm also going to bring in additional resources that can help monitor and model atmosphere changes caused by the falling sea level."

Camilla asks, "Dr. Reddy, given that we've been monitoring rising sea levels for so long, isn't it likely that we are already studying appropriate climate change factors?"

"Possibly, Camilla. But given the nature of this event and its manifestation being sort of topsy-turvy, we need to take a fresh look at what and how we are monitoring, modeling, comparing and drawing conclusions. But I'm glad you asked the question. I'm sure others will make the same assumption, especially given the immediate geological change problem we are addressing."

Peary looks at his iPad to make notes and wonders about the threat to vessels in the area. He finishes his entry and begins stretching his head left and right to loosen his neck muscles, then looks up to see Camilla tapping on her cell phone.

"Camilla, you must be happy to have completed your trip and not be sailing in the Atlantic right now . . . instead you're back safe and sound."

She stops fiddling with her phone, caught off guard by Dennis's comment. She has trouble finding the words. She looks back at her iPhone to see her husband's phone number queued up.

"Yes . . . well . . . almost. Gerber is sailing those waters," she can barely speak the words and steps out of the Greeley conference room. Panalla Reddy watches her leave the room unsure what to say and glancing at the others for reaction.

The meeting goes silent for a minute. Dennis Peary scratches his head, trying to find something to say, having said the wrong thing, being up to this point still unaware of Eddie and Helle onboard *The Kiss* and their predicament. He decides that it's more important for him to return to his office to examine and identify any marine traffic at risk, issue alerts to the International Maritime Organization (IMO), NOAA, the US Navy, etc., and to begin preparations to secure the area and support the IPCC efforts.

CHAPTER 15

It Takes a Cowboy

D ennis Peary hurries through the labyrinth of connected buildings along Water Street, returning to his office located in the bowels of Woods Hole. When Dennis decided to join the Woods Hole Oceanographic Institute, or "hoo-ee" as it is referred to by its WHOI acronym, the board was so delighted that it went through the extra expense of constructing his office below sea level with a twenty by twenty foot wall of tempered glass exposed to an artificial reef where local fish and marine life thrive, and from where various biological, engineering, and other oceanographic related experiments are conducted.

As Peary enters his office, still viewing his cell phone in hand, several displays on the interactive wall opposite his desk begin to synchronize to the information he's browsing on his phone. He swings into the large leather chair behind his desk not noticing the school of three-foot-long wolf fish passing along the reef. The alerts that he's just issued to NOAA's Ocean Prediction Center, and the US, Spanish, and Portuguese Navies, populate a section of the display. He begins composing a brief to NATO headquarters in Brussels concerning the alert, and switches to his notebook computer as he completes and releases the brief for immediate distribution to member nation ambassadors or permanent representatives, advisers, officials, and committees.

The alert warns all ocean-going vessels to immediately change course from that quadrant of the Atlantic Ocean 260 nautical miles off the coast of Morocco, N35 degrees and 12 minutes, to N34 degrees and 48 minutes latitude, W11 degrees and 30 minutes, to W12 degrees and 12 minutes longitude, an area of approximately 800 square miles of ocean. Vessels bound for or departing through the Strait of Gibraltar are advised to examine and adjust course to be clear of the quadrant. Vessels north of the islands of Madeira, southeast of the Azores, and off the coasts of Morocco, Spain, and Portugal are to examine and adjust course to avoid sailing the specified quadrant.

Dennis's next action is to bring up the worldwide marine traffic tracker application that he helped develop when first joining WHOI fifteen years earlier. The Marine Automatic Ship Tracking system (MAST) is an automated tracking system used extensively in the maritime world. Using MAST he's able to see all global maritime traffic, each vessel's type, position, heading, port of origin, and ports of call.

He grimaces and a look of frustration comes to his face as he rubs his forehead with both hands. He sees that the alert quadrant is a very busy part of the eastern Atlantic Ocean. The shipping lanes from the Americas pass very close, with many Mediterranean destinations via the Strait of Gibraltar. Traffic northbound and southbound along the coasts of Europe and Africa is heavy as well, with a large density of vessels sailing to and from the Azores, Madeira, and Canary archipelagos.

Dennis increases the display zoom to focus in the general area of the alert quadrant and the Strait of Gibraltar. Roughly 100 vessels populate the display chart, the majority being cargo ships and tankers making way to and from the Strait.

Near the alert quadrant he sees two cargo ships, both passing safely north of the area, one eastbound, one westbound. The eastbound Tong An Cheng is bound for Gibraltar and directly north of the area by just a few miles. It reported its position just eleven minutes ago and is steaming steadily at twelve knots. The *Voc Rose* cargo ship is also making way for Gibraltar, currently just north of Madeira and still 250 miles from the alert quadrant.

He makes note to check its position in thirty minutes to make sure it changes course to the south, thereby avoiding the area. A third cargo ship, the Celine, is also in the area making way to the Canary Islands, and is directly east of the quadrant. Its present position, reported just nine minutes earlier, and course appear to have it passing safely to the east.

Another section of the wall-size display alerts Dennis to an incoming call. He slowly takes his glance from the marine traffic display and sees the image of Camilla. He takes the call and pushes back into his chair.

A few seconds go by, and the call is connected and he sees Camilla on the display screen. "Camilla, I'm glad you called—is everything OK?"

Camilla is looking down at her hands folded in her lap. She is a little ashamed thinking that she is about to ask Dennis Peary for his help.

"I was concerned when you left the meeting suddenly. I didn't mean anything about the sailing remark."

"No, I know . . . Dennis . . . I had to step out and call Gerber. I was upset. I'm still upset," she blurts out and finally raises her head to look at Peary.

"Are you and Eddie having some trouble?" he asks, furling his brow, not believing that Camilla would bring marital problems into the workplace. He thinks something else must be going on. "Camilla, how can I help?"

A calm comes over her. "Dennis, when you asked if I was glad to be done sailing those waters, it shook me because Gerber is still sailing in those waters."

He pulls himself toward his desk, as if to get closer to Camilla's image. "I thought . . . didn't you both sail back together?"

"No," she blurts out. "He and a friend are sailing back . . . I flew back weeks ago while there were some delays preparing the new boat in Málaga. From there Eddie and our friend Helle left Málaga several days ago for Madeira. They stopped in Gibraltar first and plan to sail to Madeira, the Canaries, and then from there to the Caribbean."

"Columbus's sailing?"

She smiles at him and shakes her head yes. "I've been talking to Eddie and he's complained about the autopilot not keeping them on course. I'm a little worried after the meeting we just had and the lost *Nereid* and Drs. Lin and Cooper's report."

Dennis turns his attention away from Camilla's image, focusing again on the marine traffic display. He zooms in on the quadrant and there, inside the quadrant at N35, 6" latitude, and W11, 54" at 13 knots, *The Kiss* has turned to the southwest, bearing 214 degrees.

"Camilla, is he sailing the vessel *The Kiss*?"

With an expression of surprise, her eyes wide open Camilla pulls her head back, not understanding how Dennis could possibly know *The Kiss*. A broad smile comes to her face. "Dennis, how in the world could you possibly know they are sailing *The Kiss*? I don't recall mentioning it."

"I'm on the global marine traffic website. It tracks everything on the water. I can see virtually every vessel, its position, speed, destination, heading, the time its position was last reported, past track, forecasted route, and much more. Your not familiar with it?"

"*Mmmm,* OK . . . yeah, I do recall it. Eddie assured me when we began sailing in deep water that it was safe inasmuch as we could be seen, I mean tracked, like how the FAA tracks air traffic."

"Yes, sort of. He may have exaggerated a bit. The air traffic control system is much, much more interactive. I mean, there's always an air traffic controller watching, and the system is a lot more aggressive about issuing warnings and alerts and involving the controllers. Much of that is missing in this. Just the big shipping lines are actively tracking their freighters, cruise ship, etcetera, and the system doesn't give any alerts."

Dennis brings up another section of the display wall to enter a new reminder to enhance the marine traffic application using the FAA's air traffic control system as a model.

"So . . ." Camilla is thinking about the implication of what Dennis has just said. "While smaller craft can be seen, no one is actively monitoring their progress, status?"

"You've got it, Camilla . . . and now that I'm examining that particular area of the Atlantic, I can see the sailing vessel *The Kiss* on the marine traffic map."

"I see it!" she says, navigating herself to the website.

"Dennis, it looks like this position was reported more than an hour ago; and . . ."

Camilla pauses as they both look at the data. She raises her eyebrows, looking surprised.

"Wow . . . yes, they are off course for Funchal in Madeira.

Why so far west? Eddie complained several times about the current taking them west, but it appears they've finally been able to turn south toward Madeira."

Camilla sits back in her chair feeling more at ease despite *The Kiss* being off course to the west. Just being able to monitor their progress makes her feel empowered to possibly help Eddie and Helle sail safely from danger.

Dennis clicks on the map icon for *The Kiss* and sees new information, reported six minutes earlier from its autopilot. Now at 34, 53N and 11,57W at 18 knots, it's clear to Dennis that *The Kiss* has made a quick move to the south. A worried look comes to his face as he reads the new heading of 112 to the southeast, and their speed has increased to 18 knots.

Is the information accurate, he wonders. *Of course it is,* he thinks as he clicks on the MAST icon to display the past tracking for *The Kiss.* He sees that *The Kiss* sailed along the northern part of the alert quadrant in a southwesterly direction for two days, zigzagging as the two men attempted to steer the boat south. Then around 11, 54W, *The Kiss* moved decidedly to the southwest.

"*Mmmm,* their speed is now eighteen knots."

"What do you make of it, Dennis?"

"I don't know . . . yet, Camilla. *Ahh . . .*" He stops short, feeling uncomfortable about telling Camilla that *The Kiss* is caught in whatever caught *The Nereid* sub. Instead he clicks on the icon to bring up the Route Forecaster function of the MAST app, which takes the position, heading, speed, wind direction, and sea current to forecast the route of *The Kiss.* Dennis is stunned to see the bull's-eye shape of the forecast and vessel speed.

CHAPTER 16

The Zug Connection

Lisbeth sits alone with her lunch on a park bench near the shoreline overlooking Lake Zug. A late summer breeze whips under her nose, reminding her that soon enough the snow will fly. She enjoys the egg salad–filled baguette from Nussbaumer Bakery Café, which is a short walk from her office at Chollerpark, Sumpfstrasse 15. Steam rises from her tea as she lifts the lid and places it next to her on the bench to cool.

This solitary bench along the lake is her favorite place to enjoy some quiet time and lookout across the beautiful lake and admire the snow-topped Swiss Alps in the distance. A large cherry tree shades her from the midday sun as she enjoys the baguette and watches a small fishing boat motor its way out from an adjacent marina. She sips the hot tea as the breeze blows a bang of her dark hair across her nose. Further down to her left, along the lakeshore, she watches the midday bustle of the Zug municipality.

The city of Zug is a medieval, walled storybook town filled with brilliant examples of Gothic churches, castles, and towers. Its history as a fishing village is more than 5,000 year old. Zug comfortably blends a sizable modern metropolis of office buildings, residential apartments, and malls with the city, which dates back to the 1500s and is called the Altstadt,

complete with cobblestone streets, plazas with colorful outdoor cafes and places for people to meet, medieval houses,
and the romantic Swiss cow-laden countryside, which is just
a mile or so from the clock tower, or Zytturm, situated at the
entrance to the Altstadt.

The Zytturm was built in the mid thirteenth century simply as a passageway through the oldest part of the town wall
of Zug, founded by the noble Kyburg family. From 1478 to
1480, Hans Felder, Zug's master builder of the renowned St.
Oswald's Church, extended the buttressed shell of the tower,
adding side battlements and a turreted pent roof inclined on
one side toward the town, so making it the town's most significant tower. In 1557, the tower was given its present shape
with the watch chamber, the turret-shaped bays and the steep
hipped roof. In 1574, a clock was installed.

More than ever in the past, the region of Zug (the city of
the same name its capital) comfortably retains its reputation
as a tax haven and as a haven for those wishing not to be
found. Like the notorious Marcel Reich in the previous century, other white crime criminals often find Zug a good place
to disappear while fleeing from a host of federal and sovereign
charges. Mr. Reich, better known as Marc Rich, successfully
escaped indictment by the United States on federal charges
of tax evasion and illegally making oil deals with Iran during
the 1979 Iran hostage crisis, by fleeing the US and alluding
capture while hiding out in Zug until President Bill Clinton
pardoned him in 2001 before leaving office.

The tempest that is modern-day Zug is filled with electronic smugglers, hackers, tax evaders, money launderers,
currency counterfeiters, illicit security traders, organized
transnational criminals, etc. The Zug yellow page directory

might well be organized by "type of white collar crime," which would be to Lisbeth's liking. Having been cut from that cloth, she feels the need to be close to friends and closer to enemies. Coming to Zug and leaving Gibraltar after more than a decade of conducting her business transactions from there, she no longer feels the need to "hide out" on that tiny outpost strip that juts out into the Mediterranean Sea.

Now owning numerous legitimate business interests around the world, Lisbeth finds Zug appealing due to its world-class investment banking as well as access to the murky underground part of the earlier life that she has left behind, but will not fully detach herself.

She finishes her egg salad and sips the last of her tea as a small sailboat drops its sail and serenely begins to motor toward its marina slip. Her black leather slacks and jacket feel good to her as she stretches out the stiffness from her legs, arms, and shoulders while thinking of how to approach Camilla with the information she's uncovered earlier in the day.

Her phone rings—it's Camilla. Smiling, she sits erect on the bench and answers the call. "Camilla, hi. I was just thinking of you. It must be early there."

It was not yet half past six in the morning in Greeley, Colorado.

"Hi, Lisbeth. You were thinking of me?"

"Do you recall when you visited me here in Zug I told you about how I made a lot of money back north?"

Camilla had been unable to sleep much the night before, worrying about Eddie, Helle, and *The Kiss*. The meeting and *The Nereid* data are still twisting through her mind.

"Yes, but I have to talk to you about Eddie on *The Kiss*."

Lisbeth listens intently as Camilla runs through an abstract of the prior day's session in Falmouth, Massachusetts, about *The Nereid* going missing, the discovery in the Eastern Atlantic, and the threat to *The Kiss*.

"Life can change so fast, Lisbeth. It's just a few weeks since I was there with you and we were enjoying Zug and the Alps. Now..." She trails off as a sense of helplessness and not knowing what to do comes over Camilla.

* * *

Just a few weeks earlier, Camilla made a stopover in Zurich en route to the United States for a visit with Lisbeth. Their lost love for each other had quickly been reignited. Both women recognized the chance and desire to know and love one another as only sisters can, and, after so many years apart, both felt the joyous realization that suddenly they each had "family." They loved this idea of having family after so many years without.

Their short time together in Zug was a blessing. Enjoying each other's company and the beauty of the lake, mountains, Swiss cuisine, and Lisbeth's Porsche Spyder made for three days of heaven.

It was during these days that Lisbeth revealed to Camilla her "secret" skills of breaking Internet barriers and corporate firewalls, hacking into places to either save herself, or at times, for a wealthy paying client looking for information. Camilla being Camilla began asking questions as they approached Lisbeth's awaiting Spyder.

"Wow, Lisbeth . . . that's an expensive car."

"It's a Porsche 925 . . . I can drive it either electric or use the engine. I like using the engine around the lake and in the mountains. Come . . ."

Lisbeth sat comfortably behind the wheel, lightly juicing the accelerator. "Get in. I want to show you this beautiful part of Switzerland." A warm smile from under her Bulgari Flora Sunglasses made her offer irresistible to Camilla.

The Porsche gurgling its 925 horsepower engine rolled its passenger side door toward the sky and Camilla jumped in. The shoulder harness and midsection restraints quickly locked in position. Lisbeth gunned the engine; the rear tires chirped, and without the slightest rear-end wiggle, the Porsche jettisoned as straight as a bullet down Mattenstrasse, reaching sixty miles per hour in under three seconds. In minutes, they were riding alongside the lake on E41 toward the small town of Arth twenty-five miles south on the opposite end of the lake. With a top speed of 250 miles per hour, it was a quick trip around the lake the long way to Lisbeth's favorite restaurant, Sternen Walchwil.

"I haven't been in anything but driverless cars in quite a few years," Camilla chuckled. "Is it easier to get a license in Switzerland?"

"I'm not sure. I had my license amended when I took residence here a year ago or so."

"You had a license in Gibraltar?"

"Yeah; a motorcycle license. I changed it when I came here and bought this car. It's nice, isn't it? I just love the Cartier timepiece." Lisbeth points to the jeweled circular clock in the middle of the dashboard.

"I guess they have to let you have a license if you can afford this car?" Camilla asked.

Lisbeth was quiet, feeling uncomfortable with the

question. With the center roof panels removed from the top, an occasional breeze runs through the compartment. The hum of the V-8 exhaust gently surrounded them and filled the quiet. Lisbeth didn't want to hide anything from Camilla. She overcame her natural propensity to keep her personal life locked up, and said, "I had the license before the car."

Camilla waited to hear more.

"I changed it myself."

Camilla wondered what she was getting at.

"I made the change myself; issued it to myself and had it sent from the Strassenverkehrsamt on Hinterbergstrasse in Steinhausen."

"The what?!"

Both of them laughed at "Strassenverkehrsamt on Hinterbergstrasse in Steinhausen."

"That might be easy for you to say, Lisbeth. The Strassen-what on Hinter-something-strasse in where?!"

The two women were laughing out loud as Lisbeth maneuvered the 925 through a series of hairpin turns as the road ascended up the side of a mountain.

"The road traffic department. What . . . *sprechen sie kein Schweizer?*"

Still laughing, Camilla let out a big "No!"

"The road traffic department in Steinhausen," Lisbeth said as her laughter subsided and she became serious. "It's just on the northern side of Zug a few minutes from my office."

Lisbeth began telling Camilla how she had been able to hack into the department database and change her license from a class 'M' motorcycle license to both motorcycle and passenger class, and then have it reissued and mailed to her apartment on Baarerstrasse.

Camilla was awestruck by this and by Lisbeth's description of her supporting network of hackers who collect and sell information to clients, and how in the years following her adolescence, she relied on these skill and resources to first save her life, and then to make a living legally as an investigator, eventually becoming a successful businesswoman.

*   *   *

But now, as Camilla describes to Lisbeth the situation Eddie and Helle are confronting aboard *The Kiss*, the thought of those three days in Zug are like a dream and fading away.

The cell connection drifts as the breeze off Lake Zug blows the sandwich wrapper from her lap. "Hello? Camilla, can you hear me OK? Maybe I can help . . . like I said, I was going to call you . . . with some information."

"Information? Are you OK?" Camilla asks with the voice of concern one has when everything seems to be going wrong.

"Yes; I'm fine, but . . ." She hesitates. "The LET session with Ron—how did that go?"

Camilla thinks about the question. Having been distracted by the Falmouth meeting, she hadn't thought of the LET test. "Actually, it was sort of a big bust. The *Nereid* meeting has sort of distracted me, but actually it didn't go well at all. Several components didn't function as planned. I'd sum it up by saying that Ron and his team, including me now, have a lot of work yet before any kind of rollout or demonstration to the public."

Lisbeth gets up from the bench and discards the remaining baguette in a nearby trash container and begins walking briskly toward town and her office. "Go on. What were you expecting . . . to roll it out, right?"

"That's right. I probably told you about it when I was in Zug. Panalla was bringing me on this project to roll it out, so ... I don't think we're even close to that."

"I did a little snooping into Ron Billings and the LET project."

"You did what? What do you mean ... snooping?" Camilla felt a little stepped on.

"Camilla, I only began looking at some of Ron's background. His earlier work is interesting; the AVE, and then the marine traffic app. I was curious, and then, purely innocently, I took a look at his wealth and found a few things of interest I didn't expect."

"Ron worked on the marine traffic app . . . MAST?" Camilla's voice expresses surprise.

"Yes."

"I guess he and Dennis know one another pretty well then. I didn't know that, but . . ."

"Well if Dennis is Dennis Peary, I'd say so."

Too many surprises, Camilla thought.

"Yes, Dennis Peary. He was the project manger I believe."

"Yes, and he and Ron have since then been in other business ventures, landing lucrative contracts and supplying the IPCC with a breadbasket of equipment and services from shell companies they've owned since the LET project got underway."

Camilla was stunned and immediately furious.

Lisbeth felt bad that she had to be the one to tell her sister. "Camy, I'm sorry to have to be the one to tell you about this, but I'm glad I did. Especially with this news about Eddie and Helle being in danger and those two rascals involved."

Lisbeth goes on to describe the money-skimming scheme

Ron Billings and Dennis Peary are running, enriching themselves using shell businesses to acquire large IPCC contracts and provide sub-standard or nonexistent materials to the LET. From those companies, they are charging consulting fees, making gifts to themselves, buying properties, enriching themselves.

"Dennis Peary is running operations with the IPCC," Camilla adds. "Now that they've uncovered what's happening at the bottom of the ocean, the IPCC and NOAA are in charge. They're still looking at solutions, but this is a huge environmental problem they won't act on too fast less they do something to make it worse. Meanwhile, since Peary and WHOI have a lost *Nereid* at the hands of the IPCC, Panalla sees him as their go-to guy for any oceanic operations."

Lisbeth reaches her office on Sumpfstrasse. The elevator door opens, and she gets in, saying, "Third floor. . . . That sounds like a perfect setup for Peary; a new opportunity to acquire foreign resources for the IPCC through their shell businesses in Europe. Are they planning any further operations at this point? And what about *The Kiss?*"

"Lisbeth, they're still working through this, but Dennis and the others are assuming they're going to save Eddie and Helle with a helicopter rescue . . . but they're not sure if there's enough time."

"Camilla, if that is what they're talking about, I'm pretty sure they're going to do that even if it's unsuccessful. They'll scheme a lot of money from it regardless of whether it'll work or not—and it's likely doomed to fail and cost them." Lisbeth stops short, not wanting to say it would mean that *The Kiss* would be lost.

Silence fills the line for a few seconds as it begins to sink in with Camilla.

"Camilla, I have an idea. Do what you can to keep Peary from getting the nod from Panalla and the IPCC. He'll make it look like he's ordering a top-end SAR helicopter, and instead have an older less costly rescue helicopter sent via one of their shell companies in Europe."

"But how will *The Kiss* be saved?"

"I'm pretty sure I can get a SAR helicopter there faster than they will. Have they any idea of how *The Kiss* can be steered clear or at least lengthen the time we have?"

"Well, Dennis has asked his associates at NOAA to help him determine if there's a point in *The Kiss*'s current course where they'd have a chance of being blown clear, or if there is another course of action that will result in saving them."

Lisbeth chuckles at this as she searches for the IPCC files on the lost *Nereid.*

"Another course of action?" Lisbeth is stumped, and then it comes to her just as Camilla says, "Abandoning ship. They've asked Eddie about using the small Sunfish they have in tow and abandoning *The Kiss.*"

Yes, onboard *The Kiss,* Eddie had tied together a pair of old Sunfish Lasers built around 1997, and lashed them from the transom davit. A small sailing dingy, fourteen feet in length, the Sunfish was commended by the American Sailboat Hall of Fame for being the most popular recreational sailboat . . . ever. Eddie liked to sail the Sunfish in the bays while in port. Helle, of course agreed with the idea, so when they had stumbled upon a pair of solid 1997 fiberglass hull Lasers in Málaga, they jumped on them.

Brilliant but dangerous, Peary and NOAA are looking

outside the box, or in this case, literally outside the boat. They examine the tentacle-like current of the giant whirlpool, the ocean currents in that part of the Atlantic, and, most important, the wind, to determine if an optimal point exists where *The Kiss* could be abandoned for the Sunfish, and skip enough like a leaf on a windy day dances across the Great Ponds of Martha's Vineyard in order to gain time. Exactly how much a Sunfish is going to dance is the part of the equation that's most speculative to Peary.

Ron Billings had agreed saying, "If they can just steer clear enough, they might escape, or possibly just gain valuable time while a helicopter races to save them." Peary liked the idea, particularly since it involved a helicopter rescue . . . and he'd run the operation.

"Camilla, do you think it can work? I haven't any sailing experience."

"I think the idea has merit; an examination of the wind, currents and the boat drag will tell if it's a good idea. The key is the wind. If they find that somewhere along the circular current, the lighter boat having only a daggerboard for a keel . . . it could do just what they're thinking and skip across the water like a leaf escaping the current."

"Sounds a little scary out that far in the ocean in that small boat. Couldn't *The Kiss* do the same with the right wind direction?"

"The weight of *The Kiss* and its heavy cast iron keel make it much, much less likely of escaping the current without significantly greater wind; and, the size of the Sunfish is irrelevant . . . it's practically unsinkable."

Lisbeth is on her computer messaging in her network of associates. "Camilla, it sounds pretty frightening."

"Believe me, I'd be scared out of my wits! I mean . . . leaving, abandoning *The Kiss?* It's a forty-six footer and loaded with lots of navigation, radar, communications . . . the Sunfish would be like jumping onto a piece of plywood with a sail on it. Eddie told me they've been in a fog for several days. How would you like to abandon ship in the fog? Helle says he won't do it." She chuckles with a sly grin. "He thinks he can sail *The Kiss* clear. Gerber is trying to convince him that the Sunfish will give them a chance of escaping or and being saved."

"Camilla, honey, I need a little time, but I'm sure I can contract an EC Airbus SAR helicopter and get it out to them, but you'll have to go to Panalla and tell him about Dennis and Ron and let them complete the operation plan. We'll then have to engage with the NOAA operations staff to get the SAR into position and make the rescue. Panalla can tell Dennis Peary that the Spanish are executing the rescue and are already in position. Let's talk in an hour. I'll have the SAR ready to go."

Camilla hangs up and calls Panalla for an update and to let him know about the criminal activities Dennis Peary and Ron Billings are engaging in.

CHAPTER 17

The Last Straw

ennis Peary is up late in the evening examining reports of the trade winds. He believes they set the prevailing pattern of surface winds as far north as 37 degrees north—i.e., the southern coast of Portugal. And it is because of this, he and the NOAA team feel that *The Kiss* will not make another revolution around the northern part of whirlpool, but be lost midway across the northern perimeter. They decide the crew of *The Kiss* must abandon ship for the Sunfish as it passes the southern part of the whirlpool, just where its current begins to turn to the north, at its easternmost point. The computer picks 34°56'39.35"N, 11°42'5.51"W despite the five miles per hour lighter wind of just nine to ten miles per hour.

Peary is surprised, thinking the western part of the current that turns south will have the best wind for the Sunfish to be blown to safety. But he quickly realizes that the extra time needed to get to those coordinates makes the eastern point a better choice. The Morón Air Base is just 60 kilometers east of Seville, or 325 miles from the coordinates, which are well within the range of a Super Puma SAR Airbus Helicopter having a top speed of 191 miles per hour and six hours of flight time. Peary calculates the operation has three and a half hours of flight time, leaving two and a half hours to rescue

Eddie and Helle. However, the helicopter rescue team feels 1 hour will be plenty of time to pluck their quarry from the sea. In either event, everyone is in agreement that it is a sound operating plan.

A short time later, Peary and Ron Billings finish assembling their rescue operation resource team when Dr. Reddy informs Dennis that NOAA has already arranged a SAR helicopter rescue and will execute the plan. Dennis can do nothing because the IPCC and NOAA have given the job to the Spanish Air Force. Peary looks around in disbelief as Dr. Reddy calls from Greeley, Colorado, to give him the news.

"Yeah?" Dennis looks at him with a questioning look. "OK, OK. I've also prepared a plan and readying a team from Nouasseur; I'm pretty sure it's closer."

Nouasseur Air Base is near Casablanca in Morocco and was formerly a United States SAC Air Force Base. The USAF closed the base in 1963 and the government of Mohamed V took it over, and now it is known as Mohammed V International Airport. It also is home to a helicopter squadron of the Royal Moroccan Navy.

"Thank you, Mr. Peary, that won't be necessary."

Dr. Reddy looks sadly at Dennis Peary, knowing that the rescue task is not without peril, and deep down he wishes it was in the hands of Peary; however, Camilla has convinced him that Peary and Billings have other interests and can't be trusted. He's confident of the plan's probability for success with the resources that NOAA has arranged with Lisbeth's help.

"I'll be in my office observing the operation." Peary disconnects the call and walks out of his office with that cowboy strut of his—hands in his pockets, head looking up with an expression of wonder on his face as he thinks about what's just happened and the money he'd miss out on.

Final preparations are underway at the Morón Air Base east of Seville as Helle emerges from the shower, drying his long salt-and-pepper hair with a towel as Eddie is hanging up a call with Lisbeth.

"Señor Eddie," he calls out. "What's new? What does NOAA propose we do to get out of this?"

Helle tosses the towel aside and begins combing his hair, readying it for its usual ponytail. It's grown quite a bit since leaving Málaga and now combs out below his deltoid muscles. In dark glasses, he looks like a rock star.

Eddie places the phone down and looks up from the navigation table. "Abandon ship."

Helle collects his hair and pulls it back into a ponytail, then double wraps a scrunchie around it midway to keep it in place. He smiles and walks over to Eddie at the table.

"Ah! . . . *muy divertido!* Very funny, Señor Gerber."

Eddie looks down toward the chart at a new position he's pinned and noted as an *obstacle*—the approximate position of the whirlpool.

"Helle, I'm not being funny . . . and neither are NOAA and the Coast Guard. They've declared *The Kiss* to be manifestly unsafe for voyage and ordered us to abandon ship. Either we can take our chances and wait on *The Kiss* to be rescued by helicopter or increase our chances of being rescued by sailing the Sunfish east. Either way, we're getting off *The Kiss* before we get sucked down the whirlpool like insects down the kitchen sink drain. They say our chances are better by sailing the Sunfish east toward the helicopter where the current is moving slower, the fog less thick, and they'll reach us sooner. We have to go as soon as we can prep an emergency bag."

It is not expected that there is enough time to wait for a daytime pickup, so it will be at approximately 3:17 a.m. Seville time. The dense fog and the speed that the Sunfish and the rescue helicopter will be moving make the pickup anything but routine, even with wave heights rolling at a gentle five feet.

"It's suicide!" Helle reacts with emotion and begins to laugh at the idea. He sees that Eddie is still thinking it through. Sounding incredulous, he asks, "You're not thinking of doing it?"

Eddie looks up, still going over it in his head and begins pacing. Helle continues to rub the sleep from his eyes. "Are you telling me you're going to get into that Sunfish"—he points to the stern where the Sunfish dangle from the davits—"a few hours from now, in the middle of the night, and expect to steer clear of this whirlpool?"

Standing in the middle of the cabin, with arms outstretched, Helle loses his balance as *The Kiss* rocks to starboard and finds a cushion to sit on. He calms himself by trying to come up with another solution. *My god*, he thinks . . . surely he's gotten himself out of worse situations: storms, rough seas, off course for days with little food and water, run aground dozens of times. But nothing quite like this where the clock is ticking and just hours are left before being plunged a mile to the bottom of the sea. He looks across at Eddie and asks, "How are we going to navigate direction?"

Eddie is still going through it in his mind. "It might work . . . we'll navigate direction using the compass on the phone and use it to communicate with the helicopter. They think we need to extend our time by sailing east at least an hour. We need to take a few items with us . . . iPhone, the Sunfish oars, an emergency bag." Eddie looks at his watch. "In about an hour and we go. We'll reach the eastern most part where the whirlpool turns the current to the north. We need to abandon *The Kiss* and sail the Sunfish as far east as we can while the rescue helicopter comes for us."

It has become as certain as coming down the Niagara River to the falls that *The Kiss* will go over in three hours given the current wind conditions. At the current wind speed, in less than three hours, the speed of *The Kiss* could exceed thirty-five knots making the likelihood of a successful helicopter rescue just twenty percent.

"Eddie, I've sailed through many difficult situations. I'm not sure about this idea that the Sunfish will skip like a leaf in a pond. I think we can gain the time we need by tacking *The Kiss* to the east once we reach the coordinates . . . and run the engine . . . we'll get some speed—" Eddie cuts him off.

"Helle, the problem is the weight of *The Kiss*; its keel is nearly ten thousand pounds. It's like a magnet in this current. See the speed we're getting here? We're getting twenty-two knots with an eight-mile-an-hour wind. You know as well as I do that this ship is going to follow the current, given the wind speed, but I think the Sunfish has a better chance of using the wind and sailing away . . . so get a fucking emergency bag together."

"I'm not getting off. You go, Eddie. I'm sailing *The Kiss* out of this at the coordinates."

"Sorry, buddy, but the Coast Guard and the Spanish Navy have *ordered* us to abandon ship." He looks Helle in the face and says slowly, "I'm fucking ordering you to fucking abandon *my* fucking ship . . . OK?"

Helle looks at him for a few seconds without answering. He then walks forward and from a lower cabinet pulls out a pair of life jackets and wet/dry bags. From another cabinet, he begins to assemble several survival pieces: flares, flashlights, snorkels, fins, and diving masks.

"Hey, Eddie!" He calls out.

Eddie has located and is on deck walking the Sunfish oars toward the stern where the Sunfish dangle from the davits. He stops and turns toward Helle, who is now standing at the top of the stairs looking at him. Pointing to the bag, Helle says smiling, "Don't forget to throw some fresh underwear in here."

Eddie smiles back at him. "Good idea. I'm sure to shit the bed going over this fucking whirlpool. So start packing. There's no reason to try to save face, I hope you're not serious about *not* abandoning ship. There's a lot of resources committed to rescuing us so . . . go find your tighty-whities."

The two men chuckle over the idea of packing fresh undies. Then together, they continue to assemble the items they need to take with them aboard the Sunfish.

"Are you scared, Eddie?" Helle asks.

"There's no time for being scared, Helle. It's more a sense of reality . . . maybe some sadness."

"Yeah, we're scrambling instead of fishing to stay alive."

They continue to ready themselves to abandon ship.

* * *

In Woods Hole, Dennis Peary slips into the first unoccupied conference room he comes upon. He closes the blinds and sits in the dark room with the door open and takes out his cell phone. Looking down at the phone in his lap, he brings his favorites list up and is ready to push "Ron" but stops and instead clicks the screen blank. He pushes back from the conference table and places the phone on the table, running his hand through his hair.

Don't rush into anything, he's thinking. *Take a minute . . . step back and survey the situation. It might be prudent to not call Ron right away . . . you don't want to raise any red flags to set him off.*

He waits another few seconds, and then decides it's best to focus on supporting the operation and not risk stirring Ron up. He thinks that perhaps he is jumping to the wrong conclusion and it's just that the IPCC has made its decision to execute the operation using the Spanish Navy purely on logistics or for any number of reasons, perhaps a political one.

You don't know what you don't know, is the last thing he tells himself as he leaves the empty conference room. *Need to talk to Ron about the operation . . . and get a sense about his latest interaction with Dr. Reddy.*

Back in his office, he calls Dr. Veerabhadran. "Dr. Veerabhadran, Dennis Peary. I'm checking in to see if there is anything I can help with."

"No, no—the SAR helicopter is in the air from Seville."

"Yes, I can see that on the mission operations screen."

The mission operation access allows any of the resource groups to selectively see any of the operations information displays available to the operations group, which Dennis Peary, Dr. V, Panalla Reddy, and other key players are part of. All of them, including Camilla, Ron Billings, and anyone else participating in the operation can see the information systems supporting the rescue task. Dennis will periodically keep an eye on marine traffic to see that no other vessels wander into the alert quadrant. The Spanish Navy is tracking their Airbus SAR; Dr. Veerhabadran is watching the computer estimation of size and movements of the great maelstrom and the track of *The Kiss*.

"Dr. V, I'm not sure if you've noticed on the marine traffic display that there are two very large vessels near the rescue operations area. They might be useful if needed."

"I did see them, Dennis. The *Daewood* tanker, and the *Nerval* container ship. They're pretty far away though."

Several seconds of quiet goes by as Dr. V focuses on the marine traffic display to collect additional information about the two vessels near the rescue area. He calculates their distance.

"The *Nerval* is about ninety-five nautical miles from the quadrant, passing to its north on their present course headed for Gibraltar."

"They're about four hours from the area," Dennis mentions.

"Yeah, OK . . . good to know. Hopefully the SAR helicopter will save those on *The Kiss* . . . my god, I am concerned for Camilla," Dr. V says, his tone saddened.

"I know . . . she's such a beautiful lady, Dr. V. I'm praying for her that the rescue is a success."

"By the way, Dennis, I have some good news . . . *The Nereid* . . . it's transmitting. We're once again receiving signals from it . . . just moments ago."

Ron Billings had, just a minute before, informed *The Nereid* operator that *The Nereid* had started transmitting new data from its location near the quadrant. *The Nereid* operator sits in the Woods Hole operations room just feet away from Dr. V.

Dennis Peary enlarges *The Nereid* tracking display to see the location of *The Nereid* near the northeast corner of the quadrant, emanating a red blip. "Hot damn, it *is* alive! That is good news."

"And you can see we're able to see how the shape and strength of the maelstrom is changing and chart *The Kiss* and the SAR helicopter. The data collection devices on *The Nereid* appear to be working fine. Ron Billings is working on extracting new data about the trench collapse size for Dr. Cooper's group from new data being transmitted from *The Nereid* . . . that's an amazing piece of equipment you've got there Dennis."

"It is. I'm not that surprised to tell you the truth, Dr. V."

"Dennis, it's been quite a few hours since we heard from it though."

"I'm sure it was surprised by the quick and extreme change in velocity and got swept away in the powerful current . . . it probably smacked into something and temporarily lost control. Once it propelled itself out of danger, it parked somewhere safe on the surface, then linked up with the com pod, and began checking its gyroscopes, power, navigation, and other systems before reconnecting with a dozen or more satellites roaming the globe. At least that's what it's suppose to do in such events."

The nuclear-powered electric engine *Nereid* had struck more than one mountainous obstacle as it tumbled temporarily helpless toward the great opening in the trench floor. This condition lasted briefly, and in short order, it recovered its engines and thrust itself from harm's way using its sixteen engines and props, each with 350 horsepower, resurfacing miles away from any danger from the maelstrom.

"It's amazing, Dennis."

"I'm going to talk to Ron to see what he thinks about the condition of the data and *The Nereid* connectivity."

"Sounds like a good idea, Dennis."

"I'll be back to you shortly, Dr. V."

Dennis terminates the audio portion with Dr. Veer-abhadran while bringing up a window display of *The Nereid* autonomous glider systems and the dataset for the East Atlantic mission. Each attribute in the data collection is indeed again being transmitted.

"Hi, Ron. I see *The Nereid* comm has come back."

"Yeah, I was just going through it with Dr. Cooper and his team about the data we're getting. I have to get back to them and see if there's something else they need before the SAR mission is due to pickup *The Kiss*."

"OK, the operation of *The Nereid* should be normal now if the data is rich. I'm assuming it's navigable?"

"Well you might want to check that with Dr. V; I'm just working with the data connection. I don't think anyone has tried or needed to have it leave its present position."

"That's OK, Ron. It's just treading water. I'll check with Dr. V and confirm its navigation system."

Dennis hangs up the call with Ron and thinks, *Everything is OK—didn't sense anything out of the ordinary with Ron . . . perhaps Panalla Reddy is just trying a new partnership with the Spanish Navy.*

* * *

It's almost time for Eddie and Helle to abandon *The Kiss*. The sun won't even begin to cast its haze for at least another hour. The SAR helicopter is still more than ninety minutes away.

Eddie has pulled the Sunfish alongside *The Kiss* and readied its sail, daggerboard, and lashed its oars. Any fear he had is gone; the thrill of the adventure and his drive to survive and beat the threat have overtaken him. He's tingling with excitement about their prospects of survival in the face of disaster, and he gets to do it with his old friend the Sunfish. His first sailing experience at the age of fifteen was in a Sunfish, sailing the great ponds on Martha's Vineyard.

"Helle, I just got off the phone with Veerabhadran's operator. We're just about to *kiss off.*"

Helle is poring over the navigation map display. They're receiving data now from Woods Hole enabling him to display the size and ferocity of the whirlpool and to plot alternate courses.

"Eddie, look at this. Maybe we don't have to abandon ship. I think if we run to the north with the turn of the current and increase speed, we can hit the northeastern edge and burn the rest of the fuel to get us clear."

"Helle, we don't have time for this any longer. The current isn't going to let us steer north and steer clear as you plotted here. Let's go."

A pair of Spanish Typhoon fighter jets scream across the sky, collecting and sending position, speed, wave length, and other data back to the operations staff. Eddie and Helle are stopped in their tracks as the jets scream overhead. They can't see them, but the sound is deafening.

"Eddie, I'm certain I can sail clear. It's all timing. Here look." He gestures for Eddie to take a closer look at the display on the nav table. "See, our speed is nearly twenty knots now and will continue to increase. Once we're about thirty miles further north, we'll be at twenty-three to twenty-four knots before the current turns us to the west. Just before that point,

I think we can burn the engines and get another five, maybe as much as eight, knots more, and then turn the rudder heading to the northeast and burst through."

Helle emphasizes this by punching the air, saying they'll *"Burst through!"*

"Unfortunately, this fucking current isn't going to let you get to that point, Helle." Eddie is ticked off and begins marching off to the stern. "Here . . . look . . . here." He walks back to the nav table and puts his finger on the display where the projected course indicates the current will take them too far west and closer to the center of the vortex for his plan to work. "See, you won't get to the northern coordinate. You'll be too far west and doomed." He switches off the display. "Let's go," he yells and walks toward the stern again.

"I can tack us and work the engines to that point. It'll work, Eddie . . . believe me."

Helle has decided he's not getting off. Eddie can get off if he wants to, but Helle is bent on sail *The Kiss* into Funchal, Madeira.

"You're fucking crazy, Helle."

Eddie grabs one of the large X-LED flashlights on the cabin table and stands ready to step up and out of the compartment and onto the deck where the Sunfish waits.

"Last chance! Don't make me leave you here . . . Camilla is going to be pissed . . . at both of us . . . you . . . fuck!" He hesitates and watches Helle switch the nav display back on.

He wishes Helle good luck and ascends to the deck. He boards the Sunfish and unties it from *The Kiss,* sets the sail, and heads to the east in the predawn hours. The flashlight is strapped to the bow by a bungee cord. His phone compass is in a plastic bag and taped to the mast in front of him.

Wind speed is just eight knots to the northeast and steady, with gusts to twelve knots. The ocean swells are relatively calm at five feet. The Sunfish performs as planned and is blown full tilt toward the east under Eddie's skilled hands. He soon pulls the daggerboard rudder out, eliminating the drag it creates and picks up even more speed; it's an old trick he learned racing Sunfish on the great pond in the Vineyard as a teen. He lets the sail full out and heels the boat, steering the Sunfish downwind without the rudder, using his body weight and balance to steer and a degree of heel to change direction.

"Yeah, baby, find that groove," Eddie says aloud as the boat picks up speed. He looks back to see that he's already, in just seconds, put a hundred yards between the Sunfish and the illuminated ball of floating cotton, which is the stalled *Kiss*. One of the Typhoon jet fighters passes overhead in a thunderous roar. He looks toward the sky and begins singing Christopher Cross's "Sailing," as if praying.

An hour passes and the Sunfish performs exceptionally, exceeding Eddie's expectations. He's used the powerful current with the wind to move more than twenty miles to the east-northeast. He continues pushing the Sunfish following the compass. Another twenty-five minutes go by along with 4 a.m. The first glow from the sun begins to illuminate the eastern wall of fog and soon he hears the chop of the Puma.

Pilot Diego Banderas is on the radio with the Morón Air Base in Seville, relaying conditions and the location of the Sunfish. The fog is so thick and the Sunfish is moving so fast that, even with their radar, powerful searchlight, and brightening sky, it takes fifteen minutes before Banderas locates the moving Sunfish. They text Eddie to pull in the sail to reduce speed as much as possible. Hitting a moving target in the fog is hard enough without having to do so at nearly twenty knots. Eddie pulls in the sail, and the Sunfish soon comes to seven knots.

Banderas takes several minutes evaluating the conditions and discussing the rescue with his swimmer, Raffy Nadal, the flight engineer, Jose Cruz, and Eddie. No two rescues are ever alike, and there's nothing simple about this one: the target cannot be seen in the pre-morning light and swirling dense fog; it is moving at seven knots and is rocking back and forth in an eight-foot sea with a ten-foot mast waving in an unpredictable pattern. Banderas asks Eddie if the mast and spar, which hold the Sunfish sail, can be removed and tossed overboard now that the sail has been lowered. But Eddie is reluctant, fearing that in the process of untying the rigging and removing the mast, he will end up in the water and lose communications with the Puma, making the rescue even more difficult.

They consider dropping the rescue swimmer into the water several yards in front of the Sunfish and then having him swim to and board the sailboat as it approaches. But in the thick fog and early morning light, it will be very difficult for the swimmer to swim to the moving Sunfish. Banderas decides to attempt to lower his rescue swimmer to within a few feet above the Sunfish, and utilize a secondary cable with a belt that Eddie can wear around his waist, and once he secures it, Nadal can hook it to the main cable, and they both will be hoisted aboard the Puma. If the secondary cable should become entangled in the mast, it can be discarded and another secondary cable attempt can be made. Everyone is in agreement.

Raffy Nadal is a ten-year veteran and has done several rescues involving African migrants on overcrowded boats, in addition to a major rescue involving a cargo ship. His profession of rescue swimmer came about when, early in his Naval career, he participated in saving the twenty-two–man crew of a listing cargo vessel in rough seas in the Bay of Biscay. He is in his neoprene wetsuit, and now Banderas tells him to get ready. He straps on fins, pulls the mask over his head, and places the snorkel in position in case he ends up in the water. He buckles on a life vest, pulls on his gloves, and signals to the flight engineer, Jose Cruz, that he's good to go.

All three men are in constant intercom communication. Cruz helps him to the jump door. Just outside the jump door, the rescue basket that will lower Nadal to the Sunfish is ready with two sets of secondary cables and belts. Banderas tells him they're hovering at ten meters and moving at nine knots. Once Nadal is in the basket, Cruz will lower Nadal just three meters in hopes that he will be able to lower the secondary cable to Eddie.

Eddie texts that the Puma sounds to be directly above him. Cruz lowers the basket three meters, and Nadal calls out. Eddie hears him and calls back, but neither man can see the other. Cruz lowers the secondary cable, but Eddie is still several feet away and does not see it. Nadal retrieves the secondary cable and instructs Banderas to move the Puma's position two meters forward and lower the basket sixty centimeters.

Eddie and Nadal can hear each other's shouts clearly. Nadal is convinced he's in perfect position and can successfully lower the secondary cable. He reaches for the cable lying in the basket and *whack,* the mast strikes the side of the basket solidly, almost knocking Nadal out of it and into the water. He instructs Cruz, "Up thirty centimeters and hold position."

Nadal tells Cruz and Banderas to hold position, but they have to wait for the basket to stop swinging before he lowers the secondary cable. He shouts to Eddie, telling him to be ready, and slowly begins lowing the cable. Another two meters of cable goes out when Eddie yells out, "I got it! I got it!" and he pulls the cable till there's enough slack to rest on the top of the Sunfish. He straps the belt around his waist and texts Banderas, "UP."

Banderas instructs Nadal to hook Eddie to the main hoist and bring him up when ready. Nadal shouts to Eddie to confirm he's ready, and one minute later, Eddie and Nadal are comfortably aboard the Puma.

Nadal and Cruz are getting ready to retrieve the second man, not knowing that Helle opted out of the Sunfish.

"Señor Gerber, the other man is not with you?" Cruz asks.

"That's right. He's still on *The Kiss*."

Cruz relays this to Banderas. "I see the boat on radar about twenty-five minutes to the northwest and moving . . . ah, twenty-four knots. I'm afraid we don't have fuel enough to attempt it. Tell Señor Gerber I'm very sorry, but we have to return to base. I'll request another Puma be sent."

* * *

Onboard *The Kiss*, Helle is using every bit of his sailing skills to tack to the northeast. The wind at just six or eight knots is not sufficient to bring *The Kiss* clear of the increasing velocity of the current, which holds the weighty keel of the boat as if on a train rail. Time and time again, he corrects course and makes a move to the east, but in fifteen minutes time, *The Kiss* is again west, considerably north, and quickly further west again.

An hour passes, and Helle feels he's got one more shot to

burst through. He corrects the course again to the northeast, starts the motor and guns it. The boat makes firm headway to the northeast, but as with the earlier attempts to correct course, the seventy-five horsepower engine makes little difference and is unable to increase the speed of the forty-six-foot *Kiss*.

"A good blow will do it," Helle tells himself. "If the wind speed would get to twelve or fourteen knots, it could press through."

But Helle's prayer is unanswered, and even if it were to be answered, it is too late to push through thirty-five miles of powerful current and reach manageable waters. The current continues to suck *The Kiss* to the northwest and forty minutes into running the engine, the fuel is depleted and the engine quits. Helle looks at his position and realizes that *The Kiss* is doomed. He rests his head on the navigation table and tries to think of a way to escape, and for the first time, he notices the roaring of the water. He sees through the portal that the day is dawning and walks to the stern and steps on deck, sensing the velocity of *The Kiss*. He sits on the deck, grasping a cable and rests his head for a moment on his extended arm.

Looking out into the fog, he is first struck by the terror of the whirlpool he is approaching. But then he begins to reflect on how magnificent a thing it is to die in this manner, after all his hundred-plus years. He decides to give up hope and rid himself of the terror.

"How foolish." He laughs. "How can I be so selfish to be thinking only of myself where one of God's wonders manifests itself here right in front of me ... I'm blessed," he calmly says and looks out into the fog, wondering about the whirlpool and ready to make the sacrifice to explore its depths.

The Kiss's speed approaches twenty-six knots, and Helle begins to sense the pitch of the great whirlpool along with an occasional rocking as the ocean water's turbulence increases. The sun breaks through, and soon the fog lightens to a mist as Helle looks out, still unable to see anything distinctly. The waterfall-like roar of the whirlpool continues to grow louder, and suddenly, the mist parts for several seconds and he catches a glimpse of the great funnel, now less than a mile from *The Kiss*. Again a brief clearing, and he sees its glistening sides and the broad tower of moisture escaping up toward the sky from the center of the whirlpool feeding the cloud and engulfing fog. The sun flickers for a few seconds off the shinny interior surface of the funnel and then again the image disappears as *The Kiss* is engulfed again by fog.

Helle rests his head again and begins to pray: "Holy Mary, Mother of God, pray for me, a sinner, now at the hour of my death." Helle's eyes are closed as he goes on to the Lord's Prayer and awaits his destiny. The sail flaps loudly as a gust catches and snaps it taut; a turnbuckle pings against the mast.

Helle continues with his eyes closed, taking in the sounds and reciting the prayer, "On earth as it is in heaven. Give us this day our daily bread, and forgive us our debts, as we also have forgiven our debtor."

He suddenly stops short of finishing the prayer as he detects through his closed eyelids a bright light flashing as if a strobe is flashing on and off. Turning his head and stretching to see off the starboard side of *The Kiss*, through the fog a flashing object is approaching.

The vessel reduces its speed and pulls along starboard, keeping pace with *The Kiss*. It moves to within six feet of the boat and then extends a mechanical arm with a clawlike piece of apparatus to capture one of the deck tie-down cleats toward the bow of *The Kiss*. A second arm extends from the rear of the vessel and captures another cleat to the rear of *The Kiss*. The arms then pull the two vessels within twelve inches of one another. Together, they move in unison along the doomed course. Helle moves closer to the four-meter long vessel and sees written near the front of its hull *Nereid* and just below that at the waterline, *Woods Hole Oceanographic Institute*.

The Nereid AUV is a completely autonomous underwater vehicle with a depth capability of 10,000 meters, or 32,808 feet; and, theoretically, due to its S10G nuclear reactor and propulsion system, it is capable of an infinite submersion time. It has already traveled 62,000 miles over the past fifteen months since being placed in service by WHOI, propelling itself at an average speed of thirty knots, without refueling. Its fourteen brushless DC electric thrusters on pivoting wings enable its powerful propulsion.

Helle stands at mid-deck, staring at *The Nereid* not knowing what to expect. He calls out to it, "Hola . . . soy Helle Pinzon! *Usted está en aguas peligrosas!*"

As Helle begins to move toward the bow to have a closer look, a hatch slides open from the top of *The Nereid* and a voice addresses him: "Hello, sir. This is Jeb Arnold at the Woods Hole Institute. I'm operating *The Nereid* vehicle remotely. If you will please board the vehicle through the hatch, we can get underway and leave these waters."

Helle can hardly believe his eyes and ears and looks back in the direction of the funnel and thinks about the excitement he felt just minutes ago at the thought of going over the edge in *The Kiss* and the ride to the bottom of the sea. He then hesitates no more and steps onto the platform of *The Nereid* and lowers himself into the single-seat cockpit. The hatch door closes above his head and a series of hisses are heard as the hatch is locked and sealed. A twelve-inch display in front of him contains the image of *The Nereid* operator Jeb Arnold.

"Sir, if you would please find the shoulder harness belts and buckle yourself in, we'll be underway. Is English OK? My Spanish is pretty limited."

"Yes, English is fine." Helle finds the belts and begins strapping himself in. Jeb Arnold is meanwhile busy releasing *The Kiss* from the grip of the robotic arms, and retracting them to their compartments within the hull. Helle can see through several other smaller displays that *The Nereid* has slowly moved fifteen or so yards from *The Kiss*.

He sees her for the last time as *The Nereid* quickly submerges to fifty feet below the surface, turning away from *The Kiss* and toward the Northeast. A sinking feeling comes to Helle as he wonders if he will ever see Eddie and Camilla again.

In less than a minute, *The Nereid* is 200 feet below the ocean surface and achieving thirty knots, slicing through the strong current like a knife through butter at a summer picnic. Helle is too emotionally exhausted to talk to *The Nereid* operator. He reaches behind his head and removes the scrunchie holding his ponytail, allowing his hair to fall around his shoulders. He rests his head back and tries to sleep, but his thoughts are still filled with images of earlier in the day: his argument with Eddie as he abandoned *The Kiss*, his unsuccessful attempt to sail *The Kiss* clear of the whirlpool's current, and the sights of the great funnel.

Feeling composed after several minutes, Helle asks, "Mr. Arnold, can I talk to you . . . can you hear me?"

"Yes, sir."

"Can you tell me what's happened . . . is happening? You're aware of Mr. Gerber's abandoning the vessel I was on . . . was he rescued?"

"Yes, sir. The SAR helicopter was successful. Mr. Gerber is being taken to Morón Air Base."

"Ah, Seville."

"Yes, sir. I believe you are right."

"And where are we going?"

"Well, sir, we're going to intercept the vessel *Nerval*; it's a container ship headed for Gibraltar. She's only about ninety minutes north of your current position. Have you ever been to Gibraltar, sir?"

Helle rests his head back in disbelief . . . *Gibraltar.* "Yes, Mr. Arnold. I've spent some time there."

"Well, I think you'll be there in time for supper, so, if you'd like to nap, I'll wake you shortly before we approach *The Nerval.* I can pipe in some satellite music if you'd like."

"That would be nice . . . but keep the volume low . . . please."

"What would you like?"

"Opera . . . please." Feeling weary he again requests, "But low."

The gentle, soothing sounds of violins, flutes, and horns fill the cockpit as Wagner's overture from *Das Rheingold* begins. Barely audible but discernible, the piece brings a smile to Helle's face, and he begins to relax as *The Nereid*'s engines hum and make way for safer waters and toward *The Nerval.*

Soon out of the clutches of the whirlpool, Jeb Arnold gently turns *The Nereid* to the north, on a direct course to intercept *The Nerval.*

Helle is at first unable to fall asleep; his mind is still imagining what is happening or has already happened to *The Kiss*. As he slips into a light sleep, in his mind he is still on *The Kiss* as it finds its way to the edge of the abyss. Round and round it races in dizzying twists and throws, moving hundreds of feet in just seconds, completing full circles, moving downward at each revolution, along with other objects in the clutches of the current—sea junk, pieces of boats, shipping containers, large masses of timber and trunks of trees along with pieces of furniture, broken boxes, barrels, bottles, metal drums, tires, tangled netting. Helle is there in his dream as they all make the final plunge and disappear.

He wakes to the voice of Jeb Arnold. "Mr. Pinzon, Mr. Pinzon; it's time to wake up. Mr. Pinzon . . . Mr. Pinzon . . . Helle."

"Sí, . . . OK . . . gracias, Mr. Arnold. I'm awake now." Helle lets out a few yawns. He is still recalling his dream of *The Kiss* going into the whirlpool; he's feeling scared as if he were actually there and then suddenly awake as Jeb Arnold brings him back to *The Nereid*.

Now fully awake, he asks how much time before he's on *The Nerval*.

"Ah . . . less than twenty-five minutes."

"Thank you, Mr. Arnold. You said earlier it's a container ship. Where is it from . . . its crew?"

"It's sailing from the US . . . let me see . . . Charleston. It will stop in Gibraltar, and then onto Port Said, Egypt. It's of Maltese registry."

"Ah . . . good . . . a crew speaking a language I know."

Resting his head back again on the cushioned headrest, he can't believe he's going to survive. "And Eddie too . . . on a

Sunfish! Amazing." He chuckles under his breath to himself with a big cat's grin on his face as his favorite tenor, Beniamino Gigli, begins to sing *"Tu che a Dio spiegasti l'ali"* from Donizetti's great tragedy, *Lucia di Lammermoor*. He thinks that he, Helle Pinzon, unlike Donizetti's Edgardo, will survive yet another one.

CHAPTER 18

New Beginnings

Aboard the SAR helicopter, Nadal and Cruz move Eddie into a net-style seat that allows him to relax in comfort while remaining mainly upright. He lies back into the netted seat, collapsing in relief. "Oh . . . thank god," he gasps.

Someone hands him a bottle of water, which he gulps down. "Where will you take me?" he asks, still catching his breath.

"*Base de la fuerza aérea de Morón . . . está cerca de Sevilla,*" Cruz tells him.

"*Gracias, señor, y gracias por salvarme la vida,*" Eddie replies, thanking them for saving his life. He reaches out to Nadal, who is still in his wetsuit, to gently squeeze his arm, then falls back again into the netting. Lieutenant Jose Olazabal hands him a cell phone. It is Camilla.

"Eddie? Are you there? Eddie, I love you." The line is quiet, but she can hear him breathing.

Eddie is overcome with emotion; he is not ready yet to speak to her. The spanking, womping of the SAR helicopter is filling the background. Finally, he says, "I'm in the air, honey . . . they're taking me to Seville . . . I love you too, Camy."

"Eddie, I was so scared . . . I didn't know if I'd ever see you again, Gerby . . ."

Camilla is crying in happiness, unable to speak. Eddie begins to cry as well, Neither of them is able to speak.

"Me too . . ." he says after a few moments, then hands the phone back to the lieutenant.

Eddie sits quietly, slumped in the netting, exhausted from his ordeal of racing the Sunfish through the foggy Atlantic and gaining enough time to enable the SAR chopper to reach and save him. Only through his racing skills and years of experience with the Sunfish is he able to make eighteen plus knots by finding a joint and riding the current, tacking in expert fashion to escape the destiny of *The Kiss*. Using the brightening sky to the east, he had wasted little time checking course on his phone, instead relying on visual sighting once his course was set with the compass. The Sunfish escape plan proved to be the right call, as Helle is unsuccessful in his attempt to save *The Kiss* from the doom of the great whirlpool.

Eddie rests for a minute before the lieutenant is back.

"Señor Gerber? I'd like to check your vital signs."

Lieutenant Olazabal sits on a stool in front of Eddie. He nods with approval.

"Can you sit up a little so we'll remove your shirt? That's it."

Eddie reacts with wide eyes as the coolness of the stethoscope surprises him. Lieutenant Olazabal's assistant takes Eddie's blood pressure, and they check for signs of shock and concussion. "Señor Gerber, do you feel any nausea or dizziness?"

"No, just exhausted."

Olazabal checks Eddie's pupils and pulse, and soon they are done with their examination.

"Everything looks OK . . . just get some rest and we'll be at base in an hour or so. Take some more water . . . there's another bottle right here next to you. I'd rather you sit than lie down . . . we want to avoid any dizziness."

Eddie takes another sip of water and relaxes into the netting. Opening his eyes he asks, "Lieutenant? . . . Helle . . . *The Kiss?* Was he able to get out?"

The lieutenant sits again on the stool and puts his hand on Eddie's shoulder. "Señor Pinzon was rescued and is aboard *The Nereid* submersible. *The Nereid* will intercept the Maltese container ship *The Nerval* shortly, which will port in Gibraltar sometime this evening. He'll get the attention he needs once onboard *The Nerval,* but I believe he's in good shape."

"*The Kiss?*" Eddie asks.

"I don't have any information on it . . . sorry . . . I'll see if I can find out. Get some rest now."

The lieutenant walks through the curtain divider that separates Eddie from the rest of the SAR's compartment. Eddie's senses are beginning to return to normal as he catches a glimpse of the Airbus's wide comfortable-looking cabin. He notices how well the energy-absorbing systems are doing their job reducing vibration and most of the chopper's sound, which was deafening during his rescue. *Almost as quiet as a commercial jetliner,* he thinks. *I hope The Nereid is as comfortable—and . . . my god . . . The Kiss!*" A chill runs through him and again he begins to cry with the realization that, if Helle has abandoned ship, *The Kiss* is lost. He soon dozes off as the Airbus's turbine engines power its five blades through the early morning air.

*   *   *

Camilla places the phone in her purse and rests her head in her hands, pushing her long blond hair back over her shoulders away from her face. Still upset but feeling relieved at the sound of Eddie's voice, she wants to freshen up in the Boeing 777XO's spacious lavatory. She returns to her seat and tries to sleep, but her mind is full of images of *The Kiss*, Eddie, Helle, and sailing the deep blue sea. The cabin interior lighting comes awake. Checking her watch, she sees that they will be landing in fewer than ninety minutes. She is energized by the thought of soon being reunited with Eddie.

"Just coffee please," Camilla tells the flight attendant.

She turns on the television and selects the BBC news channel to see the news of the coronation of a new King of England. Standing in front of Big Ben, the reporter describes the scene, "Preceding the King into Westminster Abbey was St. Edward's Crown, carried into the abbey by the Lord High Steward of England, then the Viscount Cunningham of Hyndhope, flanked by two other peers, while the Archbishops and Bishops Assistant of the Church of England, in their copes and mitres, wait outside the Great West Door for the arrival of the King . . ." And on and on in great detail of the proceedings.

The broadcast switches to inside the Abbey as the reporter continues; "The final complement of choristers comprised one hundred eighty-two boy trebles, thirty-seven male altos, sixty-two tenors, and sixty-seven basses. Together with a full orchestra, conducted by Sir James McCartney, the total number of musicians is four hundred eighty."

"My god," Camilla whispers to herself as the broadcast continues with hundreds of royal guests from nations around the world pictured. European royal families from around the world are seen parading: the queen of the Netherlands, the grand duchess of Luxembourg, the prince of Liège, Prince

Albert of the Belgians, King Haakon IX of Norway, several Mediterranean royal families, several Asian royal families, and on and on. Finally, it is mentioned that leading the delegation from the United States of America is the vice president and the daughter of the president, who has taken time off from her junior year at Dartmouth.

Lucky girl, Camilla thinks as the Iberian pilot announces that they will be readying the cabin for landing. Camilla checks her phone for messages and sends a text message to alert the Uber of her impending on-time arrival.

She calls Lisbeth to give her an update. "Hey, sis . . . did I wake you?"

Lisbeth is sitting on the rooftop terrace of her apartment, overlooking the beautiful city of Seville, sipping espresso and gazing at the spires of the cathedral. In the distance the walls of the Alcazar are draped by the vibrant colors of its amazing gardens. "We'll be landing soon," Camilla says.

"No . . . hi, Camy. I'm enjoying this beautiful morning with a coffee on the terrace . . . and I can tell you it will take a while to get here from the airport. The traffic, as usual, is pretty bad. But anyway," Lisbeth says with excitement, "I'm overjoyed that it's worked out and Eddie and Helle are OK."

"I spoke to Eddie briefly . . . from the helicopter. He's OK—just worn out . . . he's no spring chicken you know."

"Neither is Helle. I didn't research him initially when I hired him. I went on his predecessor's recommendation. Recently though I spent some time looking. He's one interesting dude . . . I'll fill you in later."

Camilla asks, "I can't reach his phone . . . have you talked to him?"

"No, but they've confirmed his boarding *The Nerval.* He

should be in Gibraltar by this evening. How was your flight? I imagine it must have been a little nerve wracking for you not knowing about Eddie."

"I was very scared. I couldn't sleep or read; I couldn't focus on anything. I felt in a daze from the lack of sleep. I've been going since leaving Greeley! I finally turned the TV on and watched some of the coverage in London of the coronation."

"Oh yeah . . . the freaking coronation. I can't believe those pompous assholes are still doing that stuff in this age. How much of it did you see?"

"Oh god," Camilla says, feigning exhaustion, "It was endless, but . . . it was, well . . . sort of therapeutic. I mean, it got my mind off worrying about what could go wrong rescuing Eddie and Helle . . . and that beautiful sailboat . . . I just sat there watching the royals parading around through Westminster Abbey, and through the streets of London. I never saw such pomp and pageantry . . . one royal family after another and another and another . . . Denmark, Sweden, Sultans from the Mideast . . . even the Far East, Thailand! It just went on forever."

"Yep . . . all those places they colonized in barbarian times hundreds of years ago. Jeez . . . the British Royal scam will go on forever."

"Yeah, right . . . the royal Brits and the not-quite royals from everywhere else!"

The two sisters are having a royal laugh. Camilla continues, "And then the good ole U. S. of A., not quite fully colonized some two hundred fifty years ago, sending the veep; and . . . oh yeah . . . and the president's daughter is there too. Both of them appearing more down to earth . . . but there's no missing the prez's daughter—she's a beauty."

"She is . . . and I guess with her attending the coronation, I shouldn't be surprised that there's a lot of messaging about her lately. A lot of online chitchat about Jackie right now. Hey, Camilla, I'm getting another call. I think Eddie is at Morón Air Base . . . I'll be at the front entrance when you pull up . . . I'm tracking your Uber."

"OK, bye, Lisbeth . . . love you."

"Love you too, sis."

Camilla puts her phone away and relaxes into her seat, takes a sip from her coffee before the attendant approaches, holding out her hand to indicate it's time for landing.

"Thank you," Camilla says, handing her the cup. *I think that is enough coronation for now,* she says to herself and turns the TV off.

Once on the ground, she locates her Uber, and soon she is on A-4 for the short ten-kilometer ride into the city of Seville where Lisbeth is waiting in her apartment at Calle Pajaritos 6. The Uber informs her that it will take more than an hour with the usual snarled city traffic.

She switches the Uber's TV set on, and again, the coronation fills the news for most of the ride. She watches with the sound muted until the footage is of the American president's daughter arriving at a coronation party. She turns up the volume to listen to the reporter's narration, ". . . has blossomed into a beautiful young women! The daughter of the American president looks gorgeous, attending her very first state function here in London. She is wearing a stunning glamorous dress and flashing sweet smiles as she chats with people at the lavish event."

Camilla relaxes as the Uber makes its way through the snarled Seville traffic. Again her phone rings; it's Panalla Reddy.

"Hello, Camilla."

"Hello, Dr. Reddy. I was going to call you later. It must be late there in Greeley."

"Yes, a little after one a.m., but I wanted to speak to you before calling it a day."

"I'm glad you called, Dr. Reddy."

"Camilla, while you were in the air, there's been a development. I wanted to let you know that I spent several hours with the IPCC attorneys discussing how we are going to move against Mr. Peary. There's a chance he will be arrested tomorrow morning and taken into custody by federal agents out of Boston. His whereabouts, though, is a question—Ron's too."

"Dr. Reddy, I haven't been in touch with either of them, I . . . since we were all in conference with Drs. Cooper and Lin. I haven't had any contact with Ron since the LET test in Colorado Springs."

"Should you have any contact with either of them, please contact me immediately."

"Yes, I will, Dr. Reddy. I'm meeting my sister shortly at her residence in Seville and traveling to Morón Air Base to bring my husband home. I'm not sure of his condition, but I believe he'll be able to travel in a day or two. I think he's suffering exhaustion. What is the new development you mentioned?"

"Before you return to Colorado, please contact me. It may be advantageous if you were in Woods Hole depending on what develops concerning Mr. Peary. The other thing is that there's been another quake in the Iberian region. Have you heard about it on the news?"

"All I've watched on the flight, as well as what I've seen since on the ground, is about the British coronation. I haven't heard about the quake."

"Drs. Cooper and Lin notified me of it around nine pm here in Colorado . . . four-plus hours ago; it's four point seven on the Richter scale. The epicenter of the quake is off the Iberian Peninsula, sixty miles out in the Atlantic west of the Strait of Gibraltar."

"Will it affect the collapsed canyon bed?"

"Drs. Cooper and Lin are not sure yet, but they are hopeful the data will indicate some degree of closure there. They are *not* expecting that this will trigger a complete return to normalcy. Right now, they are saying it could go any way; that is, the opening in the crust could be closed, or just made a degree smaller . . . possibly degrees larger . . . or left totally unchanged. I think you were lucky that your flight was unaffected, but I guess Seville is far enough inland. Some of the Mediterranean ports were not as lucky."

"Oh no, what's happening, Dr. Reddy?"

"Nothing major; however, some of the large seaports are closed until their cargo-moving equipment, railways, etc., can be checked to ensure safety. I can tell you your husband's shipmate now aboard *The Nerval* container ship will not dock as expected in Gibraltar . . . it's closed."

"I guess they'll have to tie up and wait."

"Either that or more likely they'll continue to another port."

"Another port? Where might that be?"

"From Gibraltar, *The Nerval* is scheduled to next arrive in Port Said, Egypt."

"Dr. Reddy, excuse me. I'm pulling up to my sister's residence. I'll call you in a few hours with an update.

"Good luck, Camilla."

"Bye, Dr. Reddy."

Lisbeth is at the front entrance, waiting as the Uber pulls up. She gets into the backseat with Camilla, and the two sisters hug one another tenderly.

"Camilla, I'm so happy for you and Eddie."

" And we'll all be together again . . . how long is the ride to the base."

Lisbeth looks to the front-seat trip display. "No traffic, forty-five minutes."

They arrive at Morón Air Base and quickly pass through security with Camilla's IPCC credentials. Eddie is at the base hospital and has been released. The staff has been alerted to Camilla's arrival at the security gate, and they bring Eddie to the lobby for pickup. He sits patiently in the wheelchair, grumbling that it was unnecessary to wheel him when he's perfectly all right.

A motorcycle pulls up, and then another of the same. The two riders dismount, remove their helmets, and stand together, looking and pointing at the bikes. Eddie is reminded of his youth when he rode motorcycles. He stands and begins wandering toward the exit.

"Mr. Eddie . . . señor! Please wait in the wheelchair." A Nurse Ratched–like attendant sits in the waiting area near Eddie with the release log for Camilla to sign.

But he is intrigued by the bikes and walks through the revolving door to have a better look at the pair of 1967 Bultaco Metralla MK2 road bikes. He can't believe his eyes.

One of the riders walks past Eddie through the door toward the reception desk. Eddie approaches the other remaining with the bikes. The attendant now is up following Eddie and calling his name, "Señor, Señor Gerber. You have to wait inside, please."

"I love your motorcycle," he calls out as he approaches the man who is now sitting on one of the Bultacos, cell phone in hand.

"Gracias, Señor. *Está familiarizado con las motocicletas?*" he asks Eddie.

"Yes, around the time this bike was built, I owned a similar bike. What year is your bike?"

"It's a sixty-seven . . . yours?"

"Same year; English though. Velocette."

"No puedo creer!" the man reacts with disbelief. Eddie has his attention. *"Cúal?"*

"A nineteen sixty-seven Velocette Thruxton."

"Señor Eddie, please!" The hospital attendant, now outside, is gesturing, trying to coax Eddie back toward the revolving door.

"I'm sorry. OK . . . one minute," he says to her.

"No kidding?" The bike rider is surprised and changes to English. "Very nice . . . five hundred cc?"

"Yes. Is this a two fifty?" Eddie asks as he squats down next to the engine to take a closer look. "I love this bike. So simple . . . so fucking fast!"

"What was the Thruxton like . . . a little faster I expect?"

"It was. Mine had the race cylinder head with extra-large valves, a downdraught inlet port and a bored carburetor."

"I bet you wish you had that bike now. How many did they make—a thousand?"

"Something like that. Eleven hundred, maybe. Seeing this bike reminds me of it. I read about Bultaco bikes . . . but they were a rare sight back when I was in my teens."

"You are British?"

Eddie ignores the question. Still squatting he says, "This

bike's engine is a two-stroke, right?" To the dismay of the attendant, he scoots more closely to examine the engine, carburetor, and drive chain.

"Señor Gerber, can you come back inside until señora arrives . . . please, Señor Gerber?"

The attendant now comes and stands next to where Eddie is squatting and lightly taps his shoulder.

Eddie looks up at the bike owner. "OK, I'm coming. Can I hear it . . . can you start it? I haven't heard a two-stroke like this in quite a while."

"Sure."

Before the attendant can say anything, Eddie gets up out of his squat position, and the bike owner opens the fuel valve, straddles the bike, and turns the key position to on. With one kick of the kickstart, the two-stoke is twanging away, ringing out its trademark *inging
inginging*.

"Nice!" Eddie yells out to the rider. "I love that sound . . . it's like nothing else."

"Eddie!" A shout is heard from the parking area. It's Camilla.

Eddie looks away from the bike to see Camilla, followed by Lisbeth, walking across the roadway toward him. They meet and kiss in the driveway and stand there, looking at each other and stroking each other's cheeks, wiping away tears of joy. Then turning toward the biker and the attendant, they walk back.

"Señor Gerber! Please. I'm going to get in trouble." Then turning toward the bike rider, she yells out to turn the bike off: *"Y por favor, señor, que a su vez fuera!"*

"It's OK . . . this is my wife, Camilla. She's here to pick me up."

"Please, then let's go inside, and she can sign the release log."

Eddie, Camilla, and the attendant return to the lobby where Camilla shows her identification and signs the release log. Still arm in arm, Eddie and Camilla exit through the revolving door just in time to hear the *wing-ing-ing-wiiiiii* of the Bultaco, and watch as Lisbeth takes a ride on the bike down the air base road, then a quick turn toward A-360.

"She rides?" Eddie asks with a stupefied look.

Camilla says, "Everybody in Europe rides, Gerby. You know that."

"Well, I'm next! Hey, buddy . . ." he calls out and walks toward the biker, while looking over his shoulder at Camilla with a big smile.

Camilla catches and stops him. "Eddie, I think you've had enough excitement for a while. Let's wait in the car."

He looks at her smiling face and kisses her. "OK . . . but listen. I'm thinking of laying off sailing for a while. You know I used to own and race motorcycles just like that one!"

They walk across to the parking lot.

"Eddie . . . is there anything you haven't done?"

"Well . . ." he pauses, "I can tell you what I haven't done recently that I really want to do."

He pulls her closer to his side to nuzzle her ear. She lets out a laugh as they climb into the backseat. Eddie is imitating the sound of the two-stroke, *wing-ing-inginging, wing-ing-inginging,* which rings out in the distance as Lisbeth puts the bike through its gears.

The End

About the Author

The author, who writes under the name J. Joseph Mawek, wrote *The Last Straw* as a framework for a screenplay and subsequent film. If you would like to participate in the film production, please visit the film's Kickstarter.com project, which is planned for late Spring 2017.

When not traveling, Mawek and his wife, Patricia, reside in the town of Port Washington, New York, which is located along the gold coast of Long Island's North Shore. Mawek is a graduate of Stony Brook University and Manhattan College where he published works of both fiction and nonfiction.